Kay Mellor, th   /
drama series,   g
writer whose   e
Woman, starri   e
success. Her ITV series, *Just Us*, won a BAFTA
award for Best Children's Drama.

John Burke is an acclaimed writer whose novelisations
include *The Bill* and *London's Burning*. He lives in
Scotland.

BAND OF GOLD:
Ring of Lies

Created by
Kay Mellor

Novelised by
John Burke

HEADLINE

First published in 1996 by
HEADLINE BOOK PUBLISHING

10 9 8 7 6 5 4 3 2 1

ISBN 0 7472 5405 2

Typeset by Palimpsest Book Production Limited,
Polmont, Stirlingshire
Printed and bound in Great Britain by
Cox & Wyman Ltd, Reading, Berks.

HEADLINE BOOK PUBLISHING
A division of Hodder Headline PLC
338 Euston Road
London NW1 3BH

BAND OF GOLD:
Ring of Lies

1

Gina heard the car draw up as she leaned over Sarah trying to fasten the buckle on a shoe that was by now too small. Her four-year-old daughter Sarah needed new shoes. Joanne, who they were going to collect from school, needed a lot more than that. Michelle, wriggling in her push-chair, would keep growing and keep needing things. Trying to cope with the three of them was becoming more than a headache: a throbbing agony, the turning of a screw inside her head that grew more and more terrifying.

And here was Mr Moore again, swinging his briefcase out of his shiny red Granada like a lethal weapon and stamping up the path to the front door.

He jabbed at the doorbell. And kept at it.

Sarah jumped, nearly losing her shoe. 'Who is it, Mum? Is it that man again?' Already she and Joanne were learning fear, without knowing quite what they had to be afraid of.

Gina grabbed Sarah's hand and dragged her behind the settee, reaching out to haul Michelle in the pushchair alongside them.

Mr Moore must have caught a flicker of movement. He came away from the front door and pushed his wide, jowly face against the sitting-room window.

'I know you're in there, Mrs Dixon.' He put on that particularly gloating tone of his. 'I can wait here all day. I've got all the time in the world.'

There was a sudden snarl from the next-door neighbour's

Alsatian, and Mr Moore's face disappeared from the window. Gina wasn't going to waste a second. She guided Sarah towards the kitchen and dragged the pushchair after her. Easing the kitchen door open and praying it wouldn't creak, she nudged Sarah out and then inched Michelle in the pushchair on to the path.

She found herself confronted by the garden fence. It wasn't their fence but their neighbour's, and in fairly good repair. Left to Steve, it would have been falling apart by now.

'This way, Mum.'

Sarah was expertly removing two loose slats to make way for all three of them. Gina thought of the number of times she had told her older daughters not to play in Mrs Wainwright's garden; and then summoned up a feeble, grateful smile.

Mr Moore must be still prowling about, or sitting back in his car, as they found their way out on to the side road and hurried towards the school. They were late. She would have to take the short cut down Lambton Lane.

Even in broad daylight the women were out, teetering on high heels up and down the pavement or lounging in doorways in the hope of catching some passing trade. In spite of an unseasonably cold breeze, striking in sudden gusts from the main road beyond and making crisp packets and crumpled cigarette ends dance in the gutters, most of the women wore flimsy blouses open at the neck, tight black leather pants – you couldn't call them hot pants in *this* weather – and only the sheerest, most revealing stockings.

Gina had rarely done more than glance at the pub halfway down the lane, but now, somehow, she found herself staring thoughtfully at the open doorway. It was called The Bobbin, from the days when it had been a favourite haunt of workers in one of the now abandoned mills. Today most folk in this area of Bradford referred to it as The Hustlers' Arms. Everyone knew it was there. One of the facts of life. You didn't have to go in there or pay it any attention at all if you didn't want to. And if you weren't interested, then its regulars didn't bother you either.

A young girl, no more than a kid, pushed herself away from the pub door and stamped her feet to keep out the chill. Her legs were as blue as her lacy transparent blouse. Gina leaned over Michelle, clattering the pushchair off the kerb and across the narrow entrance to the alley by the pub.

Behind her she heard a half-bored, half-friendly voice saying, 'Hello, what do they call *you*?'

Sarah was staring at the girl's shiny black high-heeled shoes. As Gina backtracked to pull her away, Sarah said, 'Mum, can I have some shoes like that?'

'No!'

Girls like that could afford shoes like that. Gina felt a twinge of envy. Maybe . . .

Only a few years ago, even a few months ago, she wouldn't have thought herself capable of thinking it. Never in a million years. The mere idea of letting some other man, not her husband – some utter stranger, a slob she didn't even know and wouldn't ever want to know on a bet – crawl all over her, pound into her and then clear off as if he'd just done no more than relieve himself in a public toilet, was no more than a dirty joke. Dirty and not very funny. She could never get that desperate.

Never.

You saw them most days around here, and in the evenings there were plenty of television documentaries to shove the facts at you, and newspaper stories every now and then, especially when one of them got beaten up and the police said they were having a new crackdown. Only, hadn't they been asking for it anyway?

And hadn't she been beaten up herself, more than once – and by her own husband?

So what was so different?

At least you'd get cash for letting some yob heave you around, which was more than Steve had provided for a long

3

time. A husband thought he was entitled to everything just because he had paid for a marriage licence: a one-off fee for the use of her body whenever he felt like it, and the right to beat her up whenever she *didn't* feel like it.

What was so wrong with doing it for money? No strings, no live-in bully.

Only of course you'd never really let yourself be used like that by anybody else, no matter how desperate you were.

Gina was desperate.

It was unthinkable; but she was thinking it.

Urging her on was the picture of Mr Moore, coming back over and over again, sitting and watching the house or getting out and marching up to it. It was a house she had been so proud of, those few years ago: a council house they had bought and done up, with new carpets and curtains and a sort of Georgian front door she had persuaded Steve they had to have. Now the mere thought of that bastard Moore in his striped blue suit staring at it and sizing up everything about it was enough to contaminate the whole place.

They reached the school gates to find kids surging across the yard, a few already climbing into battered old cars, others being led, pushed and yelled at along the pavement. Joanne was close to the railings, hand in hand with a little dark girl a couple of inches shorter than herself. Before Gina could manoeuvre the pushchair closer to the gate and wave to Joanne that it was safe to come out now, the little girl said, 'Can Joanne come to our house?'

'I'm working tonight, Emma, love.'

Emma's mother was a slim, leggy woman with smooth skin and a complexion that was silky dark grey rather than brown. She was wearing jeans and a sweat shirt, and her hair was tied back in a tight pony-tail. A bomber jacket hung loosely over her shoulders. In spite of the casualness of her attire, she had something of the swagger of a fashion model; but you didn't get many fashion models in this corner of Bradford. Gina wondered fleetingly whether there was a potential client here for some of the cosmetics she trudged around trying to sell.

'Just for tea?' Emma was pleading.

Gina held out her hand. 'Come along, Joanne.'

'I want to go to Emma's.'

'She can come if it's all right with you.' The woman had a lazy, self-assured voice. 'Just for tea.'

It was a bit much, having nearly broken her neck to get here on time. But in the face of that enviable poise, Gina didn't want to look flustered and unsure of herself. They exchanged names and addresses, and she promised to collect Joanne before Carol Johnson went out to work.

She hadn't said what her work was. Funny if it was the same sort of thing, and she too was plodding wearily around with a case of cosmetic samples. Gina didn't really believe in coincidences like that. She would take some samples along with her; see if she could flog a few lipsticks and moisturisers.

It was a good thing, anyway, to have Joanne off her hands for a couple of hours. They couldn't go home yet, with that loan shark still skulking around. She had to sort something out, and quickly.

'We'll go and see Grandad.'

Sarah made a face. She did her best to like Grandad, only he was really her great-grandfather and too far gone to do more than mumble a few incomprehensible words and wait for someone to wipe the moisture out of the corners of his eyes and mouth. Gina tried not to force a visit on the kids more than once a week; but she knew that at this time of day her mother would be there, and she had to swallow her pride and make another appeal to her.

They went the long way round, avoiding Lambton Lane and giving her time to think what she was going to say. Or what she was going to do. Think . . . of *something*.

But what if there was nothing? No hope, no way out of this mess?

She thought of Steve, and tried not to think of him. The last time he had shown up and tried to persuade her to open the door and let him in, he had been full of remorse. Sorry for what he'd done, and it wouldn't happen again, and he was looking for a job, honestly, and there was a chance of a decorating contract up Henchard Lane. Could lead on to a lot more like it, and he could pay off a few bills for a start.

Including the mortgage, well overdue? And new shoes and clothes for his three daughters, and food and rates and the electricity bill?

She was as likely to let him back into the house as she was to let Mr Moore in. In fact Moore stood a better chance. He had made it sound so simple at the start: all she had to do was take out one loan to pay off all the outstanding bills up to date, and then repay him in nice easy instalments. Only they had proved not so easy; and before long he would be forcing his way in, bristling with warrants and repossession orders and God knows what.

Her grandfather was sitting in front of the television staring at a children's programme. That was a relief. Sarah didn't mind wriggling on to the couch beside him and watching the programme. Gina's mother tucked a teatowel into the neck of the old man's jumper and set a plate of mince and mash on the table between him and the television. She fed him a couple of mouthfuls before he insisted on clutching the spoon himself with a trembling hand.

Joyce looked at her daughter, and nodded towards the kitchen.

'All right, what is it?'

'I've got to get a job.'

'Thought you already had one.'

'Only part-time. And there's no real money in it. I mean a full-time job.'

'Well, get one, then.'

'Mum, it's not that easy. Not with the kids on my hands all day. I've got to find some way of—'

6

'Oh, I get it.' Joyce's always earnest face puckered into lines that seemed to drag her eyes and cheeks down a fraction of an inch. She pursed her lips. 'You know Bob would never wear it. He'd go barmy. He doesn't even like me spending time with your grandad. He wouldn't stand for it.'

'I'm not asking Bob. I'm asking you.'

Joyce leaned wearily against the edge of the draining-board. Her smile had once been warm and spontaneous. Now she had to force even the sketch of a smile – and a sad one at that.

'I don't want lumbering with kids now. Not at my age. I love 'em, Gina, honest; but they get on my nerves. I can't be doing with it. I've had my share, and I'm finished with all that. Why can't you sort it out with Steve?'

'There's nothing to sort out. It's finished.'

'The trouble with you is you don't know when you're on to a good thing. He's kept you for seven years—'

'He hasn't worked for nearly two years.'

'Well, that's not his fault. Not the way things are these days. He stood by you when you were pregnant.'

'He *got* me pregnant.'

'He does one thing wrong, and you throw the poor bugger out.'

'One thing?' Gina protested. 'He only broke my bloody tooth. And I had a bruise on my face like—'

'Do you think you're the only one that's ever been hit?' It was Joyce's turn to flare up. 'I stuck with your father for sixteen years, and I couldn't stand the sight of him.'

'Well, that was you. I want something better.'

'You should have thought about that before you started buying your council house. Everyone else pays rent, but you, oh no, *you* have to go one better than the rest.' Joyce sighed. 'I'm not a miracle worker, love. There's only so many hours in the day.'

She did not need to spell it out. Gina knew all too well that her mother was out cleaning by seven every morning, and that she had to fit in visits to Grandad when she could manage it. And of course she had to rush back to get Bob's tea, because Bob would raise hell if she didn't. Bob . . . Whatever faults Gina's father might have had, he was surely never as crude and selfish as Bob. And still her mother slaved for him, and tried to make excuses for him.

Gina had tried making excuses for Steve. But not any more.

Joyce was saying, 'You've got your makeup round, why can't you make a go of that?'

'I've told you. Because there's not enough in it, that's why. I've just *got* to find something else.'

Sarah called from the other room to say that Grandad had spilt something. In the doorway Joyce hesitated, then held out two ten-pound notes. 'Here, spend it on the kids. Only don't say 'owt to Bob.'

Gina wished she could have refused the money. She felt guilty at taking it; guilty about leaning on her mother and playing on her sympathies. And guilty about having to ask her another favour right now. 'Mum, I've got to go and fetch Joanne from this friend's place. And I'll collect my case on the way, and maybe make a sale while I'm there. If you could see Sarah and Michelle home . . . I'll be as quick as I can.'

'Oh, God, what Bob'll say . . .'

'Twenty minutes. Half an hour at most. Honest.'

She dashed off before Joyce could make her feel any worse than she already did.

The hall of Carol Johnson's council house was papered with a heavy, expensive floral pattern, and there was a fancy chandelier that Gina wouldn't have minded seeing in her own house. Only maybe the house wouldn't be her own for much longer.

The door had been opened by a teenage girl who said simply, 'I'm Julie,' and led her into a front room where

Emma and Joanne were sprawled on a new carpet that Gina wouldn't have let any kid play on.

Joanne looked up without much enthusiasm at her mother's arrival. 'Mum, Emma wants me to sleep here tonight, and Julie says it's all right, because she'll be looking after us.'

'We've got to get back. Nanna's waiting for us.'

'But Mum . . .'

There was a throaty laugh from the far corner of the room. A middle-aged woman with a lined but still attractive face, and hair touched up to retain echoes of what must once have been a warm bronze, was lounging back on a brand-new couch with a pink cover and luxuriously plump pink cushions. Whatever Carol Johnson's work might be, thought Gina enviously, it certainly paid off.

The woman said: 'They never stop arguing, do they?'

'Auntie Anita, will *you* ask Mum if it's all right for Joanne to stay the night?'

Gina said, 'Has Mrs Johnson . . .' A slight twist of Anita's lips made her realise that she was taking too much for granted. 'Has Carol gone out already?'

'No. She'll be down in a minute.' Anita was eyeing her case. 'Not off to organise a Tupperware party, are you?'

Gina hastened to open the case. Anita pushed herself forward on to the edge of the couch and stared eagerly in. She was just the sort of customer Gina most liked to see: one who was eager to buy something just for the sake of buying.

'I like that pink.' Anita held it up, then glanced back at the pink cushions behind her. 'Mm. Not on this couch, though.'

'You wouldn't suit pink,' said Gina authoritatively. 'You're more orange.'

'Yes, I know.' Anita looked none too pleased. 'I've had loads of orange lumbered on me. There's a young lass comes round our end, I've got a bag full. Still –' she peered even

9

more closely into the sample case '– it could be time for a change.'

There was a clatter of feet on the stairs, and Carol Johnson came in. Gina just managed to restrain an involuntary gasp. The transformation from the woman who had come to meet her little girl from school was staggering. The jeans, sweat shirt and jacket had given way to a short, tight leather skirt and a low-cut blouse. The pony-tail was gone, and her hair was loose, long and wild, threatening to snarl up in her huge dangly earrings. Her long legs were encased in high-heeled black boots.

'I want five quid off you,' said Anita. 'Two bleaches and a disinfectant.'

Whatever this might mean, Carol ignored it. 'I'm going to be late. Come on, Emma, a quick kiss – and be a good girl for Julie.'

Instinctively Gina reached out to draw Joanne close to her. But Joanne was staring longingly at Carol.

'I like your boots, Auntie Carol.'

'Thanks, sweetheart. They cost me an arm and a leg.'

A growing suspicion tugged at Gina's mind. This whole house and its contents had cost more than that – something quite different from an arm and a leg, though they might play their part as well. But it was all so smart and clean and tidy; and Carol's little girl was sweet, nicely dressed, and obviously well cared for.

She said, 'It's time we were off, Joanne. Nanna will be wondering where on earth we've got to.'

'Or Bob will,' said Joanne knowingly.

Carol was looking impatient. 'I really must be off. Can I drop you somewhere? Your place can't be far off.'

Joanne was delighted. She had never been in a taxi before. Gina was half glad to accept, half reluctant. The driver's knowing look as Carol slid into the taxi, showing a great expanse of thigh, confirmed what she had suspected. Yet there was something so warm and immediately friendly about Carol that she was quite sorry when she saw the familiar corner ahead and said, 'This'll do fine, ta. Just drop us here.' Then she glanced awkwardly at Carol. 'Thanks for the lift. I've only just realised, I haven't got any money on me. I must have—'

'Get lost. I don't want any. But I want some of those lipsticks and bath essences of yours. When do you get a delivery?'

'I could see you a couple of weeks from now. See you at the school and fix something, anyway.'

Her heart sank as she approached their front gate. Bob's clapped-out old van was standing right outside. There was no way round it, and no way of dodging down the overgrown path to the back. As she tried to hurry Joanne past, he let out a roar.

'Where d'you think you've been? I've been sat out here for bloody hours.'

'That's a bit of a—'

'Your mother's got enough to do without looking after your kids.' In the yellow light of the street lamp his face looked even more pasty and unappetising than usual. 'You shouldn't have them if you can't look after them. And another thing—'

She didn't wait for whatever it was he was thinking up next, but clutched Joanne's hand more firmly and led her indoors. It was hard to decide when Bob was at his most repulsive: when he was snapping and snarling, or when he was trying to imply that things could be better between them if she could only relax a little and let him be nice to her. Behind her mother's back, of course.

Joyce, washing up two cups and saucers in the kitchen, seemed to have been infected with some of the rasp in Bob's voice. 'I've been worried sick. Where the hell have you been?'

'You know where I've been. Out trying to earn some money.'

11

As Joanne went upstairs to bed, Joyce dried her hands hurriedly. 'Right, that's it. I'm off. Oh, and you've had a gentleman waiting to see you for the best part of an hour.'

Without waiting for another word, she went out of the back door just as Mr Moore came into the kitchen from the sitting-room.

Like Joyce, he wasted no words. 'You owe me two months' money. I want a hundred and eighty pounds off you.'

'No, that's not right. I owe you a hundred and sixty.'

'Accumulative interest, love. It's gone up.'

The screw was tightening again inside her head. She couldn't believe what she was hearing. 'You can't have it. I haven't got it. You'll have to wait till the end o' the week.'

'That'll be another week, then,' Mr Moore smirked. 'That's extra time again, and it'll cost you another—'

'You can't have what I haven't got, can you?'

He jerked his head back towards the room where he had been waiting for her. She could have strangled her mother for letting the evil, hulking bastard in. 'You've got a nice telly and a video in there. Sell 'em.'

'I get my commission at the end of the week.' She improvised madly. 'And they've just told me I'm gonna be made up to area manager. So I'll be able to pay the whole lot off next month. I'll get a car, and commission, and everything.' To distract that stony stare of his, she opened her sample case. 'Here, take one of these. You can give it to your wife.'

'I don't have a wife.'

'Well, your girlfriend, then.'

'I don't have a girlfriend either.'

'A nice bloke like you, without a woman?'

Even in her own ears it sounded feeble. Mr Moore did not even bother to summon up a self-deprecating smile. He ground the words out loud and clear: 'I'll be back on Friday.

12

You make sure you have that money for me, or else I'll take what I want. And I do mean what I want. Get it?'

It took her two days to find Steve. Always bobbing up when she least wanted to see him, but not around when she needed him. It was not until the Friday morning that she found him a good three streets away from Henchard Lane, up a ladder painting an upstairs window, while another man worked on the front door below. Sarah had spotted him first, and ran ahead as Gina pushed Michelle in the pushchair up the slope.

Steve waved. He looked delighted to see them. She wondered how delighted he would be when she demanded some money; and wanted it here and now.

'Well, now.' He was marching towards them as if he expected a forgiving kiss and a hug.

Gina said flatly, 'I need to talk to you.'

'Sure. Great. Look, I'll be knocking off for me dinner soon. Can you hang about? Or I can ask Dave if he'll—'

'Have you got any money?'

'Just a couple of quid,' said Steve warily. 'Why?'

'I thought you'd be getting a deposit. An advance, or something.'

'Well, yes. But we had to buy the paint, didn't we. Why – what's up?'

She had tried all along to make him believe she was doing all right without him, and paying all the bills. Just to put him in his place and make him feel ashamed. She didn't want to let on the full awfulness of the whole situation; not all at one go.

'Sarah needs some new shoes,' she said feebly.

'Well, I should have this finished week after next. Then we can sort it out.'

'That's too late.'

'Why? What's so urgent about a pair of shoes?'

'She needs them now, not in two weeks' time.' Gina

was yelling so loudly and angrily that Steve's mate looked apprehensively over his shoulder. 'I can't keep stuffing her feet into shoes that are sizes too small for her.'

'What d'you expect me to do?'

He was so plaintive that she could have hit him – preferably with one of his own cans of paint. What had she really expected him to do? Nothing, as usual. She ought not to have bothered coming here in the first place. It wasn't going to solve one single damned thing.

'Is that all you came for?' he was bleating. 'Just money?'

Just money. It sounded so trivial.

Gina steered the pushchair so fast downhill that it was in danger of running away with her.

As they approached home she was half expecting Mr Moore's red Granada to be parked slap outside the house. In fact it was on the opposite side of the road, leaving room for a small van into which a man was loading the television. Gina stumbled into an erratic run with Michelle, while Sarah let out a whimper and huddled against the hedge.

'What the hell d'you think you're doing?'

'Me job, love.'

'That's mine.' In the back of the van she saw the video. 'They're mine.'

'Not any more.' He jerked his thumb towards the side door of the house. 'Ask the man.'

As they entered the kitchen, Mr Moore was unplugging the microwave. Gina lunged at him, catching hold of one arm and trying to grab the microwave with the other hand. 'You can leave that where it is, you bastard. I'm going to ring the police. You're trespassing.'

He was enjoying every moment of this. 'I'm just taking goods to the value of the money you owe.'

'You've broken into my house. You've got no right.'

'You should have been in, love. I did say Friday.'

'Get out. Go on, get *out*.'

The van driver put his head round the door. 'Are we all done?'

'The microwave,' said Mr Moore with some relish.

'Don't you touch it.' Gina had a firm grasp on the lead.

Mr Moore wrestled with her for a moment, then decided either that it would be undignified or downright dangerous to go on struggling for possession.

'All right, leave it. But we'll only get a couple of hundred for the telly and the video, so you'll still owe a grand.'

'Get out.'

'See you at the end of the month. One hundred and eighty pounds. Don't forget.'

As the door closed behind him, Sarah flung herself against her mother's side. 'It's all right, Mum.' Her face was pressed into Gina's coat. 'I don't really want any new shoes.'

Gina looked over Sarah's dark head, unseeing, at the wall and beyond it. She wasn't going to break down. Wasn't going to howl in despair. She was quite clear now what had to be done – and done quickly, before she had time to back away in fright.

2

Carol had just disentangled herself from her regular Friday five o'clock punter when there was a knock at the door downstairs. Behind her, Sidney swung his skinny legs off the bed and made an apprehensive grab for his pants. Carol waved him to silence and carefully parted the thick lace curtains. She could see nobody.

The knocking came again. She opened the window and leaned out.

'Who is it? What d'you want?'

Nobody she knew would come round at this hour. Even the occasional punter fancying a repeat performance wouldn't risk it without having fixed the time with her first, just the way Sidney had. And Julie had been paid as usual and knew exactly when she was supposed to bring Emma home from the park.

Gina Dixon stepped back from the doorstep and looked up.

Carol was in no mood for a casual visitor; nor for a delivery of cosmetics. 'What d'you want?' she demanded again, as off-puttingly as possible.

'It's me.'

Carol could see that.

'It's about your order.'

'Yeh, well, I—'

'I'm not doing cosmetics any more.'

It seemed an odd hour of the afternoon to come round just to make such an announcement. Carol said curtly, 'I'm a bit tied up at the moment.'

'I'll wait. 'Cos I've got to talk to you.'

Carol turned back into the bedroom and indicated to Sidney that he should get a move on. Reluctantly she slipped on a baggy shirt and went downstairs to open the door.

Gina started babbling nervously right away. 'I'm sorry to disturb you, but I had to come and ask if you could . . . that is, I thought you might . . . you see, I need to earn some proper money, so I'm looking for something else. You weren't in bed, were you?'

'No, I were just . . .' Carol changed the subject quickly, looking down at the case Gina was carrying. 'What's wi' the case, then, if you've packed it in?'

'My mother's looking after the kids. She thinks I'm out selling. Only I'm not. I've got your bits, and that's it.'

There was the sound of the toilet flushing. Carol steered Gina into the sitting room and hurried back upstairs. She was furious at anyone using her toilet. Even a regular like Sidney. Using her toilet, and her washbasin. She snapped savagely at him in an undertone, and bustled him downstairs and out of the front door.

Gina watched her from the sitting-room door.

Carol wasn't going to wilt under that wide-eyed gaze. 'Let's get one thing straight. I aren't ashamed of what I do. Them that can do it becomes whores, and them that can't become whore-wives. Right?'

Gina nodded mutely.

'I don't ponce off the state, I earn my money. I bet you thought we lived in slums, didn't you?' Carol waved her arm about the room. 'I decorate right through once a year. Come on, let me show you.'

She was glad to get back upstairs and start running the shower and the bath, not just to show off but to have the chance of digging out the brush and the disinfectant Anita had brought her, to scrub vigorously round the lavatory and the washbasin, and tip bleach down the pan. It really pissed her off when they went to her toilet. Gina looked surprised

18

at the energy she was putting into the cleaning; then turned to admire the gleaming new tiles and the shower fitment.

She said, 'I owe money.'

'Don't we all?'

'I dunno, you don't seem to be doing too badly.'

Carol slotted the brush neatly back into its holder, adjusted the flow of the bathwater, and led the way into the bedroom. If the kid wanted to get the picture, let her get the whole thing.

At first sight the rumpled candlewick bedspread on the large double bed was out of keeping with the rest. As Gina looked doubtfully at this hustling cover, most likely conjuring up all sorts of pictures in her mind, Carol pulled it off to reveal the bright satin duvet cover beneath.

'So you've had some nasty man knocking on your door, have you? Demanding money with menaces?'

Gina had a pert, pretty little face with lips meant for laughter. They weren't laughing now. 'I was hoping to pay all my other stuff off. I thought if I just had the one payment each week I'd be able to manage.'

'But Mr Heavy—'

'Mr Moore.'

'All Mr Moore wants is more, right?'

She saw that Gina had been briefly distracted by the handcuffs attached to the curlicues of the ornamental brass bed-head. 'Do they fasten you up in them?'

'No way. I fasten *them* up.'

She remembered with a mixture of reluctant affection and seething dislike the one-time detective inspector who had supplied her with the cuffs as a sort of payment in kind. They had saved her quite an outlay on rope and stuff; though the bed-head itself was taking some stick.

It was time to get back to the bathroom. She shed the shirt and climbed in, reaching for the soap and starting to scour her flesh with a scrubbing brush. Gina sat timidly on

19

the lowered lid of the toilet, still watching her every move as if hypnotised.

At last she found words. 'How much do you . . . I mean, how much will they . . .'

It was difficult to explain the going rates and the possible extras to a naive outsider like this. There were subtleties and crudities and gimmicks you could only learn on the Lane itself, or when you'd actually got the punter panting in your bedroom. Only from experience could you find that it made good sense to start with twenty-five quid, and not many of them argued about that. After all, Carol prided herself that she still looked pretty good and could go on looking good for a few years yet. Maybe you had to settle for twenty sometimes. But then when you got them back home you could get awkward and tell them you weren't taking your clothes off for twenty stinking quid: it would cost them another fiver, and if they were hinting at a blow job then they were looking at a tenner on top.

'I usually finish up with thirty-five a punter.'

Gina was watching the thrusts of the scrubbing brush.

'Doesn't that hurt?'

That was difficult to explain, too: that she *wanted* it to hurt.

Carol heaved herself out of the bath, grabbed a towel, and led the way back to her bedroom.

'So when's he coming back, your loan shark?'

'End of the month. I've got to find a hundred and eighty quid. And that's just for this month.'

'Tell your old man.' Carol writhed into a black bra and pants, and reached for a scarlet lustre jacket. 'Let him do the worrying.'

'He hasn't got any money, and anyway I don't want him to know. I'm going to sort it out for myself.'

'And how you gonna do that?' When she saw the kid looking meaningly round the room, Carol realised that she was getting too many bloody stupid notions in her head.

Fiercely she said, 'D'you think I'd be doing this if I had a husband?'

'Yes. It's better than—'

'Crap. You know nothing, you. I tell you, in the end it does your head in.'

'I only want to do it till I've paid my loan off.'

Oh, they all said that. Till this, till that. 'Till you feel your bones banging,' she rasped, 'and there's no one there any more.' Carol smoothed her hands over her hips and tugged the jacket down a fraction of an inch. She made up her mind. She would take the silly little bitch on a conducted tour, rub her nose in it, and by the end of the evening there'd be no more talk of making what she thought would be easy money with no after-effects.

'I'm twenty-three,' said Gina defiantly as they crossed the estate towards Lambton Lane.

'That's old.'

'Well, how old are *you*?'

Again, you could hardly begin to explain. Some things crept up on you, others seemed to have been fated right from the start. Carol had started hustling when she was thirteen. Her mother had been a hustler, her sister was at it in Manchester, and her brother had two girls working for him. She had never seriously thought of any other occupation. And when Emma came along, she could fit in looking after her with working hours to suit herself, and make sure the money kept coming in.

They passed a woman who dodged across the street to avoid them. Stupid cow. It really got to her that Carol had a council house, and in this very street. It was one of her sort who had grassed Carol up and had her social security stopped. Gina wanted to save up enough money to pay off a piddling little debt. Carol wanted enough to buy the house outright and stick a red light in the window, just to piss the whole lot of them off.

They had reached the end of the Lane, and the yellow

lights were coming on above the heads of the regulars. Gave some of them quite a halo. Carol slowed her pace as she began giving Gina a rundown on the girls, laying it on with a trowel.

A car was crawling beside the kerb. Tracy stepped out of a doorway and stooped to look inside. She was only fifteen, and relied mainly on those punters on the lookout for the young ones. Not just a child, but childish with it: a sweetie girl, doing it for a packet of jelly babies, a couple of quid a trick.

Carol remembered her own first time. He had been a long-distance lorry driver. Must have weighed twenty stone, and he stank. She couldn't get her knickers back on fast enough, and out of that lorry. She ran like hell and was well away before she looked at the note he had shoved down between her breasts. At first she was fit to burst with misery. A foreign note . . . only it turned out to be a Scottish tenner.

She pointed across the lane at the girl hunched against the iron grill of a video shop. Here was a good object lesson for Gina Dixon.

'That's Amanda. She got beaten up last week.'

'By a . . . a punter?'

'No. By us. For going without a rubber. And her on the corner over there, she's Asian. She does well with her own kind. Has 'em queuing up for her. Old ones give her some stick, though. They shout names and throw stones at her.'

She had had some names chucked at herself, too, in her time. You got used to it. You had to, especially with a skin her colour.

They had reached the pub door. The thumping of the music throbbed out through a swirl of cigarette smoke. Gina stared in. 'Do they . . . is this where you . . . find business?'

'Listen,' Carol set herself on the step to block the way.

'Go back home to your kids. Let Moore take what he wants. They're only things. You're not bad-looking, you could go to any pub, pick up a well-dressed fella and get him to give you some money. Get it all at one go. You don't have to hustle.'

'I don't see the difference.'

Carol sighed. All at once she was dying for a drink. She turned and went inside, with Gina doggedly following.

They were met by the usual hubbub. Familiar figures clustered round the bar, twosomes and threesomes leaned across tables to argue, and there was a scattering of lonely punters pretending to look at their evening papers every now and then. One unfamiliar face stood out, topped by faded sandy hair in lank curls which might have suited a certain sort of girl but looked weird on a man. The expression was common enough, though. You got to know that sort of haunted look, the hunger mixed with self-contempt, capable of weird fancies and sudden swings of temper. Could be pitiful or dangerous.

Carol pointed Gina towards a space just vacated by a girl heading out on to the Lane, and went to the bar. She found herself trying to squeeze in between a man with some ornate tattoos on his neck and Rose, sitting on a bar stool – or, rather, swaying on it. She was wearing tight black stretch trousers which emphasised what a large bottom she'd got, and a knitted top which kept sliding off one shoulder. Rose had another five or six years in her at most, Carol estimated, and then it would be a steady decline, lucky to get custom even on the canal towpath in a thick mist. You had to admit she carried her thirty-odd years pretty well, and her blonde hair had a nice sheen; but her bossiness towards the rest of the girls was beginning to twist her mouth permanently into a peevish shape.

She was staring past Carol at Gina. 'Who's that?'

'Nobody you'd know. She's straight.'

Making her way to the table with two gin-and-tonics,

Carol was aware that the ginger-haired weirdo had focused his attention on Gina. His bottom lip went slack as he went on watching.

Gina didn't seem to have noticed him any more than any of the others. 'Everybody's looking at me.'

''Course they are. Wondering what the bloody hell you're doing here.'

Suddenly the sandy individual was blotted out. Rose swayed above them, glaring at Gina. 'So what's your name?'

'Gina.' It was little more than a whisper.

'Gina what?'

'Just Gina.'

Rose looked drunkenly suspicious. 'Really? Hm. Nice name, Gina. I suppose you're a nice person, too.'

Carol said, 'Leave it, Rose.'

'No, I'm interested, that's all. I haven't seen you in here before.'

'She doesn't come from round here.'

Rose ignored Carol and went on staring at Gina. 'Where do you come from, then, love?'

'Butterworth Hill.'

'Which end?'

'Top.'

'Very nice too.' Rose's tone was growing more menacing. 'What you doin' in here?'

'Having a drink with me,' said Carol.

Rose spotted the case on the seat. 'What's in there?'

'Makeup.'

'Need a whole bag of it, do you?'

Carol smelt trouble brewing up. 'Lay off her, will you.'

Rose lurched forward and grabbed the bag. Gina jumped up. Carol tried to reach past her and get a grip on the bag.

Rose backed away, triumphant. 'She don't mind me having a little look, do you, love? I mean, if it's only lipsticks and that.' She unzipped the case and rested it against the edge of the table. 'She's right.' There was a tinge of disappointment in her voice. She took out a perfume bottle, read the label, and then began rummaging in the case again. Gina managed to grab a corner this time and wrestled to free it. Rose held on with one hand and tossed a handful of eye shadows towards the door just as Anita came in.

'My samples!' Gina howled.

'Any pinks in there?' Anita giggled.

Gina wrenched the bag clear. Rose leaned further across the table, lost her balance, and kicked the adjoining table so that two glasses slid off and gin and beer went spraying everywhere. Gina was trying to fasten the catch on the case as Rose regained her balance and grabbed at her hair.

'Get off her,' Carol yelled.

'It's my makeup,' Gina shouted into Rose's contorted face.

'And this is my patch.'

Carol dragged them apart. She knew how ugly Rose could get. Maybe this would show the silly little girl the sort of aggro she was liable to walk into: not as easy a way to make money as she had been hoping.

'All right.' Rose let go of Gina's hair. 'But what's going on? This isn't a perfume counter. So what's the idea?'

Carol said, 'She thought she might want to work the Lane.'

'I still do,' said Gina.

Rose snorted. 'As if I didn't know. You've had it written across your face all along. Well, nobody works this Lane without my permission. You wanna work the Lane, you ask *me*.' She turned to go back to the bar.

Gina said, 'I'm asking.'

Carol felt a pang in the pit of her stomach. The bloody stupid creature really meant to go through with it.

Anita was explaining the financial arrangements for use of

her spare bedroom. She spent a lot of time making round-about excuses for herself, denying any personal involvement in anything even halfway dodgy. It was just that she needed a little extra money to keep herself going. The flat wasn't hers but George's – George being a respectable married businessman who could visit her only on Thursdays but who might, Anita hinted several times, soon be leaving his wife and moving in here permanently. Then of course she would have to stop helping her friends, but until then they could have the use of the room any time except Thursdays.

She emphasised that it was a great privilege for Gina to be accepted into this group so early in her career. She would be better off here, much more comfortable than outside with some of those loonies who were in too much of a rush ever to do things properly. It was a bargain, really. It cost two quid for half an hour: though, Anita confided, Gina would soon find how easy it was to get them out in fifteen minutes.

So it was a deal.

And the next step . . .

Carol had reluctantly agreed to ease her into the ways and means of it all. If she was determined to go ahead, then at least she should have a preliminary warm-up before hitting the Lane full-time. Carol would pick out somebody suitable and set up the meeting, and then it would be up to Gina.

In the end Carol personally escorted the man to Anita's place and kept him waiting outside the bedroom door while she ran through a final briefing with Gina.

'His name's Ashley. You got nothing to worry about. I've done him meself, and he's fast. Won't keep you busy for long. I've told him you're something special, not what he usually gets on the Lane, and he'll be the first. Nobody else has ever had you. Right? I got twenty off him, but I reckon you can get at least another five.' She noticed that Gina was shaking, and patted her on the shoulder. 'Come on, you'll be all right. Oh, and if he asks, I've told him you're seventeen. And you're a virgin.'

That at least made Gina laugh. A virgin! After the kids, she'd got stretch marks that anyone would be bound to notice.

'Listen,' Carol went on. 'They believe whatever you tell 'em, because they *want* to believe it. You have to use your gob one way or another in this business, so best use it to gab with. You can gab money right out of their pockets. Well, are you all set, then?'

All the talk about using her gob stabbed home to Gina. 'What if he tries to kiss me? I'll throw up.'

'Tell him you save that for your boyfriend. Either that, or it'll cost him thirty. He won't ask again.' Carol went to open the door. 'Well, have a nice time.'

Ashley's left cheek had a faint nervous twitch, and his fingers fumbled as he began unbuttoning his shirt. He looked rather silly as he stood first on one leg and then on the other to haul his trousers off. Crazily Gina wondered if he would take the loose change out of his pocket and clatter it on to the dressing-table, the way Steve always did.

She had never been naked with any man other than Steve. They had married so young that she had never had the chance to shop around. Not that she had ever wanted to. Now she spread herself on the bed and tried to pretend that this would be no different from that very first time. If she closed her eyes she might be able to believe it was her husband.

Ashley had bad breath. She caught a waft of it as he mounted her, kneaded her breasts for a moment or two, and then began pounding into her. She gave up pretending. It wasn't Steve. Wasn't anybody or anything. Just an impersonal nothingness of pulsating muscle, and a loud grunting, and a few drops of spit on her left shoulder.

Carol's voice echoed in her head. *Till you feel your bones banging and there's no one there . . .*

But at any rate Carol had been right about something else. Ashley was a fast one. There was no hanging about when it was over. He got his clothes on a sight faster than

27

he had taken them off, without sparing her a glance. Only at the last minute did he hesitate, look at her again, and then take a fiver from his pocket and chuck it on the bed. He mumbled something as he went to the door. It might have been a 'Thank you', or it might not.

It was a shock to find Steve in the house when she let herself in. He was propped in his usual armchair listening to the radio but switched it off the moment she came into the room, and smiled ingratiatingly.

'It's all right. They're sound asleep.'

'Where's Mam?'

'I told her to go. It's not her fault. I came because I wanted to talk to you. Didn't realise you'd be out working.'

'I'm trying to earn some money.'

'Did you do all right?'

'They've got this special offer on,' Gina improvised. 'If you buy a body lotion or bath gel, you get a talc free.'

Steve was trying to look interested, but hadn't really taken any of it in. She could have told him almost anything, and it would have floated in one ear and out the other.

They believe whatever you tell 'em . . .

'I'll always sit for you,' Steve was saying. 'After all, they're my kids. You don't have to ask your mam. Look, shall I come tomorrow? Straight from work.' When she did not reply he took some money from his pocket. Second man this evening to hand over some cash. 'I borrowed thirty quid off Dave. Will that get Sarah some shoes?'

Gina was afraid she was going to cry. All she could do was nod, and take the money.

Steve said, 'I'll never hit you again. I swear to God.'

'You said that last time.'

'I mean it this time.'

He tried to touch her arm, but Gina drew away. 'I don't want you back,' she said flatly.

'I'm not asking to come back. Not yet, I mean. I

know I did wrong, and I've got to give you time to get over it.'

'Goodnight, Steve.'

At the front door he said, 'I love you.'

'Yes,' she said wearily. 'Oh, yes.'

He tried to kiss her. Again she dodged.

It'll cost him thirty.

Only when the door was shut and he had walked down the path did she let herself slump into a chair and lean forward with her head in her hands.

Bloody stupid. She couldn't wait to get rid of him, to turn him out of the house, and now . . .

Steve had been the best-looking lad on the estate. Every girl fancied him. When he asked Gina out, she couldn't believe it. And then there came that time when Rita Fairley picked a fight with her in the school toilets because Steve had finished with her to go out with Gina. When Gina told Steve about it, he had gone right up to Rita, in front of everybody, and told her that if she ever touched Gina again he'd smash her face in.

When I told him I was pregnant, she silently recalled, I thought he'd do a runner, smash the place up, something like that. But he just smiled and put his arm round me and said he'd always wanted to be a dad.

So do I still love him, really?

No. I wouldn't have done what I did this evening, if I did.

All right, I loved him once. But he's squashed that out of me.

She hunched even further over, hugging a determination to go ahead and prove she could, after all, look after herself and the kids. She wasn't going to back down now.

3

Gina set her mind on one goal. A hundred and eighty quid, and that would be it. Every time she pulled a trick she took out a crumpled slip of paper from her bag – actually the cosmetics agency form with Carol's order and address ticked off, getting a bit crumpled now – and scribbled twenty or twenty-five pounds in a wobbly column. It didn't add up as quickly as she had hoped. There were still daily running expenses: food for the kids and herself, stockings and a few lurid trimmings for her new occupation, drinks with Carol and the occasional drink to keep Rose sweet. And of course the payments to Anita for the spare bedroom. But gradually she was getting there. Learning to make the right noises, put on the right 'come-on' expression . . .

'You're getting really good.' Carol made it a friendly, admiring compliment. Gina felt absurdly pleased. 'We make a good team, you and me. You can do without giving Anita a rakeoff for her place. We'll organise our own arrangements, right?'

Gina was amazed by the number of men who enjoyed having a twosome around. It was comforting, though. Less risk of something nasty happening if one or the other of you was leaning against the side of a van while the other was being done inside. 'We work together,' became their catch-phrase. 'So it's both of us or neither.' Even with that weird woman. That was something Gina hadn't expected: a smartly dressed woman leaning out of her car and quietly asking 'How much?' And looking even happier at the sight

31

of Carol coming protectively up to the window as well. Fifty quid for the two of them – it was a bonus for her, and for them. All the same, it was the creepiest twenty minutes so far for Gina. She hadn't realised what one woman could demand of another, or how it could somehow be more eccentric than what the men got up to.

But it was business. What they wanted, they got. She was learning.

Then there was Ian. Carol had been approached by Ian in the street, and was quick to make arrangements. A gentleman this time, she assured her partner. Way out of the ordinary, and with his own place in St Paul's Street, way off their usual patch. Only he was a bit awkward, and she couldn't help thinking this was his first time.

Ian frankly admitted to his inexperience. He was a well-built man in his early fifties, and with his slightly affected gestures and voice Gina would not have been surprised to find that he was queer. But once he got going, he really got going. If it was his first time, he certainly intended to make a meal of it. Then when it was over he pulled his trousers on and smiled at her almost apologetically.

'I've never done this sort of thing before.'

'Neither have I.' She supposed this was what he wanted to hear.

He handed her some clean, folded notes. She could feel that there was more here than they had agreed.

He said, 'Can I see you again?' It was like a shy youngster making his first date. Only in this case, a second one. He went on, 'Look, there's a good new pub, down by the canal. Have you been in there?'

'I don't think so.'

'Maybe we could try it.' He opened the door and they went through to the large front room where Carol was studying a bronze statue of two naked boys, flanked by an ornate inlaid table with a Chinese box in the middle.

Ian looked dubiously at her. 'Perhaps if your friend would care to join us—'

'We must be off,' said Carol. She tried to soften the blow by waving her hand at the marble Madonna over the mantelpiece. 'Lovely house you got here. Big, though, isn't it? What do you do?'

'I'm in security.'

For some reason Carol twitched, and said more urgently, 'Right, are you ready, Gina?' She picked up Gina's sample case. 'Got all your deliveries to finish, haven't yer, dear?'

'I could give you a lift if you like,' Ian offered.

Carol took Gina's arm and hurried her outside. As they reached the gate in the late evening sunshine, she said, 'Run!' She set off down the street. Gina, baffled, followed and caught her up.

'What's the rush? He only wanted to have a drink with us. He was quite nice.'

'Never let yourself think things like that. Never get attached to a punter.'

'I thought getting attached was the whole idea.'

Carol laughed raucously. 'You're coming on, girl. But you know what I mean.'

They made their way towards the Lane. Rose was just coming out of the pub as young Tracy, pathetically pale and fragile on the edge of the kerb, leaned out to proposition the driver of a battered Transit. Rose's voice blasted across the Lane. 'Police are out looking for you!'

There was a roar of engine and a squeal of tyres as the van raced off.

'Stupid cow,' Tracy yelled back.

'If I see you on here again, I'll knock seven sorts of shit out of yer. Go play with your Wendy house – go on.'

Carol said to Gina, 'There's another example for you. Dim little kid, hooked on her dreadful Dez.'

'A punter?'

'No. Her pimp. Nasty bit of work, treats her like dirt –

33

and she still wants him to love her. All she gets is kicks and the odd lifter to keep her on a high.'

They went into the pub. Smoke bit at Gina's throat as she headed for a vacant table. And something jabbed in the corner of her eye. She glanced across the room to see that silent, morose man who had sat and stared at her before: a man with greying ginger curls, and eyes that had a disturbing effect on her stomach.

Carol thumped two glasses down on the table. When she had sat down, she nudged Gina's knee under the table and passed a small wad of notes on to her lap.

'What's this?'

'Nice place that Ian feller had, eh? And loads of money.'

'But he paid me while I was there.'

'Extra,' Carol grinned.

Gina counted the money below the table level. It added up to fifty quid. She couldn't believe it. 'Did he give you all this?'

'Oh, yeh, sure. He said "Here y'are, Carol, I want you to have this." Did he hell. I took it out of that little wooden box. If he's stupid enough to stuff his loose change in fancy boxes – well, he's asking for it, isn't he?'

Gina felt dizzy. She had liked the man. It had been one of the easiest sessions she had had so far. He hadn't done anything wrong, and she wouldn't have minded seeing him again. That certainly wouldn't happen now. She didn't want stolen money, not even if it helped her to pay her loan off a bit more quickly.

She shoved the notes back at Carol and stormed off to the ladies'. The head of the man against the far wall turned slowly to watch her.

In the loo she got out the cosmetic agency's receipt on which she had been totting up her earnings, and added the latest figure. Only thirty-five to go, and she would be there.

As she came out, Carol had moved to sit beside

the sandy creep. His attention veered immediately to Gina, and she could see he was asking Carol about her. Carol shrugged doubtfully, but raised an eyebrow in her direction.

Gina shook her head, snatched up her samples case, and marched out.

Only thirty-five quid to go.

A car pulled in to the kerb. The driver, a young chancer in a greasy T-shirt, leered out and jabbed a thumb towards her case.

'What y' selling, love?'

She offered him her best smile. 'Anything you want.'

'How much?'

'Thirty-five.'

'Are you practising to be a comedian, or what?'

'That's the price, mister. Thirty-five or nothing.'

It was going to be nothing. He snorted, and drove off.

Gina was burning with impatience. The thought of being that close to what she needed urged her on. No question of waiting till tomorrow, setting up something else with Carol, making two twenties add up to five quid more than she actually needed. She wanted it now: thirty-five, this evening, and that would be the end of it.

She hurried round to Anita's door and pressed the bell.

Anita looked far from pleased to see her. 'You can't use the place tonight,' she hissed. 'It's Thursday. I've told you, Thursday's not on.'

Gina had completely forgotten. 'Sorry, but can I just leave my case here?'

'Till when?'

'About eleven.'

'Two quid that'll be.' Anita's tone altered abruptly, becoming loftily friendly as there was a heavy footstep at the top of the stairs. 'Thank you, Ginette.' She looked back at the man who was staring suspiciously down. 'It's

35

all right, George. Just my makeup lady, she's brought me some samples to look at.'

Carol was getting impatient. This wispy-haired oddball was proving pretty slow to arouse. It had become almost a challenge. He wouldn't be in this pub on his own, gawping around, if he hadn't come here for the usual purpose. And when she rubbed her stockinged knees together he licked his lips and she could tell that he knew what it was all about. Yet at the same time his attention was wandering, as if he was looking for somebody else, or his courage was failing, or he was just plain disgusted with himself.

If he wanted something, she could provide it. And it was high time she got a few more notes to shove in her bra.

'D'you know, you've got lovely eyes,' she tried. Bloody lies, of course, since he had hardly looked at her. 'Are you here on business, or just visiting?'

Ginger – or maybe she ought to call him Curly, since there was more curl than real ginger at his age – abstractedly took out his wallet, extracted three ten-pound notes, and handed them to her. Carol instinctively took them. Grabbing money was a reflex action after all these years.

'What's this for?'

He was still staring abstractedly across the room. 'Where's your friend gone?'

'How the hell should I know? Look, do you want—'

He was on his feet. 'We'll sort it out another time. I'll see you in here – right?'

'Yes, but . . .'

He drifted towards the door and was gone.

And where the hell had Gina got to? Crazy to feel responsible for an amateur hustler who was soon going to desert you, after all you'd done for her. But they had got on so well together. Carol was surprised at how fond she had become of the girl in such a short time. And now she was getting uneasy. There had been something desperate in

Gina's expression. Quite capable of taking stupid risks and getting herself into a stupid mess.

Carol went out into the drizzle. Typical Bradford evening. Moisture dripping from leaky gutters above, a sheen of water across the lane throwing back smears of street lighting and the occasional swirl of car headlights.

No sign of Gina. And no point in getting wet. Unless somebody useful came along soon she might as well pack it in for the night.

A white car with tinted windows splashed along the kerb and came to a stop beside her. Carol brightened, and was about to go round to the passenger door when the driver began to get out, reaching purposefully for her.

It was Dez Sadiq, Tracy's pimp. He never looked very friendly at the best of times. Tonight he looked foul. 'Right, Carol. A word, right?' It was years since his parents had left the Middle East, and his accent was as Bradford as anybody's, but with a sinister lilt he had cultivated deliberately.

She ran towards the corner, her heels slithering on the damp pavement. Behind her she heard the car accelerate. The full blaze of the headlights washed round her and seemed to pin her to the wall.

Dez was out of the car, seizing her arm and wrenching her into the gaping darkness of an old warehouse that the receivers had been trying to sell off for the last seven years. Carol stumbled again, but Dez caught her with one hand and pushed her hard against a rusty joist. A knife appeared in his other hand, its tip resting against her throat.

'I want you to stop pestering her. Or else.'

'Jesus, I . . .' Carol gagged, not daring to say another word for fear the slightest movement of her throat might open it up around the knife.

'You know who I'm talking about, don't you?'

Carol did not dare to nod.

'Say it.' Dez's voice was at its most mockingly wheedling.

'Go on, Carol, say it. Otherwise I'll shove this in a bit further.'

'Tracy,' she whispered.

'That's right. Who is it you and your friend Rose have got to leave alone? Leave *alone*?'

'Tracy.'

'Got it. Good. Any more taking the mickey, or interfering with her work, and –' the knife jabbed '– you'll be permanently out of work yourself.' Suddenly he shoved her violently away, her arm scraping against the rusty metal. 'And you can tell Rose I'll be having a word with her when it's convenient.'

Carol waited until she heard the car reverse and hiss away through the rain before she scrambled shakily to her feet. All she wanted was to be safely home, warm in bed – alone. But she had to get to Rose and warn her.

As to Gina, they'd have to have a talk tomorrow: settle things one way or the other. Whenever she got back from whatever she'd been doing.

Gina paced impatiently back down the Lane. Somebody had to show up. The persistent drizzle might damp some men's appetites, but it was a mild enough night, and surely there was somebody who couldn't do without it, no matter what the weather?

She thought of dropping in again at the pub and seeing if Carol had any ideas; but one of those ideas might be connected with the creep she had been chatting up, if he was still there, and in spite of her desperation Gina had no stomach for that particular character. He was the type you read about in the papers: scruffy and insignificant, and yet the sort who would . . .

No. She wouldn't let her mind run along those lines. She would find her own punter, make her own decision, fix her own price, and be off this Lane for good tomorrow. Finish tonight. It had to be finished tonight.

Another van cruised along the kerb, and again she quoted the price of thirty-five quid. And again there was an abusive retort, and off went the van.

Come on, come on. Silently she appealed to the evening sky.

A red car passed her and slowed, coming to a halt a few yards ahead. She quickened her step. It looked a whole lot smarter than the van, anyway.

One of the things Carol had warned against was getting into a car with a stranger, on your own. But it was crazy; you wouldn't do much business taking a chaperone along. Some punters had already shown they got a kick out of it, but a lot wouldn't.

The passenger door swung open as she drew level.

She was in a hurry. And with a smart car like this, she could be dealing with someone who would pay off that final instalment all at one go.

Whatever he wanted, she'd go along with it for that money.

It would all be over within the next half-hour.

There was a blob of what might be damp cornflake on his sagging moustache.

'Mr Dixon?'

'That's right.'

Newall showed his warrant card. 'Detective Chief Inspector Newall. And this is Detective Sergeant Kershaw.' He raised an eyebrow at her. 'Perhaps you can look after the little girl for a few minutes, sergeant. Is there somewhere we can go, Mr Dixon?'

'Go? Why, what's wrong? Is it . . .' He released the girl, sensing fear and not wanting to pass it on to her. 'Run along with the lady, Sarah. Won't be a tick.' Then he led the way into a sitting-room cluttered with children's toys. 'It's not Gina?'

'I'm afraid so.'

There was no way of breaking the news gently. And Newall had never been very good at the softly-softly approach. He told Dixon what they had found up on the moor, watching his reactions all the time. He didn't look the type to murder his wife. But few of them ever did. The way he kept saying, 'No, no, that's not possible,' sounded convincing enough. As did the story, which Newall had to extract from him piecemeal between a sudden outburst of trembling and an even more convulsive shaking of the head in hysterical denial, that he had been here all night. Worried stiff about Gina. He had been babysitting while she did her rounds, but he hadn't been expecting her to be out so late. Or so early, or whatever. And no, he hadn't rung the police.

Why not?

She had these rounds of visits as a makeup saleswoman, and he didn't know whether she might have caught up with some friends, and she'd have been upset if he had stirred up unnecessary trouble.

Newall tried to assess this. Husband and wife separated, wife out till all hours, maybe a regular boyfriend somewhere. Enough to make the discarded husband jealous? Jealous enough to commit murder – out and back while the kids were still asleep?

Steve Dixon suddenly let out a great, shuddering groan. 'But who'd ever want to kill Gina?' He began crying in stomach-racking sobs, making thrusting movements with his hands as if to push the whole insane idea away.

And that of course was the question. Who on earth would want to murder a part-time cosmetics saleswoman? Unless, maybe, while this dim bloke let himself be used as babysitter in spite of them breaking up, she was selling something other than cosmetics. Not a bad cover for drug-pushing. Yet somehow it didn't ring true.

Newall could tell he would get no more out of Dixon right now. His end of the story did seem sound enough so far as it went. He tried the sort of soothing noises Kershaw was so good at. Was there anybody they could ring, to come round and help out with the kids and talk to him? Sergeant Kershaw would stay for a reasonable time and would take a statement if he was up to it; but it would be better to have a relative in pretty soon. Wife's mother, yes, that sounded a good idea.

And while Kershaw was on the premises she could pick up any vibes that might prove significant in the long run.

Newall set off for his next call, at an address he knew all too well.

There were two lads at the front door as he arrived. One of them spotted the car arriving and legged it down the street. The other was too slow. As Newall's hand fell on his shoulder he had just finished writing WHORE across the glass with a red felt-tipped pen.

'Right,' said Newall. 'Now you can start cleaning that off.'

'What with?'

'Your snot-rag. Or your tongue. But get busy.'

Rather than interrupt the brat by bringing Carol to the

door, he prowled along the side of the house. He could hear a faint thump from the kitchen and the slam of a cupboard door. She was in, all right. Still he hesitated. Why the hell had he chosen to come back to this dump? After he had been made up to DCI he had been given several choices. Why accept this one if he truly felt such contempt for her way of life, and for his own obsession? Must be something twisted, something psychological about it. They had done several lectures on criminal psychology at Police College, but they hadn't covered the kinks of CID officers.

He forced himself to walk round the corner to the open kitchen door.

Carol was bending over her washing machine, inspecting each sheet and pillowslip as she loaded it in. Finding a stain on a towel, she reached for a small cleansing stick and rubbed it fiercely in before letting the towel go in with the rest. She could have been any fussy middle-class housewife with a fetish for cleanliness. Only Carol Johnson was not your typical middle-class housewife.

Newall eyed her long brown legs as she stooped to close the door of the machine. It was no good. He still felt the same about her.

He tried to keep it light. 'So how's Carol these days?'

She started, swore, and then propped herself against the machine. 'Well, look who it is.' There was no way of telling whether she was pleased to see him, or apprehensive.

'Keeping busy?' he said.

'A girl's got her fines to pay.'

Well, that was the way of life she had chosen. No use expecting sympathy. Already she was studying him with a slight tilt of her head like an inquisitive bird, sizing him up, wondering if he had come here for another free screw after all this time, and maybe with something worthwhile to offer her in exchange – like those handcuffs she probably still had.

He was going to disillusion her on that point. He reached

into his pocket and held out the photograph of Gina he had acquired from the dazed Steve Dixon. 'Know her?'

Carol took the photograph. Newall had a hunch that she had known who it would be before he even handed it over. She was playing for time. At last she said, 'Yeh. On the morning news. She's the poor girl that got murdered last night, isn't she?'

'That's all you know about her?'

'What else?'

'Thought you might have something helpful to offer.'

'Never met her. Not in our line of business.'

'No, I don't suppose she was.' Newall kept her waiting for a few moments, then took the photograph back and replaced it with the makeup order form. 'What you got to say about this, though?'

Carol moistened her lips. 'Of course. That's who it was. Y'know, I did think, that picture . . . and then I thought no, it couldn't be. I mean, who'd want to kill a makeup lady?'

'We intend to find out. And her line was just makeup, was it?'

'What else?' asked Carol again.

'Cover for drug handling, maybe?'

'No!' It came out in a surprising explosion. 'She wasn't that sort at all.'

'You sound mighty sure of it, considering you hardly knew her.'

'Just wasn't that sort. You can always tell. And I'm telling you she wasn't.'

'This makeup round of hers would be a damn good cover.'

'She was flogging makeup to pay off a loan shark. That I do know. Look, I only met her 'cos her little girl goes to the same school as my Emma. Took pity on her, you might say.'

'Always did have a soft spot for the downtrodden, hey?'

As he turned towards the back door, Carol said, 'What

46

would you know about the downtrodden? Climbing up a sight too fast for that, I'd say. In charge of a murder investigation now. I wonder what next?'

They stared at each other almost hungrily. She knew he'd be back. And he knew there would be plenty of excuses he could dream up for coming back.

A car passed the open door of the pub and steered in close to the pavement. Tracy stepped towards it, stooping to see who was inside and what the deal might be. Abruptly Rose's hand was on her shoulder, dragging her away and propelling her down the Lane.

'Gerroff me,' Tracy squealed. 'What d'ya think y'doing?'

'Do you want to end up dead – like Gina?'

Between them, Carol and Rose forced the girl into the pub.

Jan, the barmaid, was eager to greet them. 'Coppers have been in and out, asking about her that got murdered.'

'What did you say?'

'Never clapped eyes on her.'

By the time Carol and Rose had bought drinks, Tracy was sitting at a table with Anita, who was murmuring how awful it all was: poor Gina, what sort of maniac was on the loose? It just showed you that going off alone in the night and getting into cars on your own was simply asking for it. 'Now, if she'd only stuck to using my place, it would never have happened.' And now of course there was a vacancy in that spare room of hers. Room for anyone else who had the sense to choose a safe, comfortable place. 'Two-fifty for half an hour,' Anita coaxed. 'From Monday to—'

'Bloody hell.' Rose reached the table. 'When did that go up? It used to be two quid.'

'Listen, I've got all the sheets and towels to wash. And there's the wear and tear on my bed.' Anita concentrated on Tracy. 'Anyway, you can take it or leave it, that's what I'm charging. I have to make it worth my while, I'm not running a frigging charity.'

Tracy's lower lip pouted. 'Dez won't buy that.'

'So don't tell him,' said Rose. 'Just put your prices up.'

Carol glanced warningly at her. One encounter with Dez had been enough for her. Even Rose, bossy as she was, ought not to risk it. But Rose was going on: 'Ten quid for a hand job, twenty for a straight jump, anything else is extra. Make it up as you go along.'

Anita had no wish to be distracted by such coarseness. 'You'll be *safer* in my place,' she emphasised. 'It's warm and clean.'

'You're selling yourself short,' Rose persevered. 'Going with 'em for four or five quid, it's degrading. And you're doing the rest of us down.'

'And there's not much call for stiffs on the Lane,' said Carol, 'they can take a shovel to the cemetery for free.'

Anita wrinkled her nose in distaste.

Tracy said, 'That Gina – I only saw her the once, was she really hustling?'

'Doing it just a week or two, that's all.' Carol took a sip of her drink. 'But the coppers think she were straight.'

'And that's the way we want to keep it,' said Rose. ''Cos if they thought she was on the game, they wouldn't be nearly so concerned.'

'If she'd gone on using my place –' once Anita had found herself a theme, she did tend to harp on it '– it'd never have happened.' Suddenly she spluttered over her drink, and clapped a hand to her mouth. 'Oh, shite.'

'What is it now?'

'Her case. That samples case of hers. I'd clean forgotten.'

'Forgotten what?'

'She left it with me. Just before she went out and . . . when she went off on her own and . . . Look, I've still got her bloody case. She was supposed to be coming back for it. What am I going to do with it?'

'Dump it,' said Rose tersely.

'But how—'

'If you hand it in they'll work out Gina was hustling, and that'll be that. What's one dead prostitute? Let them think she's straight, and they'll be all out to get him. They'll have to.'

'They'll find out,' Anita whimpered.

'Not from us they won't.' Rose glared across the table. 'We've got to stick together on this, d'you hear? Haven't we, Carol?'

Carol was deep in thought. 'I did try to put her off. At the start. Honest I did. And I did tell her, must have told her fifty times, about working in cars. Oh, Christ – what's going to happen to her kids?'

Anita seemed just as preoccupied. 'What am I gonna do with that bag?'

Carol dragged herself back to reality. 'Oh, forget the bleeding bag.'

'All right, come on.' Rose had her arm round Carol's shoulders. 'Let's just keep calm and we'll sort this out.'

Carol was staring ahead again. Croakily she said, 'I bet I know who it is.'

'What?'

'Who killed her. I bet I know who did it.'

5

Whatever their money problems, they had managed to provide a hearse and two men in the regulation mourning garb. There was no procession of funeral cars, though; only a battered van with a disgruntled-looking man in the driver's seat and the victim's mother beside him. DCI Newall stood discreetly to one side of the crematorium gates as the coffin was unloaded on to a trolley and Joyce Webster got out of the van, smoothing the creases in her old black dress. From where he stood, Newall could see that there had all along been someone else in the cab, between her and that scruffy fancy man of hers. It was Sarah, the middle one of the Dixon kids. She was making no move to follow, but staying in the van with Bob Clayton. The older one was presumably at school, and some neighbour must be looking after the baby.

For a moment he thought Steve Dixon was not going to show. He hadn't cleared off, had he? Then the panic was over. Steve was approaching along the path from behind the chapel, his head down, as if he had been there quite some time and was still brooding.

He tried to take his mother-in-law's arm, but she shook him off and walked shakily towards the vicar waiting in the chapel doorway. Was she blaming Steve for something – having the same nagging doubts about him that Newall was experiencing?

Newall had already collected as much information as he could about the whole family. There was nothing out of the ordinary. You had only to look at Joyce Webster to see that she had always been the worker. The last two years of her husband's life had been spent in a debilitating illness; and he had never been much of a provider anyway. She had got a job in George Ferguson's office-cleaning business, and still kept it, largely to support that layabout Bob Clayton. The job couldn't have been much fun. Ferguson was notoriously a bastard to work for. Newall was surprised that he had even allowed her time off to come to the funeral; and he must have made her suffer every time she wanted to beg an adjustment in hours so that she could babysit with her grandchildren. And that wasn't going to get any better, now their mother was dead.

Joyce and Steve sat at the front of the chapel, in the same pew but far apart. There was one other mourner, a neighbour of Gina's. Newall sat well back, concentrating not on the service but on the back of Steve Dixon's neck.

Could he have murdered his wife? And if he wasn't the one, then who the hell else would have had any motive? Some pervert, maybe: there were plenty of them about. But the pathological killers usually picked on a different sort of woman. You didn't take a makeup lady up on to the moors and strangle her. In the first place, how did you get her into the car?

'We are gathered here for two reasons today,' the vicar was intoning. He was an earnest young man with a deeply friendly tone of voice which he had spent many hours cultivating. 'Firstly to say goodbye to Gina, and secondly to thank God for her life. Gina was blessed with a good family. Her mother Joyce, who gave birth to her, loved and nurtured her. And her devoted husband Steve, with whom she chose to share the last seven years of her life . . .'

She would only have got in a car with someone she knew. Had Steve arranged to pick her up and drive her home; but then taken her up on the moor? Or killed her in the town and then taken the body up to dump it?

An examination of that secondhand banger of his wouldn't be a bad idea.

'But the Lord said "Blessed are those that mourn, for they shall be comforted." So when we think about Gina, let it hurt, because in that hurt we remember her love, her touch, her warmth. She is alive in our hearts. So can we now close our eyes and bring Gina back before we say our last goodbye.'

Steve Dixon's shoulders were shaking uncontrollably. That didn't mean he was innocent. Remorseful killers often shivered and shook and expressed disbelief in what they themselves had done.

Yet Newall still couldn't buy the idea, even though it was the only one that came anywhere near making sense.

The curtains parted, a tape of an organ played, the coffin slid through, and the curtains closed again.

Newall was out of the chapel, waiting, as the other three came out. Joyce glared at him, resenting the intrusion; but Steve simply blinked, wiped his reddened eyes, and waited dumbly, almost as if expecting to be arrested.

Newall put it bluntly: 'I'm making a public appeal for witnesses at a press conference. And it'll go out on the early evening news. I think you ought to add your own bit. It always goes down well.'

It sounded callous, but he didn't care. One way or the other it might shake Steve into some sort of response.

In the end the television appeal went off better than he might have hoped. Steve Dixon was trembling as Newall spoke crisply at the camera; but the DCI's words really did seem to get through to him.

'We're doing house-to-house inquiries in the area we believe she was working on the night she was murdered. Any information which members of the public can provide will be welcome. No matter how trivial you may think it, please don't hesitate to bring it up. But –' he leaned forward and spoke more aggressively, to grab the attention of anyone and everyone watching '– we're particularly anxious to locate a blue soft zip-round bag containing makeup samples. We know she left home with it. We want to know where it is now.'

They left a dramatic pause before the camera swung towards his companion. For a moment Newall thought Steve wasn't going to be able to get the words out. Then they came, hoarse and unsteady. 'If anybody did see her, or think they saw her, then please . . .' His voice cracked. The trembling began again. 'Please tell the police, so that . . . so that we can get him. She had long dark hair, she was wearing a blue and white dress and a jacket . . .' He faltered, either forgetting the colour of the jacket or stricken by a sudden picture of Gina in his mind. 'She was delivering her orders,' he went on in a sudden rush, 'so she must have knocked at somebody's door. I just can't understand how this could have . . . I mean, she never did anything wrong, kept herself to herself, never bothered anybody, hardly ever went out except for that round of hers, and . . . *please* help us, somebody.' His eyes and his voice were full of tears as he turned helplessly to Newall. 'I'm sorry, I can't . . .'

Carol and Rose were on their second drink when Tracy edged uncertainly across to join them. It was as if she were trying to pluck up the courage to wheedle her way into their good graces. That would mean shaking Dez off. Carol wasn't sure she cared to risk being a part of that.

Jan followed her from the bar and plonked a half of lager in front of Carol. 'Present for you.' She jerked her head towards the bench against the far wall.

Carol gulped. It was Curly, the weirdo. The one whose eyes had kept following Gina. And maybe not just his eyes. He had got up and left right after Gina left.

Yet he had given Carol thirty quid. For nothing. That wasn't normal, was it? And he'd got eyes like a shit-house rat, she thought. Even when he was talking to her, he had never really stopped looking at Gina.

She began to get up.

'Where you goin'?' asked Rose.

'To talk to him.'

'You're mad.'

Carol reached for her glass of lager and took it with her across the bar. Curly made a space for her beside him, grinning – a sly, distant sort of grin as if pleased that things were at last working out.

She said, 'You're back, then.'

'Yes.'

'That's nice. Work round here, do you?'

'Sort of.'

'What do you do?'

'Frozen chickens.'

'That's nice.'

For a moment her attention was distracted. Dez had just come into the bar. His already dark face further darkened by anger, he pushed his way through a cluster of drinkers and leaned over the table, thrusting his face into Tracy's. 'I've been looking for you.'

'She's having a drink,' said Rose, loudly enough to turn people's heads and stifle any other conversation.

'Shut yer face, bitch.' Dez stood up very slowly. 'Finish it. Quick. I'll be waiting outside.'

He went out without looking back.

'He'll kill me now.' Tracy gulped down the remains of her lager shandy. 'I shouldn't be in here with you lot.'

'Worried we might tell you a thing or two, is he?'

'He doesn't like me going into pubs. I'm under age.'

Rose gasped. 'You should be on the stage, you. You're a right comedian.'

'He cares about me.'

This time Rose howled with outright laughter. 'He cares about the money you can rake in, you soft bitch.'

Carol became aware that Curly was repeating something, plucking at her attention.

'So how much this time?'

Wondering what she had missed, Carol said, 'Y'what?'

'Money. How much do you want?'

No hint of what he wanted for his cash. 'Are you rich?'

'Yes.'

'A lot, then.'

Only what the hell was he really after? She didn't like to guess at what sort of thing he needed to turn him on. He'd have a pricey car, of course. Might be waiting round the corner right now, just the way it might have been waiting . . .

Tracy squeezed past on her way to the door.

Curly's gaze followed her. 'A friend of yours?'

'None of your business. What if she is, anyway?'

'No reason,' said Curly in that creepy, insinuating little voice. 'I'm just asking.'

He reached for his glass, and she saw that there was a fine network of scratches surrounding a large scab on the back of his hand. How had he managed to get such a wound, and a pretty fresh one at that?

Catching her glance, he pulled his sleeve down to cover the mark.

'Her ponce is outside,' said Carol. 'He looks after her. Watches her all the time.' She hoped that Curly might assume they were all of them, always, a watchful lot.

He said quietly, 'How about a hundred quid?'

He was bad. She could smell him. He made her skin crawl, and those scratches on his hand grew more and more meaningful in her head although she could no longer see them.

'Thanks for the drink,' she managed to say. 'I'd better go back and have a chat with me friend.'

She had half expected him to protest; but he nodded complacently and sat there finishing his drink. After a couple of minutes he got up, smiled through the haze of

56

smoke at her, and left. She gave him plenty of time to get clear, and then headed for home.

On the corner of the alleyway along the backs of the houses, a dark figure emerged from the shadows.

'Jesus!' Carol groped for support, but there was none.

'Did I frighten you?' said Curly with gentle amusement.

'What do you want?'

'A hundred and fifty?' he offered.

Carol stumbled past him, fumbling for the key of her front door.

'Piss off or I'll scream.'

He stayed where he was, calling after her, 'A hundred and seventy-five.'

Her steps faltered. She turned and looked back. He was making no threatening move towards her.

'We could drive somewhere,' he suggested.

That sent an ice-cold tingle over her shoulders and down her spine. She shook her head, and went towards the house. She had to get in and put the chain on the door before he could reach her.

'Two hundred,' he said.

She couldn't believe her ears.

'Quid?'

'Quid,' he said amiably.

Some yards behind him, on the far side of the road, was a car which she supposed was his. He must have found her address somewhere, or followed her before, without her knowing . . . or seen it on that flaming order form of Gina's when he . . .

'I'm not getting in no car,' she said firmly.

But all the same, if it was somewhere safe, if they weren't going up to the moor or on to some waste ground, then – well, two hundred quid! And on top of that, there was what she might learn that would enable her to steer Newall in his direction.

* * *

She was up early, got Emma off to school on time, and set about filling the washing machine. Then there was the bathroom to be scrubbed clean, and a stain on the stairs that she worked away at but still couldn't remove. She was just thinking of having something to eat when there came an insistent hammering on the back door.

Anita stood outside, breathlessly brimming over with good tidings. 'Guess what? I've got you a punter.'

It was the first time Anita had ever exerted herself in this way. Carol looked at her suspiciously. Why was she so eager to make an impression?

'And George is paying,' said Anita.

The idea of George Ferguson paying for anything was just as new as Anita's voluntary pimping. Then it came out. George had fingers in so many pies, and this particular pie was beginning to give off an appetising smell. He was after a new contract, and he happened to know a certain councillor who wanted certain pleasures but was far too nervous to go looking for them of his own accord. George would fix it, and pay for it.

'And what exactly does George get in return?' asked Carol.

'You don't really need to know that, do you?'

'I suppose not. When's the date, anyway?'

'Two o'clock this afternoon.'

'Forty minutes? Christ, you don't give much warning, do you?'

'Never knew you had a long waiting list.'

'All right, all right.'

'I'll nip out the back, then. Give you time to get ready. But you won't mind if I . . . well, hang around?'

Carol went back indoors. She put the hustling sheet over the bed, had a quick look round the bathroom – for her own satisfaction, not for that of anyone who thought he'd be allowed in there – and wondered what she needed to be prepared for.

Her client proved to be a plump little man with flabby white hands and an unconvincingly sociable smile. He held out an identification card as if this would somehow make everything respectable, and set a large briefcase down on the step.

'Good afternoon. Councillor Baker. I'm canvassing this area this afternoon to try and find out what people think about the new Leisure Centre that's being built at the top of Winsford Lane. You've seen it, haven't you?'

'Why don't you come in?'

'That's very kind.'

Carol tried not to snigger at the charade. She had known plenty of awkward introductions and pretences before, but this was quite a new one.

'I'm wondering what sort of facilities you were hoping for from the Centre?'

Surely not what *he* had in mind, she thought. Straight-faced, she said briskly, 'Why don't we go straight upstairs?'

'That's very kind of you indeed.' Baker stumbled on the lower step, clutched his briefcase, and went chuntering on as he climbed the rest of the flight. 'There's a swimming pool with steam room and sauna off, and we're working on two badminton courts and a fully equipped gymnasium.'

'Swinging from the ropes?' said Carol. 'Could be fun.'

Baker paused in the bedroom doorway, then went in and opened his briefcase. 'I . . . I've brought my things.'

His things consisted of a schoolboy cap and short trousers. Now that she got the picture, Carol left him to get into them while she hurried downstairs to collect a large wooden baking spoon and a length of bamboo, relic of a time when she had vowed that she would grow runner beans in the patch of back garden, knowing she would never really have the time or the inclination to persevere.

Baker was sitting on the edge of the bed, going pink in the face and down his pimply chest. He stared at her with a mixture of hope and fear.

'Matron,' he whispered in awestruck adoration, and turned over on his face with his bottom high in the air.

Carol yawned, set herself at the left-hand corner of the bed, and thwacked the large spoon down as hard as she could manage. Baker moaned gratefully. She let fly again, then set up a faster rhythm. The effort was exhausting her more than him.

After a few minutes she said: 'You've been a very naughty boy, haven't you?'

'Yes. I'm sorry, matron.'

'Not nearly sorry enough. I think you deserve much more severe punishment, don't you?'

'Oh, yes, matron. Yes, I do.'

'Then we ought to get a bit closer. A lot closer.'

Carol went to the window to make sure it was tightly shut. When she came back he was writhing in anticipation. She got her hand into the waistband of his short trousers and dragged them down. Reaching for the bamboo, she slashed a bright red weal across his quivering cheeks. He squealed; but didn't try to escape. And the next time she made the bamboo whistle as it descended, and to herself she was saying in a savage rhythm: *This one's for Gina . . . and this one . . .*

Until at last his screams became panic-stricken, and he was heaving himself towards the edge of the bed and on to the floor. He was panting and scarlet in the face as he straightened up – and scarlet in other places, too. She turned away as he packed his briefcase and limped his way painfully downstairs.

Carol took an armful of washing out of the machine and went into the garden to hang it up.

Anita was waiting on the corner of the path. 'You could hear the noise out here,' she said admiringly as she took some notes from her purse. 'Right, here's George's money. Fifteen quid all right?'

'Twenty.'

'Look, I brought him to you. I ought to get something.'

There was a lingering trace of a Scottish whine in Anita's plaintive voice.

'Ask George. He's getting his contract, isn't he?' Carol clipped on the last peg, and gestured her back indoors. 'Come on, we'll talk about it over a drink.'

'Well, no. I've got to be off.'

'What's the rush? It's not Thursday.'

'No, but . . . I've got a couple of things George wanted me to get. And a bit of shopping. Like to keep the place nice for him, you know.'

'Of course. Looking after all his comforts. And his friends' comforts as well.'

Carol settled down for a smoke before she needed to go and fetch Emma. It was unlike Anita to refuse a free drink. All the days of the week when George wasn't there she was never far from a bottle. Even when he was there, Carol suspected they got through more than a bottle between them. Perhaps the place had run dry on his last visit, and she was in a hurry to replenish her stocks.

The outer office of the police station had two posters with large photographs of Gina Dixon. There was another one lying on DCI Newall's desk. He kept looking at that face, trying to read something into it, and turning over a dozen repetitive questions in his mind. There had to be a lead somewhere. A lead to someone.

His phone rang. The desk sergeant said, 'A Miss Braithwaite asking for you, sir. Miss Anita Braithwaite.'

'What does she want?'

'She won't give me any details, sir. Says it has to be you that she talks to.'

'Come on, sergeant, you can do better than that. I'm not going to waste my time on any old crackpot who wanders in off the street.'

'Just a minute, sir.' There was a muttering at the other end, and then, 'She won't tell me anything, sir. Not a word. Says it has to be you, because it was you she saw on the telly.'

Newall froze. Then he said, 'Put her in one of the interview rooms. I'll be right down.'

When he saw the rather blowzy woman seated uncomfortably on one side of the table, looking so awkward that you immediately doubted you could believe a word she said, his early surge of hope drained away again. But only for a moment.

'It's about that bag,' she said. 'The one you asked about on the news.'

'You know where it is?'

'Well, it wasn't really anything to do with me, just doing a favour, and I don't want to be dragged into this—'

'You know where Gina Dixon's bag of makeup samples is?'

She reached down beside the chair, and put the blue bag on the table.

Newall stared greedily at it.

'But it's nothing to do with me, honest. I was just minding it for a friend. A friend of a friend, that is.'

'Which friend?'

'Just a friend. Nothing special about it. I completely forgot I'd got it until I saw you on the telly. And then,' said Miss Braithwaite imploringly, 'I thought, God, yes, that could be that bag I've got in my cupboard.'

'So this friend—'

'Which friend?'

'The one you've just said you were minding it for.' Newall was on his feet, pacing up and down. There was no way he could sit still. But he thrust a photograph on to the table under Anita Braithwaite's nose. 'And this *friend* of a friend,' he said heavily, 'was it her?'

'No, I don't think . . . I mean no, it couldn't have been her.'

'But although you've said it was a friend, you can't remember who it really was?'

'Look, it's got nothing to do with me. I wish I'd never brought the thing in now.'

Newall felt that he virtually had her throat between his fingers. A little squeeze, then another, and he would hear it all come gasping out of her. He leaned on the table. 'You wouldn't lie to us, would you, Anita? Because that would be really silly. That would be obstructing the police in the line of their inquiries, as well as withholding evidence.'

She was on the brink of tears. 'It's got nothing to do with me,' she wailed again. 'I don't even know why I'm here. I was just trying to be a helpful citizen, that's all.'

No, that was not all. She was scared stiff about something. Newall at last allowed himself to sit down. Time to offer her a cigarette and send for a cup of tea. It would be only a matter of minutes now before he got the full story.

6

They stood on the arc of the footbridge curving above the traffic in a graceful sweep towards the hotel entrance. Rose leaned on the railing, contemplating the distant figure of the doorman as he came out to greet the occupants of a BMW arriving under the awning.

'I've been slung out of there more times than I've shaved me legs.'

Carol looked longingly at the man in a dinner jacket getting out of the car and waiting for his wife, whose earrings and pearls threw back almost as much light as the mirrors of the entrance hall. That was the way it was going to be for her one fine day, Carol swore to herself: out there with a frock on, a few diamonds in the right places, and the rest of it. And they would be opening doors for her and all. One day.

She said, 'You're sure this Tommy's gonna be there?'

'Of course he is. It's his job, isn't it?' Rose glanced at her under the sour yellow lights. 'Look, you sure you want to go through with this?'

'Sure I'm sure. Otherwise we'll never find out what happened to Gina, will we?'

'So long as it doesn't happen to you.'

'That's what *you're* here for.'

They made their way over the bridge and along the side of the hotel. No way were they going to risk the front door and the knowing gaze of that doorman. Tommy was waiting for them at the fire exit door. He gave Rose a nervous little smile. Carol compared the two of them and tried to visualise Tommy at it with Rose. Must have looked pretty funny: Rose big and brawny, Tommy a skinny little thirty-year-old with hardly an ounce of meat on him. Tracy was more his size. And he was already looking nervously, admiringly at Tracy.

'Come on,' growled Carol. 'Let's get in.'

He closed the door behind them and slunk along to a brighter stretch of corridor, squinting up to check on the security video camera. When he was sure it was pointing well away, he jerked his thumb for them to get down on their hands and knees, and keep tight up against the right-hand wall. Tracy hesitated. He gave her a shy, encouraging grin, and put his hand on her arm to keep her where she was for a moment. He might be a jumpy little twit, but he was coming up to scratch on the arrangements and the timing. The other two set off.

Once they had reached the main corridor, with the wide entrance to the cocktail bar inviting them to the far end, they stood up and did their best to saunter nonchalantly towards it.

Carol had chosen a longer skirt than she usually wore in the evenings, and a jumper that had seen respectable service at parents' meetings and a Christmas concert. Her shoes were practical and unobtrusive. Rose had done her best, but was still indefinably out of place here. Carol moved a few yards away from her, then wished she hadn't. A man at the bar, all too obviously a salesman on his own and hungry for something tastier than his expense account dinner, had sized Rose up and was drifting towards her. In a moment he was buying her a drink, and Rose was simpering at him. Rose simpering was not a pretty sight. And anyway, she had no right to let her attention be distracted right now, when they ought all to be on the alert for Curly.

Carol reached into a bowl of nuts, trying to appear cool and bored while she looked round the room.

There was no sign of him. It was the right hotel, wasn't it? The Norfolk Gardens he had said. She couldn't have got that wrong, when it was so crucial. It had to be the right place. She sauntered towards a table from which a waiter was scooping up empty glasses but leaving a newspaper where it was. The folded page showed that picture of Gina which had been everywhere these last few days, under a headline:

POLICE SEEK VITAL EVIDENCE IN BRADFORD
MOTHER-OF-THREE KILLING

The police weren't the only ones. Carol wondered how suicidally close she might be getting.

Somebody was standing beside her, looking down at the headline and then at her. It was Curly, carrying a smart black briefcase.

'Christ!' Carol gasped. 'Do you make a habit of creeping up on people like that?'

'I didn't think you'd come.'

'Why not?'

'I don't know. Just didn't think you would.'

He was looking at her with growing appetite. He was pretty unappetising himself, though. Close to, in this clear lighting which managed to be soft without missing a spot or a wrinkle, she could see the faint greasiness of his skin and the pinkness of his eyes. She glanced round for support. Rose, blasted bloody Rose, wasn't even looking: too busy playing up to the salesman.

Carol tried to sound matter-of-fact, in control. 'What room are we in?'

'Three hundred and two, on the third floor.'

'Have you got the money?'

'Yes.'

'Right, then. I'm off to the toilet. Won't be a sec.'

'Can I get you a drink?'

67

'Get us a bottle.'

Passing Rose, she cleared her throat noisily; but Rose was still burbling away and looking deep into the salesman's eyes. Carol seethed with rage. She had promised the silly cow thirty quid for this evening's effort, and there she was doing business. Carol stormed on into the ladies' room, to find Tracy waiting impatiently by the end washbasin.

'He's here.'

Tracy held up a master key. 'Tommy says it opens every door.'

'Good girl. I'll see you right. Anyway, it's room three hundred and two. And see what you can do about Rose. I'll bloody kill her if—'

The door opened and Rose came in, beaming. 'Saw you come through. Tell you what – I've got me lucky knickers on tonight.'

'Tough shit,' snapped Carol. 'We've got a job to do.'

'I'm having him when we've finished this. I've told him I'll see him later.'

'You let me down and you're dead.'

'Not me, love,' said Rose pointedly.

Carol did not trust herself to answer that one. She was scared enough as it was, but she was going to go through with it. She turned to Tracy.

'Where are you gonna be?'

'Three hundred and one, or three hundred and three, whichever's empty.'

'What if they've got people in 'em?'

'Then we'll hang around outside the door if we have to.'

'Make sure you do. One scream and you're Cagney and Lacey, right?'

'Trust us,' said Rose.

Carol glared. 'I mean it. One yell, and I want that door down.' She stared at herself in the long glass above the washbasins. 'I must need me head testing.'

'Listen –' Rose was quick to seize the opportunity '– if you want to back out then just say, 'cos I've got that punter out there panting.'

'No. We're going to settle this. Get going.'

When they had gone, she washed her hands with one of the coloured soaps in a basket by the basins. She could not resist trying another one. Then she shovelled four into her handbag, applied lipstick lavishly, and braced herself to go and meet Curly.

There was a telephone in an alcove near the ladies'. On impulse she groped into her bag for some change, and rang home. It took Julie a long time to answer: probably she and Emma were sunk in front of the television with the volume full blast. When at last she got through she said all the things she had already said before leaving, about Emma's medicine and not letting her stay up too late, and making sure she cleaned her teeth – and then asked for Emma to be put on. What would it be like for Emma if she was left, like Gina's kids, without a mother? These might be the last few words they would ever exchange.

'Hello,' came Emma's little piping voice. 'Are you at work?'

Across the hall Carol saw Tracy pressing the button for the lift, with Rose behind her. Thank God for that. 'Yes,' she said. 'You being a good girl for Julie?'

'Mm.'

'I'll have to go now, because me boss is watching me. Blow me a kiss.'

There was a faint puffing noise. 'Did you get it?'

'See you in the morning.' Carol prayed that this would come true.

Curly was waiting for her, impatiently tapping his brief-case with one finger. 'Are we right?'

They walked towards the lift, but at the last moment Carol had a hideous vision of what might happen when the doors closed and they stopped between floors. Crazy idea; but then, the whole thing was crazy right from the start.

'I'm not going in no lift. I'm claustrophobic.'

The room was on the third floor, as Curly had said. They were both panting as they reached it up the wide carpeted stairs: three floors, but long, extra high flights. The thick carpeting made their footsteps almost inaudible. The only sound was the faint creaking of Curly's briefcase. He gave her a sidelong smile as he held the key out to her, as if he were doing her a great favour in allowing her to open the door.

Once they were inside and the door was locked behind them . . .

Carol's hand was trembling so badly that she could not get the key in. 'It won't go in.' It was a reprieve, a stay of execution.

'Give it to me.' He leaned over her, his breath warm and spluttery from the climb. 'You've got to be *gentle* with it.' He turned the key and stood back to let her pass.

Inside there was a Do Not Disturb sign. Curly took it slowly and deliberately to hang on the outer knob, closed the door, and pressed the button of the inner knob to lock it.

Carol stood by the bed, trying to keep her breathing steady. He kept smiling at her, at the same time handing her a brown pay packet. Carol opened it and expertly counted the money. It was the exact two hundred all right.

'Must be plenty of money in chickens,' she said. 'How many did you have to stuff to get this?'

'I don't stuff chickens.' The slack smile did not falter. 'I kill them.'

She desperately made conversation. 'I've seen them little plastic packages with all their insides in, stuffed up their arse.'

'I have women that do that for me. I just cut their throats and take the money.' Curly put his briefcase on the bed and looked around. 'It's not a bad room, this.'

Carol had got her money. All she wanted now was to be safely out of here. She began pulling her jumper off. 'Right then, shall we get on with it?' She threw the jumper over his briefcase.

'What are you doing?'

'What's it look like?'

'Put it back on.'

She thought she could guess now what he was after. She moved closer and touched his arm. 'I get it. *You* want to take them off.'

'No.' He pushed her away, looking genuinely indignant.

'Well, what *do* you want, then?'

He picked up her jumper and threw it at her. 'I know your sort.'

'I were just trying to get you going.'

'I don't like that sort of thing.'

She was baffled. 'What have you brought me here for, then?'

'That's why you girls get into trouble, that sort of thing.'

'What you on about?'

He was sitting in the room's only armchair, reaching for the briefcase. 'That's why things happen to you,' he said in a sad monotone, 'and you end up getting hurt. You have to be careful.' He opened the briefcase and took out a pair of Marigold rubber gloves. 'I could hurt you.'

She began to back away towards the door as he pulled the gloves on, squeaking each finger carefully into them. Then he took out a black nylon stocking and smiled and went on smiling with growing anticipation.

Carol reached the door and groped behind her to turn the knob. It wouldn't move. In the middle of it there had to be that button, but she couldn't feel it, and if she turned to face the door and tackle it, there was no telling what would happen behind her. She let out a sob of despair, and summoned up all her strength to

71

produce a scream that would bring Rose and Tracy to
the rescue.

Rose had pressed the button for the third floor, with Tracy
clutching the master key. They had allowed themselves
plenty of time. Tracy was not even sure there was reason
for panic. It was such a posh hotel, you couldn't really
believe anything awful would happen in it. Lovely smell
off the carpets, and from the vases of flowers at every
corner of the corridors. She wouldn't mind living here all
the time. Or even coming here every now and then. But
Dez would never wear that, of course.

He'd kill her if he knew who she was with right now,
and what she was up to.

The lift doors opened for the third floor, and they began
to get out. Rose let out a moan. Pacing towards them was
the manager, ready with a courteous smile for whichever
of his hotel guests might step out in front of him. When he
saw Rose's face, the smile twisted into a furious grimace,
and he quickened his step. Rose hauled Tracy back into the
lift and pressed the button for a swift descent to the foyer.
The man could hardly race down the stairs fast enough to
catch them.

At the ground floor the doors opened just as Rose was
reaching for another button, this time for the fourth floor.
They would have to get there and then walk down a flight,
hoping the manager would give himself a nervous breakdown trying to figure out where the hell they had got to.

Before the doors could close again, they were confronted
by Rose's salesman. He got his shoulder into the gap and
thrust the doors open enough to let him in. 'Well, what d'ya
know, I've been looking for you.' He pressed the button
for the third floor. 'Where did you get to? I got you a
drink in.'

'I told you I had to meet a friend. Brian, this is Tracy.'

'Hello, Tracy.' He eyed Tracy appreciatively up and

down. Clearly his lonely evening was showing signs of getting better and better. 'Tell you what, why don't the pair of you come back to my room, and we'll open a bottle from the fridge.'

Rose was staring up at the floor marker as it reached floor three and settled there. 'We've got to go somewhere, but if you tell us your room number we could come on after.'

The doors began to open. Brian said: 'Room three two three. Don't forget. I'll be waiting for you.'

As he moved cheerfully away, the manager moved into position outside the lift.

'We're going up,' said Rose hopefully.

'You're going out.'

'No,' said Rose, 'you don't understand.'

'I understand perfectly.' The manager stepped in and pressed for the ground floor.

'Look, if you'd just listen . . .'

They reached the ground floor, and with unexpected strength for such a well-fed smoothie he had them by the arms, Rose to his right and Tracy to his left, and was propelling them across the foyer towards the doors. He stopped only under the awning outside, giving a last twist which sent them stumbling down the top three steps.

'And don't come back.'

Tracy massaged her bruised arm. 'There's someone being murdered. Don't you care?'

'We'll ring the police,' screeched Rose, 'and tell 'em what we're telling you. We'll ring the papers, tell everybody.'

'He's killing her right now, in your hotel.'

'Shut up and clear off.'

'Same man that killed Gina Dixon,' Rose ranted on. 'You must have heard about that – well, he's up there in one of your rooms.'

'Do you expect me to believe—'

'Do you want to have your precious hotel plastered all over the newspapers and the telly?'

He didn't want to believe them, but he was terrified of what might happen if he didn't believe. While he was hesitating, Rose and Tracy hurried back up the three steps and urged him back into the foyer. The lift seemed incredibly slow this time. On the third floor, Rose erupted through the doors and was first along the corridor to room three hundred and two, almost knocking over little Tommy, on his way somewhere with a tray. She grabbed the knob. It was locked.

'Carol!' She banged desperately on the door. 'Carol, are you in there? Are you all right?'

The manager, really frightened now, said, 'Tommy, get this door open.'

'I . . . er, I haven't got me key on me right now, Mr Pierce.'

'Oh, for God's sake . . .'

Abruptly the door opened. Tracy whimpered with relief. Carol stood there before them, fully dressed, wearing black stockings and looking very self-possessed and in the best of health. She stared from one startled face to another.

'What's all the racket about?'

Rose peered past her into the room. Curly, fully dressed but wearing a pair of Marigold rubber gloves, was lounging back in a chair by the side of the bed.

The manager, at a loss, found his voice. 'Is everything all right, sir?'

'Everything's fine, apart from the noise, which we find very distracting. My wife and I are trying to relax.'

'Got that?' said Carol loftily.

'I'm sorry, madam, but we were given to believe that . . . I mean, that is . . .'

'Cat got your tongue?'

'Do you know these . . .' Pierce turned to one side, to find that the little blonde had disappeared and only Rose was still there, petrified in disbelief. 'This woman?' he concluded.

'Never seen her before in my life.'

'I'm terribly sorry. There must have been a mistake.'

'I should think so. We paid good money for this room.'

The manager swung on his heel. 'Where did the other one go?'

'I don't know, Mr Pierce.' Tommy made a great play of looking both ways along the corridor, shaking his head in bewilderment. 'She just sort of disappeared.'

'Well, find her and get her out of here. And get a bottle of champagne sent up to that room.'

He seized Rose's arm, this time a lot more roughly, and shoved her towards the lift. He was still gripping her arm with one hand as he stabbed at the lift button. 'Cockroaches and whores,' he grated. 'Can't seem to control either of them.'

'Comes of being treated like vermin,' she flung back at him.

'You *are* vermin.'

The lift doors opened, and he dragged her in and pinned her against the back wall as they went down yet again.

Curly wriggled back into his chair and said peevishly: 'That put me right off. You'll have to start again, only this time do it slower.'

Carol groaned. She was in no mood to go right back and start all over again. But she walked over to the bathroom, shut the door, and looked around. It was spotless. Just the way a bathroom ought to be – and with someone else to wash it and scrub and polish.

Curly's muffled voice said, 'Go on. Say it.'

'I'm putting them on. Ooh. They fit me just right.' While she inspected the shampoos and soaps by the bath and reached for a couple as souvenirs, she went on reciting: 'Now I'm fastening the right leg. Oh, it's all smooth and silky. And now . . . I'm putting the other one on, and it goes right to the top of me leg.' She added a bath gel to the collection in her bag. 'I'm just fastening the back. There, it's done. I'm coming out. Are you ready?'

He was crouched in the chair, his face very red, and his gloved hands were fumbling somewhere way down. She walked very slowly towards him, bored but knowing just what the timing ought to be. He stared at her stockinged legs, making no attempt to touch her: his hands were too busy for that. She lifted her left foot in the stiletto-heeled shoe he had supplied and set it on to the seat of the chair right by his thigh, rustling her fingers up and down her leg as though to straighten the seam on the stocking.

He was gasping happily to a finish, looking adoringly at her foot, her leg, her face.

Carol thought it was worth a try, 'Do I get to keep the shoes?'

7

In room three hundred and one, Tracy sprawled on the double bed watching TV with the sound down low. She had finished the biscuits and the apple left on the bedside tray, and was wondering where the hell little Tommy had got to. He was a nice little bloke and she had half thought of him as someone who might look after her better than Dez; but maybe they were all the frigging same when there was trouble.

There was a faint tap at the door. Tracy slid off the coverlet and pressed the unlocking button. Tommy came in triumphantly with an ice bucket containing a bottle of champagne.

'Had to pretend I was looking all over for you,' he apologised.

Tracy looked greedily at the champagne. 'Shall we get into bed and drink it?'

With a flourish Tommy opened a door in the long wall cabinet to produce a packet of mixed nuts, and for the first time she realised that behind the panelling was a well-stocked refrigerator.

'It's like a proper house, isn't it? I mean, you could pretty well live here.'

'Some people do.' He began easing the cork out of the bottle, gripping it so that it did not shoot across the room. 'There's one woman on the second floor, she's been here nearly a year, and it's over a hundred quid a night.'

As he handed her a glass and she suppressed a sneeze over the bubbles, she said, 'Put your arm round me.'

He settled uncertainly on the edge of the bed. It was so warm and cosy and private here. She wished it would go on forever. 'I like it here.'

She tried to kiss him, but he looked as awkward as a kid trying to nerve himself to do it for the first time. 'Better get this drink down us, and then get moving.'

She moaned a sulky protest, but he was filling her glass to the brim again, and glancing nervously at the door. She didn't want to leave. Even less did she fancy the way they had to slink down the stairs and along that narrow corridor to the fire exit door. She tried to kiss him again, but he was reaching past her to release the bar of the door.

'Right, make it quick, before somebody sees you.'

'What time do you finish?'

'Eight o'clock. In the morning.'

'I could wait for you if you like.'

'No, I'll be going home after that to get some kip.'

'I could come with you.'

He twitched with alarm. 'I live with me mam, she'd have a fit.'

'Don't you like me?'

It was all a bit sudden for him. 'Yeh, of course I like you, but I can't—'

'I could earn money for you,' she pleaded. He would be so much nicer to her than Dez, she was sure of it. If only she could persuade him. 'I can earn lots of money, honest.'

She was outside, and the door was closing. She felt terribly exposed. Somewhere out here Dez would be looking for her.

Carol swaggered up to Rose's door with several cans of lager from the off-licence. She waited until Rose had opened the door, then fanned herself with twenty ten-pound notes before thrusting them under Rose's nose. 'Smell that!'

'Look, if you think you're going to bribe your way in here after that bloody exhibition—'

'What did you expect me to do?'

'We expected you to be hollering for help.'

Carol chuckled. 'I don't fancy I'll be needing much help with this one. Come on, let me in and let's open these cans. And I owe you for being around tonight – even if I didn't need you.'

When they were settled in the cramped, untidy room – Carol could never have let any of her own rooms get into this state, or put up with the stale smell from the hallway – she let out a sigh of contentment and told Rose the full story. Certainly no killer, her Curly. A pathetic little drip really, more likely to weep peevish tears of frustration than commit murder. When it was all over he had spent ten full minutes telling her his woes: all about being engaged years ago to a school teacher, and the night before the wedding he had told her that he liked women to wear black stockings. She called the wedding off straight away and put it about the village that he was a pervert. Poor sod, it had pretty well done his head in.

And now all he wanted was regular sessions like the one tonight: once a week, at a hundred and fifty a throw. Money for jam. Without him laying a finger on her.

'You're made, girl,' said Rose enviously.

'Mind you, he's got his mean streak. Stupid prat wouldn't give me them shoes.'

'You've got enough. But what about those scratches on his hands, then?'

'He's got a skin complaint. Comes from freezing all those chickens. That's why he had to wear gloves, or he'd be scraping himself in some sensitive places.'

Rose tipped back her can of lager. 'Are you still gonna do the Lane, then?'

That was something Carol had not yet decided. At a hundred and fifty a week, she could get by quite comfortably.

And she could spend a lot more time at home with Emma. Yet it also meant she was tied to just one bloke, who might go off her at any time – or become such a bore that she'd want him to clear off anyway.

She'd wait until the morning to decide, when her head was a bit clearer.

'Where's Tracy?' asked Rose drowsily.

'Dunno. I thought she'd still be with you.'

'Hope she hasn't gone back to shit-face.'

Carol grunted assent. But where else did Tracy have to go to, anyway? She opened another can of lager and stared into infinity. The pleasure of the evening was wearing off. As usual at this hour, she began to grow maudlin. 'What's gonna happen to them three kids?'

'Gina's?'

'Poor little sods. And all because . . . look, why did it have to happen to someone like her? I mean, you're always expecting it if one of us . . .'

''Cos we're whores,' said Rose dismally. 'We don't matter. Use us and then do us in. We're just scum.'

'To wash down the plug-hole.'

'Cockroaches.'

Carol was none too keen on that simile. She began to heave herself out of the chair. 'Reckon I'd best be getting along.'

'To be squashed,' Rose went on. 'Wiped out. Exterminated.'

'Back to Emma,' said Carol. 'Let Julie get away.'

When she had gone, Rose gathered up the empty cans and dropped them in the kitchen pedal bin. She knew that would never have done for Carol. However late it might be, Carol would wrap the cans in newspaper or the plastic bag from the off-licence and go out to the bin by the back step, just in case the smell of stale booze hung about the room.

She was starting up the stairs when there was a knock at the door. Probably Carol had forgotten something.

Rose opened the door. And Dez Sadiq came thrusting at her, throwing her back against the wall as he slammed the door shut behind him. His left hand bit into her shoulder and held her steady as his right hand brought a knife up against her left cheek.

'All right. Where is she?'

'Let me go. I don't know what you—'

'She's been with you, hasn't she? So where is she now?'

'If you mean Tracy—'

'Oh, I mean Tracy all right.' The point of the blade was like a wasp sting into her flesh. 'Where is she?'

'I don't know.'

'Let's try again.' He put pressure on the blade, and Rose felt a further stab of pain, and a trickle of blood down her cheek. 'Tell me where she's been and where you left her, or I'll go all the way down.'

She told him.

It was hardly the time of night to go visiting, but Newall had two very important calls that simply had to be made. One of them might be quite entertaining. The other was not the kind of thing he fancied at all, but his blood was up and there was a tingling in his fingertips which he nearly always got when clues began to come together and there was the hope of a pattern emerging at last. That was what this job was all about.

He went on his own to see Carol Johnson, parking his car in the next street and walking round to her house.

The landing light was still on, and the bathroom light glowed from behind frosted glass on the first floor. Newall felt his heart pounding absurdly. He had known he would be coming back to Carol's, but hadn't expected it to be so soon, or with the information he now had.

He reached for the bell push, only to find as he touched the door that it swung gently open under his hand. Carol, of all people, forgetting to put the chain on! She must have been well and truly on the juice this evening. He let himself in, and began to pad silently up the stairs.

On the landing a loose board creaked under his foot ten times as loudly as it would have done in the daytime.

He heard a sudden splashing of bath water and a mutter of alarm from the bathroom. He dodged through an open doorway into a darkened bedroom, praying it wasn't the kid's, as Carol came out of the bathroom wrapped in a towelling robe. A smell of expensive bath gel wafted out as she went downstairs a cautious step at a time.

'Hello?'

He heard her curse as she realised she had forgotten to put the chain on, and then the rattle as it slipped into place.

When she had come back up and gone into the bathroom again, he gave her a few minutes and then crossed the landing and flung the door open.

Carol screamed.

'You lied to me,' said Newall. 'Who's been a naughty girl, then?'

She clutched the edge of the bath and grabbed a towel from the top of the clothes basket beside it, struggling up and stepping out. Newall had no complaints about that. The towel was pretty useless when it came to covering her long legs and the corner of her right breast.

'You bastard. Get out of here.'

'Don't be like that.' He caught her moist, dark arms and relished the feel of them slithering between his hands.

'You've no right to—'

'Thought you'd try and get one over on me, did you?'

'I don't know what you're talking about.'

'She was hustling, wasn't she? Gina Dixon – you were working with her, weren't you? What *am* I going to do with you?'

She was still struggling, but it was a halfhearted sort of struggle. She knew just what he was going to do with her. As he unzipped his trousers and swung her against the washbasin, she tried spluttering a protest, but it carried no conviction. It was all part of a remembered ritual, a sort of primitive dance they had so often danced before, way back. And now it was starting again. And when at last she let out a long howl, it was not a howl of agony.

He stood back and zipped up his trousers. 'Still a good screw.'

'Still a bastard screw.'

'You really missed me, then?'

'Time you were out of here.'

He ambled towards the door. She found her bathrobe and wrapped it right round her this time, following him downstairs and overtaking him to open the door.

'Don't bother coming back,' she ground out.

'Now, what would you do if I didn't?'

'Celebrate.'

'You should always keep your chain on,' he taunted. 'You never know who might be lurking about.' Then, on the step, he thrust his face closer to hers. 'Oh, and about that other matter. Gina Dixon. She *was* on the game, wasn't she?'

'Who told you . . . I mean, where'd you get such a stupid bloody notion?'

'She *was*,' he insisted, 'wasn't she?'

Even in this uncertain light he could see in her eyes that it was true.

Now for the next call. It wasn't one he cared to make on his own. He picked up DC Jameson at the station on the way, and let Jameson do the knocking on the Dixons' front door. It took quite a time for Steve to answer. When he did, he blinked vaguely out into the night. His pale face looked paler against the dark stubble of his chin, and his breath would have attracted the attention of any officer equipped with a breathalyser. In the room

beyond a cheap portable radio squawked some DJ's shrill
ecstasies.

'Can we come in, sir?'

'This is a hell of a time of night.'

'I'm afraid we have some bad news, sir.'

Steve snorted mirthlessly. 'Couldn't be any worse than
what you've already brought me.' But he stood back
and blundered ahead of them across a floor littered with
children's toys and a couple of crisp packets.

Jameson switched off the radio and leaned uncomfortably
against the mantelpiece as Steve slumped back on to
the sofa.

Newall unemotionally told him the bleak facts.

At first they did not seem to register. Then slowly Steve
wiped a hand across his eyes, blinked at him, and said, 'No.
You've got it wrong.'

'Why would she leave her case where she did, then?'

'I don't know. There must have been a reason.'

'Oh, there was a reason, all right. The fact is she didn't
need to keep lugging her case around, because she wasn't
flogging makeup.'

'She was.'

'No. She'd found a faster selling line. One that fetched a
better price.'

'No,' said Steve doggedly. 'That's crazy.'

'Steven, she was seen working with a known prostitute.'

'You've got her mixed up with someone else.' Steve
raised his head in an appeal to Jameson, who shifted
his feet and looked sympathetic but unhelpful. 'It's not
her. You don't understand, she wasn't like that, she was
a good girl.'

'I'm afraid it doesn't look that way.'

When they had finished, Newall and Jameson sat in the car
outside for a few minutes. Jameson looked uneasy. 'What
d'you suppose he'll do now, sir?'

'I don't know. Nothing desperate, I hope. Tomorrow I'm

going to sort all this out, and we'd better have him in and throw a few straight questions at him.'

'D'you suppose that maybe he's known about this all along, really, and he . . . well . . . ?'

'Yes,' said Newall dourly. 'It had crossed my mind.'

8

Carol and Rose were in a hurry. If anyone had tried to pick them up on their familiar route down Lambton Lane, they would not have stopped no matter what the offer was. Not that there would be much trade at this time of the morning, which was just as well. Carol looked as trim as any mother who had just delivered her young daughter to school. Rose had not taken much trouble to make herself look what she wasn't, but at least for once she looked purposeful rather than just loitering along the kerb or propping herself against the wall near The Hustlers' Arms. They had only one end in view. Anita was for the chop.

'We'll just reckon like we don't know,' said Carol through clenched teeth.

'Ask her if we can look at the case, and watch her wriggle.'

They were in vengeful mood. There was only one person who could have put DCI Newall on the right track. It simply had to be Anita.

'No, sod it.' Carol changed her mind about the subtle approach. 'If anyone's gonna gob her, it's gonna be me. And right off.'

They approached the door of Anita's flat, Rose flexing her muscles in readiness for what she had in mind for that stupid, treacherous bitch. It wouldn't help Gina – nothing would help Gina now – but it would relieve a lot of their helpless fury.

Carol knocked, keeping the noise down and her voice low.

'Anita.' She made it sound cooing and friendly. No point in alarming the quarry until they had got her into their clutches.

Behind the door there was the faint click of the chain as Anita tried to twist it into place. She must have seen them coming.

'Come on, come on.' Rose pushed impatiently past Carol and grabbed the door handle, forcing it open just as Anita got the chain secured.

'What d'you want?' Anita bleated. 'I'm busy.'

'Open this bloody door.'

'You can't come in. George is here.'

'At this time of day? Where's his car, then?'

Rose got her arm through the narrow opening and groped for the chain. Anita threw her weight against the door from inside. Rose shrieked with pain as Carol tried to ease the pressure by pushing from the outside.

'Stop it, you're breaking her arm.'

'Well, clear off, then.'

'How can I –' Rose was bent at an awkward angle between the door and the wall '– with the door on me frigging arm?'

Anita relaxed the pressure for long enough to free Rose, then slammed the door finally shut. Carol rammed her face against it, shouting at the top of her voice.

'You bloody grassed on Gina, didn't you? You two-faced turd, you handed her case to the coppers. And now they know she were hustling, they'll not bother, you stupid cow.'

Rose was rubbing her arm. 'What's one dead hustler?'

There was no further sound from inside. Carol banged once more on the door in rage. 'You're bloody dead when we get hold of you.'

'Nearly broke my bloody arm.'

'When I get hold of her I'm gonna tear every bloody tinted hair out of her head.'

The door remained firmly closed, and Anita was not making a sound. But sooner or later she had to come out. She would show up in the usual places, and then they would have her.

Two uniformed policemen had picked Steve Dixon up on the bleak, exposed moor and brought him down to the claustrophobic interview room in Turton Lane police station. And another officer in a patrol car had reported the finding of another young woman.

This time it was in the back street behind the Norfolk Gardens Hotel. The back of her head was in one hell of a mess, but she was alive. Just alive.

Newall stared out of his office window into the early morning light and longed for there to be a connection between these two incidents. It would be so tidy if he could prove it and wrap the two up all in one go. Not that most investigations ever went that tidily. But at least he knew damn well where to start.

Confronting Dixon across the interview room table, driven crazy by that non-stop shaking of the man's head until he felt capable of reaching out and twisting it clean off, he was in no mood for the quietly investigatory, sympathetic approach.

'It was you all along, wasn't it? Murdering Gina, and then sneaking back for another look.'

'No. I've told you—'

'Oh, I know what you've told us. But there's a whole lot more to it than what you've come out with. Damn it, she was your *wife*! You were married to the woman. You found out she was working the Lane, not ten minutes from where you—'

'No. No.' It was the familiar moaned denial, and still the head went on shaking compulsively. 'I only found out when you told me. Will you listen to me?'

Newall was in no mood to listen to anything less than a

full confession. There could be only one kinky reason why
Steve Dixon should have driven up to the moor to the very
spot where his wife had been strangled. Whatever the motive
for this evening's second attack, the husband's follow-up to
the Gina Dixon killing was almost a textbook example of
the psychological twists in a killer's mind.

'She was doing it on your doorstep. Rubbing your face
in it. So don't give me that pathetic ignorance line. You
followed her, you saw her bobbing up and down, looking
in cars, hanging about with that other scrubber, smiling
at the punters, doing the old come-hither. You saw the
whole filthy business and you wanted an end to it – and
who wouldn't, eh?'

'I don't know what you're on about. I'm trying to tell
you . . .'

Whatever he was trying or trying not to tell, how could
he hope to explain going back up on the moor? He must
have known the police would still be watching. Was he
actually wanting to be caught? That made some perverse
sense. Wanting to confess and get it off his chest. Or was it
that he wanted to relive it all, enjoying it yet at the same time
trying to make some sense out of his own fit of madness?

'I had to go,' Steve was snivelling. 'I had to see with
my own eyes where it was. To believe it . . . to try and
. . .' His head began that damned dithering again. 'I keep
thinking she's going to walk in the door. I just can't get my
head round the fact that she's gone. You've no idea what
it's like.' He gripped the edge of the table, glaring despair
and utter loathing at Newall. 'I didn't kill her.'

There was a knock on the interview room door. Newall
was furious at the interruption, just when he thought that
in spite of the suspect's protestations he was on the verge
of cracking. Leaving Jameson in charge, he stamped out
into the corridor to confront the sombre features of DS
Kershaw.

'All right, what is it? It had better be good.'

'Thought you ought to know, sir. About this other young woman—'

'There's a tie-in? It does fit?'

Kershaw shook her head. They were all at it, shaking their heads. 'No, sir. Afraid not. The tyre tracks are different.'

'Shit. But the girl – does she fit anyone we know?'

'No real idea so far, sir. To be on the safe side I've checked the Missing from Home file, but there's nothing. I've sent a telex to all local stations. But from the look of her . . . well, she could be another one like that last one.'

'On the game?'

'Wouldn't be surprised. Not their usual location, but—'

'Their usual location is anywhere, sergeant, where there's likely to be loose change in the gutters.'

It was another excuse to see Carol Johnson. Perfectly reasonable, after establishing the link with Gina Dixon, to check whether Carol had known this one too. And as for Steve Dixon, Newall's opinion was veering wildly off course yet again. Two women attacked, one of them a hustler and the next one probably the same: it was more likely that there was some puritanical nutcase on the loose than that a dimwit like Dixon was conducting a one-man morality campaign. And Dixon could hardly have been round at the back of the Norfolk Gardens Hotel at the time of night when it had been established that he was up on the moor.

He wanted to shake something out of Dixon, some chunk of truth that would solve at any rate one case. But he hadn't enough to hold him on. The most they could do was take a few samples and let him go.

In the meantime there was Carol Johnson to be hunted down and put through another grilling – only a lot hotter this time.

She was not at home.

He realised she must by now have taken her little girl to school, and might be shopping or sauntering back along her usual route. He drove to the top of Lambton Lane and coasted slowly downwards. He was not disappointed. She was walking down the Lane with that unsavoury slag Rose Garrity. Maybe he would pull Garrity in one day and see what she could contribute; but right now his sights were set on Carol.

He drew in beside the two women and leaned over to indicate that Carol should get in the back of the car. For a moment she glanced at Rose as if to enlist her help in refusing him. Then she slid in, and he drove off.

'All right, where are you taking me?'

'On a picnic.'

'Very funny.'

'You told me you'd never been on a picnic.'

'Did I? When was that?'

'When we were . . . seeing each other.'

'When I was off me head, you mean?'

It wasn't said jokingly but venomously. He tried to tell himself it was just her brash way of carrying on, a sort of barbed self-defence; but the barbs hurt. 'Why do you act like that?' he demanded. 'As if you hated me.'

She caught his eye in his rear-view mirror. 'Because I do.'

They exchanged nothing further until he slewed into a parking slot in front of the hospital. Then she cleared her throat as if framing a question, but was too pig-headed to ask it.

He went ahead of her, pushing doors open and letting her fend for herself as they swung back. Even when they reached the Intensive Care Unit she still refused to say a word, but he could almost smell the fear on her and hear the question she was asking herself. What the hell was this all about?

The sight of a uniformed policeman sitting outside the door of the unit did nothing to reassure her. Inside, a nurse was sitting at a desk making notes, glancing every now and then at the ventilator and the pulses of light on a monitor screen. She nodded acknowledgement as Newall showed his warrant card and the authorisation from the reception desk.

He stood beside the bed, beckoning Carol to come closer.

The young woman's naked body was covered by a white sheet up to her shoulders, with a drip shunted into one of her pitifully thin, pale arms. She looked more like an undernourished child than one of Carol Johnson's crowd.

Newall said peremptorily, 'Know her?' When Carol stared in speechless horror he snapped it out, 'Carol?'

She managed a nod and a hoarse whisper. 'Her name's Tracy. What's happened to her?'

'She was found at the back of the Norfolk Gardens Hotel. Somebody coshed her over the back of the head.'

'Will she . . . is she gonna die?'

Newall was not prepared to answer that one. All they knew so far was that if the kid got through the next twenty-four hours she would stand a chance. But it would do no harm to let Carol sweat, scared enough to blurt out everything worth knowing.

'Tracy, you say? Does she work the Lane?'

Again Carol nodded.

'For how long?' he demanded.

'I dunno. A year, maybe more.'

'Who's her ponce?' When he could see she was reluctant to commit herself on this one, he said, 'Come on, it's obvious. She was on crack. They found traces of it in her blood. Somebody was keeping her supplied. You know the pattern as well as I do.'

Carol looked around for some way of escape, and found none. 'Big black Mercedes. But you didn't get it from me, right?'

'Right.'

'Sadiq, he's called. Dez Sadiq. He's got a couple of girls working for him.'

'Thanks. I'll drop you on my way back.'

Carol took a lingering look at the prone figure under the sheet, the near lifeless face with closed eyes and a tube up the left nostril, then shivered and followed him out.

It took a mere thirty minutes to track Dez Sadiq down and have him brought in to the station. He had been protesting all the way and wasn't going to stop now. He had been driving round to see his bookie – nothing illegal in that, was there? – and he'd got a box of groceries on the back seat. What right had they to grab him in broad daylight when he was going about his ordinary business? He wanted a solicitor.

'Okay,' Newall bluffed, turning to DS Kershaw, 'let's charge him.'

'What with?' sneered Dez.

'Take your pick. Attempted murder—'

'Bollocks.'

'Grievous bodily harm. Living off immoral earnings. Sex with a minor.'

'I never did none of them.'

'Drugs,' Kershaw contributed.

Newall grinned approval. 'Yes. Which one d'you think, sergeant?'

'We're spoilt for choice, really, aren't we?'

Dez's dark, veiled eyes sized them up. No doubt he was silently practising lies and evasions. He was a slimy bit of work, thought Newall – slimy skin, slimy expression, slimy habits. You could be sorry for hustlers and sorry for drug addicts. Never for anyone like this who exploited them, lived off them and made it always worse for them. It would be a real pleasure to make him squirm and then bring him down.

'Or –' Newall leaned towards that sullen face '– you can be helpful. Be a good citizen, helping the police with their inquiries.'

'Forget it.'

'A fifteen-year-old,' Newall went on. 'Working the Lane. Her name's Tracy.'

'Don't know her.'

'Well, that's funny, because she knows *you*, doesn't she, Sergeant Kershaw?'

'Knows you very well.'

'In fact she says you're her pimp,' said Newall blandly.

'Crap. She's a bloody liar. If you believe every word these young slags say—'

'So you do know her, then? Blonde hair, pretty face . . .'

'Oh.' Dez wavered, then chose what he thought would be his safest line. 'I think I know who you mean now.'

'Good. Very good.'

'I didn't know you meant her. I mean, I only asked a friend of mine if she could stay with her, 'cos she was sleeping rough. On the run from somewhere in Harrogate, I think it was.'

Newall hardly needed to give Kershaw the nod. She was already on her way to chase up someone about the Harrogate missing persons' files. It might just be that for once Dez Sadiq had inadvertently told the truth, or as much of it as suited him.

'And you gave her some drugs –' Newall went on affably as Kershaw closed the door behind her '– and put her to work on the Lane?'

'No, man. I don't know what she did. I saw her a couple of times, that's all. She only came to me if she were having a bit of bother.'

'So you were a bit like a social worker, really?'

Dez might be a smart operator in any number of ways, but he wasn't bright enough to recognise sarcasm when he heard it. 'Well, yeh,' he said hopefully. 'Sort of.'

'Somebody tried to cave her brain in last night.'

'That's bad news, man. Real bad news.'

'You could say that. So where were you last night?'

'Me? I was . . . er, out. At someone's house.'

'Whose house?'

'I don't know whose house it was. It was a bit of a party,

you know the sort of thing. This has nothing to do with me, man.'

'So what were you doing round the back of the Norfolk Gardens Hotel?'

Dez twitched, but managed an affronted, 'I wasn't.'

'I can bring people in here right now,' Newall lied, 'who'd swear that you were.'

'Who? Oh, don't tell me. Those two slags off the Lane. They'd say anything to cause bother. If anyone did Tracy over, it'd be that Garrity bitch. She's always threatening her. Wants her off the Lane. Wants her dead.'

Newall let him rant on. The angrier Dez got, the more likely he was to trip up over some crucial detail.

Carol had been home to wash and change. The clinical smell of the hospital was still in her nostrils – nice and hygienic, but too much associated with that prone, bloodless figure on the bed. All too clean and impersonal.

She found Rose on the Lane and told her the news, and what it had been like at the hospital, and what she thought Newall was thinking.

The small scar on Rose's cheek was somehow burning more and more luridly. Rose was getting frightened. 'But why would shit-face want to kill her? He's not going to earn 'owt off her then, is he?'

'You said yourself he were out looking for her.'

'Yes, but that doesn't mean he were going to try and kill her, does it? It has to be . . . well, whoever did Gina in. Somebody's out to get us. One after the other. Gina and now Tracy – and who's next?'

They sought the comfort of The Hustlers' Arms, and Rose made for the toilets.

Jan at the bar was eager for news. 'There's been another one, hasn't there?'

'Tracy,' said Carol. 'He didn't kill her, thank God. Had

96

a bloody good try, though. I've never seen so many machines.'

Her attention was abruptly distracted. Anita had just come into the bar from the side door and was ordering a Malibu with Coke, ice and lemon. She was just about to pay when she saw Carol bearing down on her. Mumbling an apology, she made a dive for the ladies' just as Rose was coming out.

'For Christ's sake—'

'Shitting yourself, are you?' said Rose vengefully.

Anita turned to run for the street, but found herself sandwiched between Rose and Carol.

'Listen,' she babbled. 'I didn't mean to grass on Gina. I only did it because I thought it might help get who killed her. And that'd help you lot, because he wouldn't be running about any more. I saw her husband on the telly, and he was crying – it was terrible. He was asking for people to come forward who knew anything, and I thought poor sod, and he were nice looking and all. I didn't say anything about her hustling, honest I didn't. I just said she was a friend of yours and I was looking after the case for her.' She turned from Carol to Rose's implacable glare. 'And I'm sorry about your arm. I didn't mean to do it, it was just I was taken by surprise and—'

'Tracy's in hospital.' Rose cut her short.

'Tracy? How?'

It was no use. The damage had been done, there was no point in beating Anita up the way she deserved. They drifted back, collected their drinks, and sat at the corner table while Carol went over her hospital visit again.

'And there's gonna be no work on the Lane right now,' Rose summed up. 'You've frightened them all off.'

'Not me,' Anita protested. 'I haven't done nothing.'

'Maybe we could find something else. Advertise, or something.'

'Do a massage parlour sort of thing?' Carol suggested.

Anita was alarmed. 'You're not using my place.'

'Why not?'

'Because George would have a bloody fit, for one thing. Anyway, what d'you think I am?'

'We won't answer that,' said Rose. 'Not that it matters to me. I've had enough. I'm off to London.'

Carol snorted. 'You're always off to London.'

'This time I mean it. There's nothing doing here now.'

Gloomily they finished their drinks and wandered aimlessly off down the Lane. It was like a morgue, thought Carol; then tried not to think of morgues. Although there wasn't usually a lot of custom at this time of day, at least there ought to be the odd casual punter or some businessman treating himself to a long lunch-hour.

She thought of Curly. There was still that offer of his. Curly would be a whole lot safer than prowling down this perishing pavement.

A police car appeared beside them. Carol stiffened, waiting for Newall to start issuing orders once more. But it was a younger plain-clothes man who got out and showed his warrant card. 'Rosemary Garrity?'

'Yes.'

'DC Jameson. We'd like to ask you a couple of questions, if you don't mind.'

'What if I do mind?'

The young detective looked momentarily nonplussed by this comeback. 'Well, I . . . look, it's nothing to get worried about, it's just a few questions.'

'Ask him what about,' Carol advised.

'If Miss Garrity will come down to the station –' he had recovered his balance '– we'll tell her. In private.'

Carol watched the car drive off with Rose in it.

Definitely time to ring Curly and say yes.

9

Sarah had been looking out of the bedroom window, clutching her doll, as her grandmother listlessly took clothes from the wardrobe and laid them out neatly on the bed. Sarah knew they were her mother's dresses, and didn't want to look.

Then she brightened. 'Daddy!' Her father was getting out of his car. She was about to run down and get a hug when another car rolled up: a red Granada, a lot newer than the Dixons' old banger.

'It's that man, the one Mummy . . .' She couldn't finish the sentence.

Steve made wearily for the path to the front door, but the driver of the Granada had already placed himself between the lopsided gateposts.

'Mr Dixon? Mr Steven Dixon?'

'If you're another bloody reporter you can just—'

'Moore's the name. Not a reporter, I assure you.' The thin smile revealed a cracked tooth which somehow made his whole face look shifty. 'Just a little confidential matter we might sort out between us. A little matter of something your wife didn't square up before . . . well, her bit of misfortune.'

'I don't get you.'

'Look, I know this must be a difficult time for you.' Moore's attempt at man-to-man sympathy rang as discordant a note as the Dixons' creaking gate. 'So I'll spell it out, then I'll clear off. Your wife took out a loan, signed a contract.

Here.' He had been holding it behind his back from the moment he got out of the car. 'A photocopy of it. That's her signature, right? Saying that she'd make regular monthly payments.'

'My wife's dead.'

'I know, and I'm sorry about that. But I can tell you're an honest man, not the sort to go back on your wife's word. So we're not going to have a problem, are we?'

Steve tried dazedly to squeeze past him and start up the path. He was dizzy with exhaustion and disbelief. But the front door was shut, and as he groped for his key Moore was closing in again.

'Look.' Steve reached out to support himself against the wall. 'I can't get my brain round this right now. So if you'll just leave it—'

'No problem. I'll come back later when you've had time to think about it. The sooner the better, really, interest rates being what they are.'

Joyce had opened the front door. She looked uncertainly at Moore, who smiled unctuously. 'I'll be off, then.'

Joyce watched him go as Steve blundered past her into the hall. 'Who was that?'

'Bad news.'

'I've seen him before.' She was heading for the kitchen to put the kettle on. 'He came when I was looking after the kids. Hung around till our Gina came home. I made him a cup of tea. But anyway, where on earth have you been? Bob won't wear me hanging about with the kids much longer. And I've got to get off to my job, or flaming Ferguson'll be going on again about docking my wages because of all the time off I've been taking.'

Steve steeled himself. 'I've been down at the police station for bloody hours. They think I killed her.'

Joyce slammed the kettle plug forcibly in. 'Stupid buggers. Dreamt that one up, I suppose, along with the one about her being a prostitute. D'you know what they've got in the morning papers? You can imagine what Bob'll have to say.'

Yes, Steve could imagine. As if Bob, the sleaziest layabout of all time, had any right to say anything about anybody.

'I've a good mind to sue,' said Joyce. It must be a phrase she had picked up from some television programme, without a clue what it entailed.

He said: 'But it's true, Joyce.'

As the kettle began a slow singing, she turned to glare incredulously at him. 'How could it be? Don't tell me they've brainwashed you as well. Our Gina, she wasn't like that.' She was going automatically through the motions of putting two tea-bags in the pot, reaching for cups and saucers and putting them side by side on the work surface.

He told her in a listless monotone what the police had told him, and why it all made awful sense now. All about Gina putting on an act that she was doing fine for herself but actually borrowing money and getting behind with the repayments, about her makeup case being found with some woman who had looked after it while Gina went out picking up men, about a known hustler she had worked with closely on Lambton Lane until she went off on her own; and about the man Joyce had seen outside – a heavy who wanted his money. Where did she think the TV and the video and all those other bits and pieces had gone? Gina must have flogged them, but it still wasn't enough for that loan shark.

'She always wanted to do things her way. Always knew better. She'd never listen to me.'

Joyce had winced as if every sentence had been a physical blow. Her eyes filled with tears as if one of them had winded her. But suddenly she hit back. 'Because you were no bloody good to her, that's why. You never had any money—'

'That's not my fault. I couldn't help being made redundant.'

101

'You could have tried to get another job. There's plenty of jobs if you look hard enough.'

'Really? You tell me where, and I'll be there tomorrow.'

'Other men get jobs. If you'd been a proper husband to her this would never have happened.'

He was punch drunk, utterly out on his feet. First the police having a go at him, then Moore, and now this. 'And if you'd been a proper mother,' he shouted, 'none of this would have happened.'

There was a click as the automatic kettle turned itself off. Joyce herself was coming to the boil. 'I did my best for her. Done my best all along. Looked after the kids, just like now. Slipped her a little money when I could afford it – and sometimes when I couldn't. And what have you ever done for her? Got her pregnant, bashed her about every now and then, and left her in debt. You might as *well* have killed her.'

'I didn't kill her. And I didn't leave her in debt. She was the one. She slung me out. And I wonder who told her to do that, eh? Same person who showed her how to screw around. What about your bloody Bob? What sort of example was that for her? Find yourself a good screw. Like mother, like daughter.'

Joyce swept her right arm across his jaw, knocked him backwards, and came forward slapping and punching wildly. 'You bastard, you bloody bastard, you *did* kill her.'

He crouched, trying to fend her off. 'Joyce, stop it. I didn't mean it. I don't know what I'm saying.' He grabbed her arm before it could lash out again. 'I'm sorry. I haven't slept, I—'

'Get off me.'

Too late it occurred to them to wonder if Sarah was listening.

Sarah was silent and subdued at a quarter past three that afternoon as he loaded her and Michelle into the car to go and fetch Joanne from school. Steve had washed and shaved but still felt battered and unclean, soiled by everything that had been piling up around him. Fragments of the loathsome revelations made by the police kept scratching at his mind. Nightmarish pictures of Gina swam up in front of his eyes, until he got a grip and forced himself to concentrate on the road. He said nothing until they had reached the school gates and Joanne was running towards him. She hugged him, and then waved at a little coloured girl her own age who was heading across the yard.

'Daddy, can Emma come for tea tomorrow?'

He couldn't have cared less. 'You'll have to wait and ask Nanna.'

As they crossed the pavement from the gates, a lean brown woman with long legs came dashing from the telephone box on the other side of the road. She put her arm round Emma's shoulders.

'That's my Auntie Carol,' said Joanna, adding meaningly, 'I've been to *her* house for tea.'

Auntie . . . ? Hints and blunt facts from that police inquisitor swirled around in a crazy whirlpool. Gina working the Lane with a West Indian hustler: that had been the story. And how had she got to know the woman in the first place? Taking his gorgeous Joanne round to her house, letting her play there while God only knew what went on upstairs or what Gina was learning from her new acquaintance . . .

He drove them home. As they went into the house Joyce was waiting, her lips tight with misery. She got the kids' tea ready without a sound, not asking him whether he wanted any or not. In spite of everything he was glad to see her. He needed her to be there for a while. After as long a wait as he could bear, wondering what the best time for exploring would be, he said, 'I'm going out.'

'I've told you, I can't be expected to hang around while you . . .'

He drove towards Lambton Lane.

He had been down it many a time without paying much attention to the women slouching up and down on either side. Everyone in the city knew where it went on, where to go if you wanted it and where to avoid if you didn't. He had never been interested himself. Now he was seeing every detail in a new, harsh light: every street corner, every girl flaunting herself or cowering back until she had spotted a reliable target. And he felt ashamed of his own hunger. He saw Gina doing things for other men that she had done for him. And he wanted her. He had been without her for too long.

Only not down here. Not with any of this lot.

Then he saw her.

He saw Emma's mother – Auntie Carol – already dressed very differently from the way she had been when she picked Emma up from school. Saw her heading for the pub with a twitch of her bottom and a calculating glance across the street just in case.

In case of what? In case she might be missing a likely client or wanting to be sure there wasn't some plain-clothes copper making notes about her?

Even he knew that the pub was a haunt of prostitutes. And DCI Newall had been crudely specific enough to make it clear that this was where Gina had come with her friend.

Steve found himself relaxing at last. He was more tired than he would have thought any human being could ever be. But now he had something to concentrate on. He would find out the whole truth: not just the salacious bits and pieces thrown to him by the police, gloating over every morsel of it, but the truth.

Starting, as it had to, with Carol Johnson.

Newall took his time, letting Rose Garrity sit there and squirm, not sure what attack to be prepared for. When he started, it was in a matter-of-fact way. 'How old are you?'

'None of your bloody business.'

'Thirty-seven?' he hazarded. 'Thirty-eight? Not so much

doing for you on the Lane nowadays, is there? Especially since all these young 'uns are coming up.'

'I don't know what you're talking about.'

Newall wondered just how many times over the last few years he had heard those words, and just how often – or seldom – they had stood up to an hour's further questioning. Sometimes it only took ten minutes to break it down.

'So what do you do, Rose?' He made it quite friendly; but when she simply sat back with a derisive 'find out for your bloody selves' glance first at him and then at Jameson, he switched off the friendliness. 'I'll tell you what you do. You try and get rid of them, because the fewer young ones like Tracy there are, invading your territory, the more likely it is that the work's going to keep coming your way. Am I right?'

Her faded, boozy blue eyes contemplated him without any hint of cooperation. Now that he had started a direct attack, she had the practice to hit back.

'You're wrong. Some punters like 'em young, some like 'em older.'

'How old?' Newall jeered.

'They take their pick. I'm not complaining.'

'No? Then why threaten Tracy?'

He could see it was dawning on her. Dez Sadiq had to have been the one to set her up. 'I never threatened her. I tried to . . . to frighten her off, that's all. She's a kid, she should be home with her mammy, not walking the Lane.'

'I see. Another caring soul.' Newall raised his eyes towards heaven. 'Funny, because her pimp seems to care about her too.'

'Does he?' Rose burst out. 'Well, I'll tell you something. It was him as did *this*.' She ran her forefinger down the faint pink scar on her cheek. 'Came knocking at my door, looking for her. Stuck a knife in my face and said he'd slit it open unless I told him where she was.'

'And you told him?'

'I said the Norfolk Gardens Hotel because that's where I left her. I thought she'd have cleared off by then.'

In spite of what he had been half hoping for, Newall found himself reluctantly believing her.

In a much more timid, genuinely concerned voice, Rose said, 'Can I see her?'

No good excuse for holding her. If she was telling the truth, as he fancied she was, the trail turned back on itself. 'No reason why not.' When she had left, he went out in aggressive mood to the custody sergeant. 'I think it's time we gave Sadiq another going over.'

Sadiq looked a trifle more subdued when DS Kershaw brought him in. A spell of meditation in one of the cells had made him less cocky; but he could still summon up a defiant grimace as Newall turned the tape recorder on.

'I'm not saying nothing, so you're wasting your time, man.'

For the benefit of the tape Newall intoned the usual incantation of date, time, place, and the names of himself and Kershaw. 'Also present . . .' He looked at Dez. 'Give your full name.'

'I'm not saying nothing.'

'For the benefit of the tape, Detective Sergeant Kershaw will read from the charge sheet.' When she had finished, he turned the full malevolence of his gaze on the prisoner and spoke very slowly and clearly. 'Dastgier Sadiq, you have been arrested on suspicion of attempted murder. You do not have to say anything unless you wish to do so, but it may harm your defence if you do not mention when questioned anything you may later rely on in court. Anything you say may be given in evidence.'

Dez tried to sprawl casually in his chair, but it had not been designed for leisure use. When he showed no sign of responding, Newall went on:

'Right. Well, we took your advice and spoke to Rosemary Garrity. She was very helpful. Guess what she told us?'

'Lies.'

'No, she told us the truth, and she's got a knife wound on her cheek to confirm it. She told you that Tracy was at the Norfolk Gardens Hotel and that's a fact, isn't it?' This time Newall wasted no more than a few seconds waiting for an answer. 'Look, this can be a long job or a short one. Up to you, really. We know that you did it—'

'You don't know no such thing.'

'We know that you did it,' said Newall inexorably, 'so all we have to do is establish where the weapon is.'

'What weapon?'

'The one you used to cosh Tracy over the head with.'

'You won't find no weapon, 'cos there wasn't one.'

'It might be in your flat. In which case we'll have to get a warrant to have a little look. Who knows what we might find? Drugs, hustlers for the use of? Maybe even something that'll help us tidy up the Gina Dixon killing as well. That would really be a bonus.'

'I don't know nothing about that stupid little amateur.'

'Creaming off the best of the custom, was she? Nice and pretty and young. Quite a rival to your Tracy, so you wanted her out of the way?'

Dez was beginning to look thoroughly scared, which suited Newall fine. 'Look, I never had nothing to do with that Dixon bird.'

'All right, let's stay with Tracy. For the time being. Why pick on *her*? I'd have thought she was your bread and butter. And where's that weapon? Come on, we'll find it sooner or later. Maybe in that nice Merc of yours? Shame if we had to carve up all that lovely leather upholstery.'

'It's not in the car,' Dez blurted out.

'Where is it, then?'

'I don't know.' Dez collapsed, his head in his hands. 'It was just a stone,' he mumbled. 'I threw it. I just wanted to frighten her, that's all. She was gonna work in that bitch's trickpad. Gonna give them all her money, and that's not fair, man. Not after all I did for her. They just wouldn't have looked after her the way I did. I just wanted to give her a taste of what could happen if she went off with them. I didn't hit her all that hard,' Dez concluded piteously.

Newall exchanged a broad smile with DS Kershaw. All round, a very satisfactory session.

Rose wiped lipstick off her mouth with a tissue, squinted to get a full picture of herself in the glass door, and fastened the top button of her blouse to make it look more respectable. Then she walked on into the hospital, trying to appear a lot more confident than she felt.

Tracy was still unconscious, but some of the tubes and connections Carol had spoken of had been removed. She looked as pale as death, though. Rose felt a searing pang of guilt. If it hadn't been for her telling Dez where Tracy was, she might not have finished up here. Because it had to be Dez, didn't it? Or was it somebody else, after all? Someone on the prowl: first Gina, then Tracy . . .

She looked at the ICU nurse at her desk, hardly daring to ask: 'Is she going to live?'

'We hope so. She's making some effort with her breathing, so that's a good sign. But we don't know how much damage will have been done till she comes out of the coma.'

A smartly dressed woman in her early forties stood outside the room for a moment, talking to a man in a white coat, then came in and glanced at Rose in surprise: a surprise which began turning to distaste as she summed up Rose's clothes and general appearance.

'Hello,' she said dubiously.

'Are you the doctor?'

'No. I'm her mother.'

The educated voice, the immaculate hair, the wedding ring and large sapphire engagement ring, the high cheekbones and velvety skin – it was all incredible.

'Tracy's?' Rose ventured.

'Her name is Naomi.' The woman was ice cold now. 'Naomi Richards. If you don't mind my asking, who are you?'

'Me? Oh, I'm, er –' Rose floundered '– just a friend of hers.'

The nurse got up from her desk. 'I'll leave you alone for a minute. If anything beeps, just press that button, will you?'

They both nodded. Then they were both silent. Rose wondered how quickly she could get out of here.

Mrs Richards said in a hushed voice, as if afraid of waking the washed-out figure in the bed: 'How long have you known Naomi?'

'I can't get me head round her being called that.'

'Well, that's the name she was christened with. The name that's on her birth certificate.'

'Yes, well . . . it's just that we always knew her as Tracy.'

'Who's *we*?'

This was getting worse. 'The other . . . people I work with.'

'Did Naomi work with you?'

It wasn't just the words but the way the woman was looking her up and down and coming to realise what it might all mean.

'It's best if you don't ask,' said Rose.

'She's only fifteen.'

'They start young these days.'

Now Mrs Richards could be in no doubt. 'You're disgusting. How can you do that? How can you stoop so low?'

Rose had had enough. She turned towards the door, but the agony in the woman's voice brought her to a halt. 'Why did she do it? Why?'

'To survive.'

'But she had everything. We live in Harrogate, you know.'

Rose hadn't known, but wasn't surprised. She could imagine the sort of house, standing white and aloof in well-kept gardens. Double doors to the garage, you could bet on that. And Tracy, the kid who had been given everything and yet had come to this – broken, battered, drained, in a hospital bed.

Rose said comfortingly, 'It must be bloo . . . must be a blow for you. But it'll be all right now. It'll be all right.'

Mrs Richards had resumed her disbelieving contemplation of her daughter. 'It's not all right, though. It's all wrong, and I just don't know what to do. I've made such a mess of everything.'

'Haven't we all?'

'But I don't see how it had to happen this way. I didn't choose for Naomi to end up doing . . . *that*.'

'Nobody chooses to end up on the Lane.'

'You've no idea what it's like to see your daughter laid out in front of you like this.'

No, thought Rose, she hadn't. Because her own kid had been taken away when she was only two months old. They had decreed that Rose wasn't fit to look after her, and that was that. But you got over it. She had told herself a thousand times that you got over it, you had to get over it.

The girl, wherever she was, must be well over Tracy's age by now.

Mrs Richards made a painful effort. 'So Naomi . . . worked with you.'

'We never actually worked together, the two of us. But I looked out for her.'

'Thank you.' It was little more than a whisper. 'I'm glad somebody did.'

The nurse came bustling back in again and headed straight for the bed, tugging at one side of the sheet. 'Are you all right, sweetheart? Want freshening up a bit?'

'Can she hear you?'

'She might,' said the nurse cheerfully. 'You never know.
I've had patients in a coma who heard everything, so I talk
to them all.' She moved round the end of the bed. 'Right,
well, I'm just going to make her a bit more comfortable.
You can either stay and help or go for a little walk. I'll be
about fifteen minutes.'

It was the cue Rose had been waiting for. She would be
glad to get out of this room and well away from this place.
'Bye, then.'

'Goodbye,' said Mrs Richards awkwardly.

There was a moment when they were both uncertain
whether to shake hands or not. Rose sensed that Mrs
Richards would look at her own hand afterwards and
maybe surreptitiously wipe it on the side of her expensive
coat, or more likely dig a cologne tissue out of her handbag.
She made hurriedly for the door, and had it half open before
looking back.

'I'll ring and find out how she's doing. But I think it's
best if I don't come again.' There was no doubt about the
flicker of relief in Mrs Richards' face. 'Anyway, good luck.
I hope things work out. She's a good girl, really.'

To herself she said a silent 'Tara, Tracy'.

Outside the hospital she felt that she still wasn't far
enough away. Time to get well away from everything.
From Dez and men like Dez, from the Lane, from The
Hustlers' Arms, from police pestering and from the shadows
that could turn murderous. She had said often enough that
she was going to London, and Carol and the rest of
them had always laughed at her. They were going to
find out that it was nothing to laugh at. Time to be
moving on.

At ten o'clock her feet had led her without conscious
thought to the echoing chill of Bradford station. She slumped
on to a bench and told herself that all she had to do was buy
a ticket. She had few enough possessions, and most of those

wouldn't be missed. Could even leave tonight, turn her back on the lot of it.

'The train approaching platform eight is the twenty-two-o-five to London King's Cross,' the announcement boomed over her head, 'calling at Wakefield, Doncaster, Newark . . .'

She hadn't got the strength to get up. Tears began running down her cheeks. She was unaware of anyone nearby until a man lowered himself on to the seat beside her and held out a handkerchief. 'Go on, have a good blow.' Through the blur of tears she made out a middle-aged face, a head beginning to go bald, and a hand that came to rest lightly on her shoulder. 'Nothing's that bad, love.'

'How would you know?' she said wanly.

The train had come breathing and rumbling in, and there was a clatter of doors opening and shutting. She thought maybe the man was going to get up and sprint away to the platform, but he stayed where he was, looking fixedly at her in what might be genuine concern or might be something else.

Rose finished drying her eyes and began to wake up. She could see him more clearly now; and recognised the symptoms.

'You from London?'

'Yes. Going back tomorrow lunchtime.'

'Not till tomorrow?'

'Doesn't matter exactly when. I've got an open ticket. I can travel any time I want. The company pays for it.'

'So you're up and down all the time?'

He began to laugh. 'Depends what you mean.' He knew all right what she meant; and incredibly she found herself laughing too.

London would have to wait. If he was prepared to pay for a taxi they could be at Anita's in ten minutes.

4

The man whose dog had found the corpse had already vomited on a tussock of moorland scrub a few feet away from the bush where it lay, staring sightlessly up into the cloudy dawn. Detective Chief Inspector Newall was a bit dubious about letting him sit in the police car and maybe do it again; but he couldn't very well leave the poor bastard out in the persistent drift of rain.

'Get this place cordoned off,' he ordered the uniformed constable by the car, and turned back to Detective Constable Jameson, who was gingerly removing the woman's handbag from her stomach, where it had been neatly, almost ritualistically, laid. Jameson handed the bag to Newall and directed the beam of his torch into it as the DCI probed the contents. Obviously she hadn't been murdered for her money. There was a cluster of five- and ten-pound notes, tucked in beside a crumpled slip of paper which he unfolded in the shelter of the car, not wanting any vital evidence to be washed out.

A sum had been scrawled on the back of the paper. On the front was a cheaply printed address on Butterworth Hill. And there was another address handwritten further down, alongside a list of items in a code which meant nothing to Newall.

But that second address meant plenty. He drew in a sharp breath.

So the victim had known Carol Johnson.

He couldn't decide whether to welcome the excuse for

41

seeing Carol again or to shy away from her. Not that there was going to be much choice. If this strangled woman with a distorted face which must once have been pretty was an acquaintance of Carol's, there could be all kinds of byways to explore. Only he had better check the Butterworth Hill address before taking any crudely obvious conclusions for granted.

The house was an ordinary semi-detached, little different from its neighbours except that the small front garden had been neglected recently, while the others were tidy and the paint of their low front gates was not so chipped and faded. It was the kind of house where nothing much ever happened except for low-key domestic bickering – never much more than squabbles, hardly ever running to outright mayhem and murder. Yet now and then there had been classic cases of a complete breakdown: a husband battering his wife to death, a wife turning on her bullying husband with a kitchen knife. For a brief while their stories made the headlines, while neighbours passed and stared and said you'd never have thought it, would you, but of course still waters run deep, and there had been that time when they'd left their windows open and you could hear . . . well, you'd never have credited the racket, but even so you hadn't expected it to come to this.

Newall jerked his head to summon Detective Sergeant Kershaw to keep close beside him. She was a broad-shouldered black girl who could cope with the worst that Bradford had to throw at her; but at the same time capable of quiet sympathy and a soothing influence on distraught relatives and witnesses. Right now it was hard to predict which of her talents would be most needed.

Newall braced himself and thumbed the bell-push.

The youngish man who answered the door looked distraught already. He held a young girl in the crook of his right arm, looking as if he had just been struggling to dress her; and somewhere within the house a baby squalled non-stop.

42

10

Once started, Steve found it impossible to slacken off. He had parked the car and walked obsessively down Lambton Lane and round the back alleys half expecting Carol Johnson to come out of the pub, or wondering if he had missed her while he was behind the warehouses, and unsure anyway what he would say if they came face to face. Nothing could bring Gina back and make things the way they used to be; yet he had to follow this thing through to an end he couldn't predict.

Finally, in the early evening, he ventured into the pub. She was unlikely to recognise him, anyway. Joanne had pointed her out as Auntie Carol but they hadn't come close and she hadn't returned his glance.

The bar of the pub was not quite what he had expected. There were only four people in it: a man drinking a pint and reading an evening paper, a man and a woman in earnest conversation at one of the tables, and a barmaid apathetically wiping the bar down. Too early, he supposed, for the sort of clientele he had heard about.

He ordered a half. 'You're quiet in here.'

'Coppers swarming up and down the Lane, it doesn't help.'

It offered a useful opening. 'Did she come in here, then?'

'Who?'

'Her that got murdered.'

She studied him suspiciously. 'Are you a copper?'

'Do I look like one?'

'They come in all shapes and sizes. And I haven't seen you in here before.'

'No, I'm just interested, that's all. She worked with Carol, didn't she?'

'Ask her yourself. She'll be back in later on.'

'I heard there was another one last night.'

'Oh, no.' The girl flung the cloth down in disgust. 'No wonder it's so quiet.'

'Usually this is where the action is, then?'

She was getting warier. 'Depends what you mean by action.'

'If you want a good time . . .'

'Look, you want to talk to someone, you come in later and do the talking direct.'

He finished his drink and went back to the car. But if Carol Johnson was coming back in later, there was no point in driving round and maybe missing her. As it began to grow dark he found a different place to park, and walked slowly back down the Lane with his hands in his pockets and his head down. A girl on the corner of the alley by the pub called out to him, and for a moment he was jolted to a halt. She was a coloured girl, wearing a shiny red lurex jacket, and in that uncertain light had so much the build and features of Carol Johnson that it might almost have been her.

But then Carol Johnson herself was walking out of the pub. She must have gone in while he was finding another place for the car. And there was a man with her, leading her towards a BMW gleaming a metallic silver in the light from the pub windows. When they were in it, he reversed swiftly down the lane.

It was probably not going far. And Steve wasn't going to let it out of his sight.

Curly said, 'I didn't think you'd ring.'

'Why not? I said I would.'

114

'I didn't think you liked me.'

Carol refrained from saying that this never had anything to do with it; but she wanted to be quite sure they understood at any rate one thing from the start. 'This hundred and fifty quid. When do I get it?'

'Whenever you like. But from now on you don't go with anyone else.'

'As if. What d'you think I'm doing this for?'

'Well, I don't really know you yet, do I?'

She didn't like the sound of that. So far as she was concerned, this was going to be a purely financial and physical arrangement: no swapping of emotions or anything of that kind. 'Are we going to the same hotel?' she asked hopefully.

'I can't afford hotels and a hundred and fifty quid a week.' Behind that cajoling, begging manner of his he could be just as firm about money as she was. 'It's up to you. We go back to the hotel and you have a hundred, or we go back to yours and you have a hundred and fifty.'

That wasn't quite the way she had wanted it. That hotel had made a nice change. But fifty quid was too much to throw away. If she had been given more time, she would have got things ready before coming out this evening. As it was, she had to put a good face on it, send Julie home, tuck Emma up in bed and tell her that Mummy had some important business to talk over with a friend, and then hurry down to spread the hustling blanket over the armchair. Curly watched her impatiently, hugging his briefcase, until she indicated that it was all right for him to sit down now.

He lowered himself into the chair and opened the briefcase, savouring every moment as he took out the black shoes and stockings and his rubber gloves.

'And me hundred and fifty,' Carol prompted.

He handed her a brown pay packet.

'Thanks.' Half joking, she added, 'I'll be able to pay me council tax now.'

The smile of anticipation was wiped instantly off his face. He stared in horror. 'You mean you haven't paid it?'

'Couldn't afford to.'

'You can get into serious trouble,' he said earnestly. 'They can lock you up.'

'I know, but what could I do?' she said with mock penitence. Before he could go on lecturing her, she clutched the shoes and stockings to her and went to the door. 'Right, I'll go put these on.'

In the hall, glancing up the stairs to make sure the door of Emma's room was shut, she adopted the cooing voice that went with the act. 'Ooh, these feel extra silky tonight. I—'

'Wait a minute,' Curly complained. 'I haven't got my gloves on yet.'

It was Carol's turn to become impatient. Curly proved to be deadly slow tonight. After she had gone through the routine twice, with a few extra gasps and moans thrown in, she collected a furniture spray can from the kitchen and went back into the room to find him panting more and more heavily but getting nowhere.

'You're taking a long time over it tonight.' She leaned across him in order to spray polish on the television set and rub it hard. 'Do you want me to take me top off?'

'No,' gasped Curly.

'You wouldn't like me to put some music on?'

'No.'

It was asking too much. Ten or fifteen minutes she could stand, but he had been at it a good half hour and these shoes were killing her corns. All at once he moaned in relief, shuddered a few seconds, and then slumped back in the chair. Carol offered up a silent thanksgiving, and without suffering another second longer took the shoes off, plonked them in his lap, and went to fetch his coat. Putting the shoes back in his briefcase, he looked at her in feeble reproach.

'I thought we might talk a bit. Just a little chat.'

'It's a bit late.'

'It's not nine o'clock yet.'

'Well, I have to be up early to get our Emma to school.'

'How old is she?'

'Seven.' He looked politely interested, but she didn't want him to be interested. That was territory none of her punters was allowed to set foot on. 'You'd better go.'

At the front door he said: 'You haven't taken the stockings off yet.'

She wasn't going to let him use this as an excuse to get back indoors. 'I'll wash 'em out ready for next week.'

'Ooh, you don't have to wash them.'

'I'm not wearing anything that's not washed,' said Carol indignantly.

Heading for his car, he turned back yet again. What the hell was he dreaming up this time?

'You won't forget to pay your council tax, will you?'

'I'll go straight down to the Town Hall,' she promised solemnly, 'after I've dropped our Emma off.'

She was half laughing, half groaning, as she went back indoors to remove the blanket and fold it up. She had committed herself to Curly and his money, but already was beginning to wonder if she'd be able to stand it. He was too grotesque. Kinky punters she could cope with; but Curly's niggling ordinariness was something else. Weeks of it might be more than she could bear.

Her throat was dry. She opened the cabinet to reach for the bottle of cider on the upper shelf. There was only a trickle left in it. She tipped it back, drained it, and went out to the kitchen to wrap it in a bit of crumpled foil and drop it in the plastic bin liner outside the back door. When she returned to explore other cupboards, it was to find what she had really known all along: she had forgotten to buy any more booze.

She took down the tin on which she had months ago pasted a label saying FINES as a joke – only it was really no joke, since she had several times had to dip into it for just that purpose – and stuffed Curly's brown paper packet into it after taking out a twenty-pound note.

Mercifully it was only five minutes' walk to the shop round the corner, with a limited selection of wines and spirits but enough for her immediate needs. Carol headed for the shelf of cider, sparkling waters and wine, and examined the wording on a bottle of Bulgarian red. It was no use: she wanted something a lot stronger than that. She squeezed round a dump bin of beer cans and reached up for a bottle of cheap brandy.

A man who had come into the shop close on her heels edged in alongside her, examining the small array of spirits. He glanced tentatively at her. 'Do you know what these blends are like?'

'No idea. I don't drink whisky.'

'Neither do I. But I'm thinking of starting.'

He was quite good looking, if a bit seedy, with a moustache that needed trimming before it ceased to be a toothbrush style and became a yard broom. The thought twisted Carol's lips into a faint grin. She covered it by saying politely: 'Had a bad day?'

'I lost my wife earlier this year. And . . . well, I saw this advert in tonight's paper – "Tina's private relaxing massage" – but I didn't have the bottle to go through with it. So I thought I'd head in here for another sort of bottle.'

It was a pretty feeble joke, but Carol found herself smiling again. 'What are you telling me for?'

'I don't know. Just that you looked like someone I could talk to, I suppose.' He followed her to the counter, and before she could push her money across he was holding out a note to the shopkeeper. 'How much is the brandy?'

'Seven pounds ninety-nine, sir.'

'That's mine,' Carol protested; but not very firmly.

The man collected his change and said: 'Right?'

She knew what he meant. 'You'll have to be quiet. My little girl's in bed.'

What was it Curly had said, such a short time ago, about not going with anyone else? The hell with that pathetic little creep. More cash in the sweet tin, and by the looks of him this punter could provide a more interesting fifteen minutes than Curly would ever manage.

Within the first five minutes she began to get frightened. She had known men desperate before, and could usually handle them competently before they got too rough. But this one, once he got going, was wild and way out. He must have been without it a long time, and she was the one who had to suffer for it. There was no slow build-up, no let-up. He hammered savagely into her as if to drive right through and impale her to the bed. And as he finished he was growling at her in sheer hatred. Hatred of himself? You got that often enough; but somehow this was different.

Carol let out a croak of pain as he rolled off her. She gave him a few minutes to get his breath back while she tugged the rumpled edge of the hustling blanket as straight as she could get it with his weight sprawled over it. She wanted him out of here just as fast as possible so that she could tidy up, fold the blanket again, and go and have a bath and clean her teeth.

He sat up. 'Do I go now?' he asked. 'Or what?'

It was a weird question. He could hardly have expected bed and breakfast. 'Yes,' she said, 'you go. Now.'

'Don't I have to pay you something?'

She stooped to pick up his trousers and throw them at him. 'Twenty quid.'

He fished two ten-pound notes out of a trouser pocket and laid them on the bedside table. 'Is that the going rate?'

'No, but you bought the brandy.'

'What do you usually charge, then?'

'It depends.'

'On what?'

'What I do. Come on, get moving.'

'Everything costs, does it?' He stood up. 'I'd like to

see the menu sometimes. No mouth, though? No kissing?'

She had told him that at the start. Why did he want it repeated? He was as bad as a copper interrogating her. She stripped the sheets off and made a big thing about carrying them into the bathroom and piling them into the linen basket. 'That's right. Come on, get yourself dressed.'

He began buttoning his shirt. Just when she thought he was nearly finished and ready to go, he came and stood in the bathroom doorway. 'What about that Dixon woman? How much did she charge?'

'I've no idea.'

'You must know. You worked together.'

'Who told you that?'

'A little bird. Was she any good?'

'It's time you were going.' He was still in the doorway, and showed no sign of getting out of her way. 'Look, can I get past?'

'How long had she been doing it?'

'I don't know. I didn't even know her.'

'You're lying. You taught her everything you knew. I've been told you did. How long?'

Carol wondered what perverse kick he was getting out of this. He was more dangerous than she had thought. Picking over the tale of a dead prostitute: was that what turned him on?

Anything to get rid of him. She said: 'A couple of weeks, that's all.'

'How many's a couple?'

'Two or three. For Christ's sake, I can't remember. What's it to you, anyway?'

'I was married to her.'

It slammed into her almost as brutally as he had slammed himself into her on the bed. In a rising tide of panic she told herself he was a liar, had to be a liar, fantasising like a lot of them did, a kinky follow-up to the rest of his ravings. But his face coming closer to hers, sweating and contorted, was filled with a loathing too real to be anything but the truth.

At last he let her pass, but only so that he could go back into the bedroom and pick up the two banknotes and thrust them at her.

'What does it feel like to be a whore?'

She rushed past him on the landing, on the way downstairs to open the front door. She wanted to scream, but Emma was on the other side of that bedroom door. Her knees were weakening by the second, and there was an ache in her guts as if she were slowly being carved apart from inside; but she had to get to that front door and get him out of here.

'Keep your bloody money,' she was sobbing as she reached the foot of the stairs.

'Oh, this one's on Gina, is it?'

'I want you out.'

He lunged down on her, grabbing her hair and twisting it until she was wrenched to one side and her head smacked against the wall.

'Here.' He brandished the money. 'Take it.'

'I don't want it.'

'You earned it.'

'Get your filthy hands off me.'

She slid along the wall, groping for the door chain. He held on, and dragged her back by her hair. They fought until she opened her mouth to howl for mercy, for anything that would stop this torture. And when her mouth was wide open, he crammed the notes in.

Then he released her and suddenly went very quiet. 'I'm glad she's dead,' he said simply; and let himself out.

Carol choked on the notes, clawing them out of her mouth and retching as she groped her way back up to the bathroom. Even more desperately than before she wanted to brush her teeth, go on brushing them, brushing everything away.

When she had finished shivering, she knew there was somebody she had to talk to. She couldn't spend the rest of the night here alone without talking it out, cleaning it all out of her system.

11

Newall had been sitting waiting for news of the surveillance his Vice Squad contacts had told him they were authorising on Anita Braithwaite's flat, when the call came from Carol. He had never heard such urgency in her voice. The Braithwaite business was Sherrington's and Unwin's affair. No way was he going to miss out on answering this personal appeal. What the hell could have got her in such a state? She was too much of a toughie to crumple easily under the demands of even the most loutish punter. He drove out of the station yard with a squeal of tyres that would have attracted the attention of any wide-awake copper on the beat. Only there weren't many of them on the beat nowadays: they were all sitting comfortably in panda cars or, like Sherrington and Unwin, in unmarked cars carrying out routine surveillance.

Newall slid to a stop outside Carol's house and bruised his fist on the front door. He had told her over and over again that one day something really nasty would happen to her. It sounded as if this might be it, at last.

She took her time opening the door, and then kept the chain on and peered apprehensively through the gap.

'Come on, Carol, let me in.' She had been hysterical on the phone, demanding that he got here right away; so why the hesitation now? 'What's been going on?'

'Nothing.'

Nothing? Screaming at him over the phone, telling him he had to come straight away, she had been bloody nearly

123

123

killed. And now she wasn't giving him the most rapturous welcome.

'Come on. Are you going to tell me what it was – *who* it was?'

Reluctantly she took off the chain and let him in. Whatever the panic had been, she was already talking herself out of it. But having been dragged this far at this time of night, Newall wasn't going to be talked out of it. He followed her into the sitting-room, where she started frenetically picking up an ashtray and putting it down, plumping up cushions, making a show of tidying the room although it was already scrupulously tidy.

'Come on, Carol, let's be having it.'

'You're loving this, aren't you?'

'Loving what?'

'Me ringing you. Asking for help.'

'Carol, I'm a copper.' He was keeping it calm and reasonable, not probing too sharply until she was ready for it. 'That's my job. Somebody yells for help, we come running. Like me, coming round here now simply because—'

'Simply because you want to control people,' she blazed. 'That's why you got into this sort of job. Only you can't control *me*, and that really pisses you off.'

He couldn't make head or tail of this. It was all so bloody warped. He had got transferred here because of her. He had had to give up working in the Vice Squad because of her – conflict of interests, they'd have called it if they'd had even a glimmering of what she meant to him. There was precious little control he had ever exercised over her, even if he had been optimistic enough to try. If anything, she was the one who had controlled him, made him dance to his tune, not the other way round.

He took out his notebook. If she was sorry she had lost her grip earlier and shown weakness in ringing him personally, he would play it strictly according to the rules and see how she liked it. Deliberately playing the dispassionate police officer, he said: 'You reported that somebody assaulted you.'

'Yeh.'

'A punter?' When she failed to answer, he persisted, 'Was it a punter?'

'No. I mean, yes.' Fear and uncertainty thickened again in her throat. 'I mean, I don't know what you'd call him. He said . . .' She whimpered, and suddenly it came out in a rush. 'He said he was Gina's husband. He stuffed money into me mouth.'

Newall forgot his notebook and the routine of questioning. In a rage of which he would never have thought himself capable he said, 'You're sure of this? Steve Dixon?'

'That's what he said. Said he was Gina's husband.' Carol was back in the mood that had led her to phone him, and now was ready to tell him the lot.

By the time she had finished, Newall was possessed by one blind vindictive impulse. He went back to the car and drove even more fiercely than before, so bedevilled that he spared hardly a second to speculate about a police car racing past him in the opposite direction with flashing blue light and siren going full blast. When he reached the Dixons' house he had calmed down just enough to think of leaving his pager in the car and locking the door on it. He wanted no official interruptions.

Steve Dixon opened the door. Before he could start bleating protests about the hour or anything else, Newall shoved him bodily backwards and slammed the door shut again.

'I think we need a little talk.'

'Look, how many more times? I've already told you all I know. You can't just keep busting in here and—'

'Why *her*?' Newall thrust him along the hall and into the kitchen. 'Why did you pick on her?'

'I don't know what you're talking about.'

Oh, not again. 'I'm talking about Carol Johnson,' Newall

raved. 'You paid her a little visit this evening, and I want to know why.'

Light dawned on Steve. He looked grimly pleased with himself rather than frightened at any possible consequences. 'Why do men usually visit women like that?'

'Come off it. That wasn't the reason.'

'All right. Because she was the one who talked Gina into doing it. You gave me the tip yourself.'

Newall pushed him back against the cooker. 'I never gave you any names.'

'No, but you gave me the picture. And I checked it out, and it was true. Gina wouldn't have done it otherwise.'

'So your wife couldn't think for herself? Had to have somebody make decisions for her, did she?'

'Somebody had to have talked her into it,' said Steve stubbornly. 'Like I said, you were the one who told me she was working with a known prostitute. Well, I started asking around. Not bad as a detective, eh?'

'So you thought you'd teach her a lesson.'

'Right. Look, what are you bothered about filth like that for?'

Newall gave up pushing, drew his right arm back, and punched Steve hard in the stomach. Steve doubled up, but managed to splutter, 'What's the matter? Shagged your bit of stuff, did I?' Newall punched him again, hauled him upright, and let him have one full in the mouth. 'Was she any good?' He spat the words into Steve's face.

Despite the pounding he was taking, Steve let out a harsh laugh. 'Yes, she was terrific.' Unexpectedly he swung a punch back and sent Newall crashing into the wall. 'Don't you understand? I had to find out for myself just what she'd been up to. I had to know what she did.'

'And what did she do? What did you learn? Tell me.'

'She was a whore.'

They stood swaying, facing each other, battered. Newall said, 'And that's why you killed her.'

126

The pager was bleeping frantically as he pushed a handcuffed Steve Dixon into the car and settled into his seat. This time there would be no let-up until he had proved his case, and put paid to the clamour in the media about a rogue killer on the loose. Get Steve Dixon put away, and there would be no further trouble.

Anita's boast that her spare room was so nice and quiet and comfortable was being contradicted by a thumping on the front door and then a heavy thud as it was flung open. Feet came pounding up the stairs. The man in the bed beside Rose, who had just confided that his name was Owen and that he had a nineteen-year-old son at university – and if he'd had his clothes on, she thought, he'd probably have been getting photographs out for her to admire – sat up in alarm. There was a moment's pause, shattered by a cry of outrage from Anita. Rose just had time to wrap a sheet round herself as a stocky man and a woman with a very blunt jaw came unceremoniously into the room.

Anita went on twittering helplessly in the background. 'Running a brothel? *Me*? Is this April Fool's Day or something?'

'We've got a record of everything that's been going on, who's been in and out, over a period. So it's precious little use denying it.' The man beamed amiably at Rose and held out his warrant card. 'Detective Constable Sherrington. And this is Detective Constable Unwin.'

'You've got it all wrong,' Anita babbled. 'This is a friend of mine, and that's her boyfriend. Isn't that right, Rose?'

'Of course it is. And I hope you don't mind if I get dressed now.'

'And you, sir?' said Sherrington politely. 'Can I have your name and address, please?'

Owen looked stricken. 'What for? I haven't done anything wrong.'

Sherrington moved aside as Rose and Owen scrambled

127

into their clothes. He found himself by the dressing-table, with a box of tissues at one end and a pottery hen at the other. He picked up the hen and peered into its wide slot.

'That's personal,' Anita objected.

'Mm.' Sherrington dipped in and took out a slim red notebook, flipping through the pages and then smirking delightedly at Unwin. 'Carol,' he read aloud, 'four pounds. Rose . . .'

'I sold her some bleach.' Rose's heart sank as she heard the hopelessness of Anita's flimsy excuses. 'I get it off a friend of mine, he's got a cleaning business. He's a very important man.'

Sherrington handed the book to his companion, who dropped it into a polythene exhibit bag.

Anita went on loudly lamenting all the way to Turton Lane police station, veering between sickly appeals to the detectives' better nature and confused threats. As they were led towards the desk sergeant she was still at it. 'I want to make a telephone call. My boyfriend knows people on the council. You're going to regret this, I'm telling you.'

She faltered only when, hard on their heels, came DCI Newall, with Steve Dixon in handcuffs. Rose remembered both faces, and Anita certainly remembered Dixon's: it had been his television appeal that had led her to hand over Gina's case. She brightened. Rose would not have put it past her to throw herself on Newall's mercy and remind him how public-spirited she had been.

But DC Jameson was rushing up to Newall. 'There's been another, sir.'

'What?'

'Another murder. Control's been trying to get in touch with you. I think you must have been in a poor reception area.' In the silence that had descended on the group by the desk, broken only by a subdued keening from a maudlin drunk in one of the custody cells, Jameson went on, 'The body was found about twenty-five minutes ago, round the side of the Social Services building. It's identical to that first one. Estimated time of death between nine and ten this evening.'

Steve Dixon laughed. It was an incongruous sound, coming right after that bit of news; but he was glaring triumphantly at Newall. 'You know where I was at that time. I was with *her*, wasn't I?'

Rose was seized by an uncontrollable trembling. Another one. There was something evil and unpredictable on the loose. She wished she had followed her impulse and just got on that train and cleared off to London.

Newall made his way round the corner into the alley beside the Social Services office. It was a gloomy, narrow cleft between two high buildings, smelling of dogs and human urine. No sensible person came here from choice, and even the hustlers used it only as a short cut between Lambton Lane and the better lit street of shops and offices beyond.

Tonight, though, the alley was drenched in brightness. Headlights of a police car were trained on the corpse lying in the gutter, and there was a sequence of flashes as a photographer paced carefully around to cover every angle.

Newall suffered a moment of sheer terror. That dark face could have been Carol's, and the glistening red jacket was the twin of one she often wore. Only when he stooped over that contorted mouth and staring eyes before they disappeared into a plastic body bag could he be sure it wasn't Carol.

No way it could have been, anyway. That bastard Steve Dixon had been right: if this one had been murdered between nine and ten, that was when Dixon had been with Carol. Which let him off the hook so far as this killing went.

It didn't mean, though, that he was in the clear over his wife's death. Newall had no intention of easing off from that one. Dixon was going to pay for *something*; he would see to that.

12

Rose knew from the moment she saw the three magistrates that she was doomed. Two men and one woman, and there might have been a chance. Men often looked tolerantly on someone like herself. But two women and one man meant trouble: no matter how tolerant the bloke was prepared to be, the two dragons would overrule him.

And she ought never to have been here in the first place. She had put Dez into the hands of the police, hadn't she? And this was her reward: stuck in a cell overnight, and hauled in here because of the misunderstanding round at Anita's, she had had her past record dragged out, plus two charges that had somehow been overlooked but were now fully operative. A misunderstanding . . .! There in the public gallery was Anita, looking as if butter wouldn't melt in her greedy mouth, getting away with it only because Rose had backed up her story. If she changed her mind under questioning this morning, it would serve the silly cow right.

The clerk of the court was on his feet. 'Is your full name Rosemary Christine Garrity?'

'Yes.'

'And your address, please?'

'Fourteen Lendon Street, Bradford Ten.'

'Date of birth?'

They'd got no decency in them, not a scrap, dragging this all out in public, when it was written down in front of them.

'Sixteenth of the sixth –' she scurried through it, lowering her voice at the end '– fifty-six.'

'I'm sorry, was that fifty-six?'

The pompous little sod. 'Yes.' And there was Anita grinning to herself.

The prosecuting counsel stood up and rustled his sheet of paper as if it was the first of a hundred, leading to one of the great perorations of the century. 'Your worships, a warrant for the arrest of the defendant was issued on February the second nineteen-ninety-five when she failed to appear in court on charges of theft.'

The woman magistrate in the centre of the three consulted the clerk. 'How does the defendant plead?'

'Do you plead guilty or not guilty?' asked the clerk.

'To nicking the telly or not turning up?'

'On the first count, failure to attend court.'

'I had tonsillitis.'

'Guilty or not guilty?'

Rose gave up. 'Guilty.'

'And on the other matter . . .'

They went on playing their games with her. There was more than one other matter, but they held back on that, hoping to take her by surprise. After the business of the television which she had flogged for ready cash while omitting to pay the rental, they sprang the accusation of using a brothel on her. She was ready for it, and unwavering in her story. If she had agreed early on to cooperate on that one and drop Anita in the shit, they might not have brought up the two older accusations. They only wanted to do her because they couldn't do Anita as they had planned. The rigmarole seemed to take half a morning, but in fact Rose was on her way out of the court, clutching the sheet of bail conditions handed to her by the clerk, within twenty minutes. The paper itself was flimsy enough, but the weight on her mind wasn't. Three hundred quid for stealing – that's what they called it – a rental company's clapped-out television; and fifty for breach of bail. With only twenty-eight days to pay, she would have to get out and earn some money.

Anita came bustling up to her and tried to squeeze her arm. Rose was in no mood for having any part of her squeezed by Anita.

'You were great,' Anita fawned. 'The way you stuck to saying he was your boyfriend – it was super.'

'I must have been mad,' said Rose dourly. 'If I'd grassed on you, I'd have been out last night and *you'd* have been banged up.'

'Well, I don't run a brothel.' Anita switched effortlessly from gratitude to indignation. 'They'd got a bloody cheek trying to swing that one on me. Anyone'd think I made money out of it.'

'But you do,' said Rose.

Anita ignored that and switched to her next obsession. She had to get in touch with George urgently. She had tried as soon as his office opened that morning, but there was a useless telephonist there who kept saying he hadn't arrived yet, and she would make sure he got the message to ring Miss Braithwaite; but Anita didn't believe a word of it. Still brooding over the need to raise money fast, Rose let the tide of twitterings flow over her without taking any of it in as they walked away from the court. Anita's swings between adoration of George Ferguson and mistrust of him were so much a part of the daily routine that you never really needed to pay serious attention to the latest outburst, whatever it might be.

Without any conscious purpose in mind, they drifted towards Carol's house, to find her scrubbing the sitting-room carpet with soapy water. 'Can I use your phone?' asked Anita, and proceeded to do so without waiting for an answer.

Rose stared down at Carol's feverish scrubbing. 'What you doing?'

'What's it look like?'

There was a ferocity in her movements that was beginning to alarm Rose. Carol was getting a fetish as weird as some of those their clients got hooked on.

'Did he give you the money, then?'

Carol stopped dead, not looking at her but briefly towards the door as if seeing someone at the foot of the stairs. 'Who?'

'Curly. Who d'you think?'

'Oh, yeh. He came round.'

'So you didn't do the Lane last night, then?'

'No, I stayed in after Curly'd been. I did nothing. Nothing.'

Anita stormed into the room. 'I'm getting sick of this. That thick little tart's still saying he's not in. There's something going on. I've a good mind to go round there.'

Rose wanted to tell Carol her misfortunes that morning, without being talked down by Anita on her pet subject. She was the one who had spent the night locked up. She was the one who had been going to London, and now she couldn't because there was a bloody probation order slapped on her. And twenty-eight days to find three hundred and fifty quid.

'All for that ruddy telly. I'd been renting it for four years, I must have paid for the frigging thing a million times over.'

'What did you want to sell it for?'

'It flickered.'

There was a knock at the front door. Rose automatically stepped out of Carol's way, to find the carpet squelching under her feet.

'Jesus! This carpet's bloody sodden.'

'I'm trying to clean it, that's why.'

'You can get stuff that you just vac up, you know,' said Anita as Carol passed her on the way into the hall.

She and Rose fell into silence as Carol opened the door. Edging to one side, Rose could just see the visitor.

It was Curly.

'Good morning.'

'What do you want?' Not much of a welcome to the man who showed signs of willingness to pay the rent and more besides.

'I just thought I'd see if you were all right.'

'Well, I am.'

'Only they've just released this story of another murder.' He handed her a morning paper. 'There's a picture of her. It's a bit blurred. I thought it was you at first, then I knew it couldn't be, of course.'

'Of course. 'Cos I was here last night, wasn't I? And I'm still here.'

'Can I come in?'

'I'm busy.'

'Did you pay your council tax?'

'Look, will you stop pestering me? I told you, y've to ring before you come round. You can't just turn up like this.'

'I've been worried about you.'

'Well, worry about somebody else. I'll see you on Tuesday.'

She slammed the door and came back in to glower at the two inquisitive faces waiting for her. Rose, having been shut away in the cell, had not seen the news story or the picture on the front page. She reached for the paper, with its heavy black headline:

MURDERER STRIKES AGAIN

'God, yes. Amanda Smeaton. She does look like you, doesn't she?'

'Thanks a lot. That does me nerves a heap of good.'

Anita fretted towards the phone again, and they heard her voice going up half an octave. 'Don't give me that. I thought you were supposed to be his secretary. Well then, where *is* he?' She returned as frustrated as before. 'There's something going on,' she whined again.

Rose shrugged. 'I don't know what you're so worried about George for.'

'I'm worried,' said Anita testily, 'about police turning up at his house and telling his wife his name's on the lease of a brothel, that's what.'

Jameson and two uniformed constables had picked George Ferguson up on the outskirts of Bradford as he left a sub-contractor's office and headed into town. He was at first unctuous; then incredulous; then irritated, building up to a mighty self-righteous rage. It was ridiculous that he, George Ferguson, respectable businessman with strong contacts with the Council and membership of many social groups not entirely unconnected with senior police officers, should be pulled up and questioned in this way. It was ridiculous: bloody ridiculous.

'I'm sorry, sir,' Jameson had said, 'but a car fitting this description was seen in the vicinity of last night's murder.'

'There must be thousands of red Jags. What are you going to do – track them all down?'

'If we have to,' said Jameson patiently, 'yes.'

Ferguson had made a big thing of phoning his office on his mobile phone, raising his voice to make it clear to the three police officers that he had been on his way to an important appointment on civic matters at the city hall, but half distracted by the sight of the two uniformed officers examining the interior of his car. As he finished, they were tugging a container of bleach and several black bags from under the driver's seat.

Still calm and courteous, Jameson said: 'Could you tell me why these were concealed under your seat, sir?'

'Ah, yes, well . . . there's a very simple explanation for those being there.'

When he had been taken into Turton Lane station, DCI Newall was a lot less calm and patient. He was willing to accept that, as the owner of a large cleaning company, Mr Ferguson would have regular supplies of bleach and black plastic bags. Feasible that he would from time to time have some of them in his car.

'But,' he barked suddenly, 'why hide them under your seat?'

'They weren't hidden. They must have just rolled under the seat.'

Newall was beginning to enjoy himself. It was a pleasing sensation to take an overweight showoff like this, so confident of his own status in the community and so oozing with expense account food and booze through his well cut if slightly bulging grey suit, down a peg or two. He said:

'It's a square container, if I remember right. I think the corners would get in the way.'

'Look, chief inspector, I can't think where this line of questioning can possibly—'

'I want to know what your car was doing parked off Mannering Lane last night.'

'It wasn't my car.' Ferguson, his face growing redder and his forehead damper, stood up. 'I've had enough of this. I've got people to meet.'

'Not at the moment you haven't, Mr Ferguson. You're going nowhere till you've answered my questions. It *was* your car parked off Mannering Lane. We've checked the registration number.'

Ferguson stood defiant for a moment; then slumped down again. 'All right, for God's sake. I was meeting someone and I didn't want my car parked outside their house. Satisfied?'

'No. I want to know who you were meeting, and I want to know where you were on April the seventh.'

'April the seventh? I've no bloody idea. What's so important about the seventh?'

'It was the night Gina Dixon was killed,' said Newall.

Now he knew that all he had to do was sit back and wait. It wouldn't take long. Ferguson's breathing was pitiful. He gasped and spluttered while all too obviously concocting a number of stories in his head and wondering which one would sound the most plausible. Out of it all would emerge something close to the truth, though that wouldn't be Ferguson's intention.

'We were watching a video.' Ferguson made his choice. 'I was in the flat – Miss Braithwaite's flat, I can give you the address—'

'We already have it,' said Newall smugly.

'What? Why should you—'

'You were in Miss Braithwaite's flat,' Newall prompted him, 'watching a video. Can you tell me what it was? And how long it took? And what time you left?'

Ferguson made an act of scratching his head, and asked how the hell he was expected to remember that. He was a busy man, he had a lot to keep in that head.

'And last night?' said Newall.

'What about last night?'

'Don't say you haven't seen the papers? There was another murder last night. Were you watching a video then, as well?'

By the time Ferguson had finished, Newall felt that a call on Miss Anita Braithwaite might prove very fruitful. There were some loose ends to be tied up; and some of them might be snarled in with the threads of one or two other matters which were coming to light.

On the way he called in at the hospital with Kershaw at his side. They had established who had bashed the back of the Richards girl's head in, so she didn't seem to belong in the frame with the other two attacks. But something niggled at the back of Newall's mind. All this sleazy lot were bound up with one another. There had to be some bits of information that would help link them together.

A middle-aged man with a pleasant face and an awkward, diffident smile was sitting on the edge of Naomi Richards' bed, unwrapping a box of chocolates. 'And I saw this little fellow, and I couldn't resist him.' The girl, sitting propped up against a pile of pillows, smiled feebly as she accepted a floppy spotted dog. 'We've really missed you, love,' the man went on with an urgent longing to get some response. 'I thought we'd never see you again. We used to drive round night after night, just looking for you.'

Newall paused beside Mrs Richards, who was asking a doctor: 'When do you think we'll be able to take her home?'

'Mm. She's taken quite a bang, but she's young. Sitting up and really taking notice. We'd like to keep an eye on her for another day or two, to be on the safe side. But she's doing pretty well.'

'In which case,' said Newall bluntly, 'we'd like to take a statement off her before she's discharged. Then we can clear off and let the family have some privacy.'

'As long as you keep it as brief as possible.'

Newall moved in closer to the bed. Her father got up but retreated only a few feet, watching apprehensively, wanting to hear yet not wanting to hear.

'How you feeling, then, Naomi? Think you could manage a statement?'

'Of course she couldn't,' Richards snapped protectively. 'She's only just—'

'It's all right –' the girl stared straight past him '– I can talk to them.'

Kershaw took out her notebook.

'Right.' Newall made it quiet and encouraging. 'That night, outside the hotel . . .'

'I was just leaving the hotel, and I remember thinking I heard something. But then you always think that when it's dark and you're alone.' Newall was aware of Richards putting an arm round his wife's shoulder; and of Mrs

Richards instinctively jerking away. 'I turned round, but I couldn't see anything, so I just walked a bit faster. And the next thing I remember was waking up in here.'

'So do you usually work the hotel or was this—'

'Really!' Richards protested. 'I do think she's had enough—'

'We'll be as quick as we can,' said Newall. He kept his gaze on Naomi's pale yet resolute face. Only the girl he was addressing was now reverting to the one Carol had called Tracy. 'Was the hotel your usual patch?'

'No, it was the first time I'd been in there. Carol, that was the woman I was with, had pulled this trick.' It was disconcerting, the way she slipped in and out between a flat little middle-class voice and the language and accent of the Lane. 'Only she thought he was the murderer, because he was new on the Lane and he was throwing his money about.'

Newall had great difficulty in maintaining his professional, unemotional attitude. The name of Carol reverberated so loudly around the depths of his mind that it was a marvel the whole ward couldn't hear it.

'She'd arranged to meet him at the hotel,' Tracy went on, 'so we could be in the next room in case anything happened.'

Her mother and father were spellbound, yet trying to look detached from it all. Newall didn't feel detached. He coaxed Tracy into finishing off the story, nodded to Kershaw that she could close her notebook, and sent her back to the station while he went off to make a very personal call on his own.

He did not bother with the front door, but went in through the kitchen. Carol was in the hall, wiping the walls down and peering at what might be a slight tear in the fabric or a smear of grease.

He wasted no time. 'I just don't understand you. Why didn't you tell me you suspected someone?'

'What are you on about this time?'

'I've been talking to Naomi. Or Tracy, or whatever.'

'Oh.' Carol's attention was concentrated on wiping round the light switch. 'Because you wouldn't have taken it seriously, that's why.'

'Right, fine!' he exploded. 'So you go into a hotel room with some man you think might be a murderer and you take a stupid little fifteen-year-old to protect you—'

'Look, I don't have to answer you.'

'Yes, you do. Because I'll pull you in if I have to.'

'On what charge?'

'Prostitution, for a start.'

'Well, that would be interesting, wouldn't it?' Carol carefully folded her cleaning rag and laid it on the hall shelf. 'I could tell them how many free shags Detective Sergeant Newall had when he was working in Vice, and then Detective Inspector Newall following in his footsteps. Footsteps, eh? Lots of free shags so that I didn't get busted.'

He couldn't believe that that was all it had ever meant to her. He wouldn't let himself believe it. He didn't want her to live this sort of life, had never wanted her to. Would she never realise? He grabbed her and dragged her towards him, thrusting his mouth down and kissing her.

She bit his lip, the bitch.

'That's my mouth,' she raged. 'I kiss my little girl with it.'

He groped for a handkerchief to dab at the blood oozing on to his chin. 'Don't lump me with *them*.'

She dragged the front door open. 'Why, what makes you think you're any better? What d'you think I did it for – love?'

Right. That had put him in a perfect mood to round off the day's work by visiting Anita Braithwaite.

She confirmed George Ferguson's story that they had watched a video together on the night of Gina Dixon's murder. No, she couldn't remember which one. He must know how easily these things were forgotten. They passed the time, and that was that. She had watched hundreds in her time.

'It could have been *City Slickers* or that one with Jamie Lee Curtis in, or *Terminator Two*, I've no idea.'

'You've taken it back, then?'

'Well –' she was obviously pleased with her own sharpness '– I'd have had a bloody big fine if I hadn't: I mean, April the seventh!'

'I was talking about last night.'

That threw her. 'What? I thought you were talking about . . . I mean, we didn't watch a video last night.'

'Sorry, I thought you did.'

'Is that what George said?' she asked warily.

'It doesn't matter what George Ferguson said. We want the truth.'

Newall could almost feel sorry for her as she fumbled, trying to guess what had been said and what he was going to spring on her. 'Well, I'm trying to remember. We might have watched something I taped last week.' She managed a wide smile. 'Yes, that's right, we did. Maybe that's what he was thinking of.' She leaned forward and inspected his lip. 'You want some TCP on that.'

'George has his own key, does he? Lets himself in?'

'Of course he does.'

'Through the downstairs door?'

'Well, he doesn't come down the chimney.'

'Only you might remember –' Newall drew it out, ready now to let her know what she was in for '– that this flat was under surveillance yesterday. Caused you a bit of an upset, didn't it?'

'It was outrageous. Accusing me of—'

'And guess what? There's no record of Mr George Ferguson either entering or leaving these premises.'

Anita was cornered, but made a last dismal attempt. 'Well,

he did. And I'm not saying anything else till I've talked to a solicitor.'

'Do you know what I think?'

'I don't care what you think.'

'I think,' said Newall, on his feet and on the way out, 'that you're lying to us. And if you are, you'll go down till it's time for your bus pass.' He grinned a farewell. 'You know where to find us.'

13

The Lane was as empty as if it had been stricken by a plague. Rose shifted her weight from one foot to another and stared disconsolately along the pavement. There was the sound of an engine coming round the corner, but it turned out to be only a brewery delivery lorry taking a short cut. If this sort of thing went on, they'd all have to combine to set up a counter in a supermarket to sell their wares. She tried to imagine what description would be printed on the aisle marker.

At last a car slowed towards her and stopped. She stooped to look in through the open window.

'Hello, lovely. You looking for a nice time?'

He was a young workman in jeans and a sweatshirt. He eyed her with waning enthusiasm. 'Do I get a rebate on account of your age?'

'Forget it.' She heard his raucous laugh as he drove off.

That did it. She'd had enough. The pub door was open, but the interior would probably be as gloomy and deserted as the Lane. Rose went aimlessly past the betting shop towards the newsagent's; then saw that every placard was screaming about a sex killer on the loose, and hurried past. Turning the corner, she narrowly avoided bumping into Carol.

She said the first thing that came into her head. 'I'm off to London.'

'Again?' said Carol sceptically.

'The hell with the bail and everything else. I'll never earn that fine here, the way things are. So I'm off.'

'Let's scrounge a drink off Anita. I'm on my way to collect some bleach from her.'

'Christ, the rate you get through it you ought to have personal deliveries by tanker.'

Anita let them in with an impatient grunt, and hurried back to the television. There were two familiar faces on the screen, tilting to and fro as cameramen jostled for position. God knows how they had all found out the exact moment of Tracy's discharge from hospital. DCI Newall was trying to carve a way through their ranks, while Mr and Mrs Richards flanked Tracy, keeping her head down as they stumbled towards a chauffeur-driven Rover.

'How yer feeling, Naomi?'

'Did you get a look at him?'

Lights flashed as a newspaper photographer tried to get an angle on Tracy.

'Clear the way, please,' yelled Newall.

'How long have you been on the game, Naomi?'

Mr Richards tried to push a man out of the way, while Newall got his hand right across a camera and eased it aside.

'She's not a prostitute,' Mrs Richards was saying haughtily. 'And none of it is any concern of yours.'

Rose marvelled at the woman's composure. She had been all of a dither inside the hospital, but faced with this sort of harassment she could really put on the posh act, looking down her nose at the lot of them.

The rat-pack turned their attention to Newall.

'Chief Inspector, could this be another Ripper?'

'As I said in my press statement, we have charged someone in connection with this case and that's all I'm prepared to say at this stage.'

'Go on' – Rose vented her frustration at the screen – 'tell 'em it were her ponce.'

The picture gave way to one of a motorway pile-up, and Anita reached for her remote control to switch off.

146

'I can't keep up with everything that's going on. One minute it's Curly, the next it's Tracy's ponce, and then they're looking for a red Jag. I mean, every two minutes it's somebody else.'

'Because they haven't got the foggiest idea who it is, that's why,' said Carol bitterly.

'Well, I wish they'd bloody hurry up and find out. It's driving me barmy is all this.'

Rose glanced at Carol. They both sensed that something was up. Apart from the brief alarm over the vice squad swoop, Anita wasn't under any threat. Not like the rest of them, out on the street. It had been the hustlers who had suffered so far, and whatever name you chose to bestow on Anita, that could hardly be it. She would never have had the energy. Yet she was even more twitchy than usual. What was it this time?

'What's eating you?' asked Rose.

'It could be anybody.' Anita put the remote control down, plumped up a few cushions as if she had caught some nervous disease from Carol, and dabbed at her eyes with a flowery patterned handkerchief. 'I mean, it could be somebody we know.'

'Go on.'

'Go on what?'

'You know summat and you're not letting on.'

It was Carol who twigged it. 'They've had George in, haven't they?'

'Only because he drives a Jag. I bet they've pulled loads of people in. Anyway,' said Anita frantically, 'it isn't him.'

'Why not?'

'Because it just isn't, that's why.'

'Well, that's easy to prove,' Rose pointed out. 'All he has to do is say where he was on the nights of the murders, that's all.'

'Exactly.' Anita sounded anything but happy about this. Carol stood over her. 'So where was he?'

147

It came tumbling out. 'He was with somebody from the Council when Amanda Smeaton got done. Only he couldn't tell the police that, because he was doing a backhander. You know how George operates.'

'We can guess.'

'So he said he was with me.'

'And when Gina was killed?'

'Well, he *was* with me that night.'

'Just a minute. I thought you said he left just after Gina dumped her case.'

Now it was clear what had been worrying Anita. 'Yes. He did.'

'Only you didn't tell the police that.'

'No. What do you think I am?'

Again there was the temptation to tell her. But Carol said simply: 'What exactly *have* you and George got round to telling them?'

Anita was never coherent at the best of times, and now she was so confused and terrified that it was hard to work out exactly what she had said to George or George had said to her, or what the police might be expected to make of it. But there was no doubt about the fear: not fear of the killer, but of George himself and what damage she might have done.

He had come straight from the police station to sort out what had got him there in the first place. And he was livid when she confessed she had told the police all about their relationship, and the flat, and him having the lease on it. She had done it for his own good, because if they were going to pull him in it would come out anyway that his name was on that lease. Only George didn't see it that way. He had been pulled in only because his red Jag had been seen near where that scrubber had been killed, so he had had to explain whom he was visiting. They would have accepted his story about the black bags and the bleach in his car being for her, without her having to let out every sodding detail about the

flat and why his name was on the rent book. To make up
for that, she'd better stand firm that he had been with her on
the night of Gina's murder and during this latest killing.

And then she'd had to tell him that they'd been watching
the place anyway, and had tried to do her for running a
brothel.

'He blew his top,' Anita wailed. 'I mean, I told him they
couldn't make it stick and everything was all right now, and
anyway who was he to complain? I mean, I helped him out a
couple of times with some of his contracts – favours for that
councillor, and a few others. You remember, don't you?' she
appealed to Carol.

'Yeh, I remember. Pathetic.'

'But the way he carried on at me . . . I mean, what does
he think I am?'

Rose said, 'Probably what the rest of us think. Bloody
stupid, that's what. Come on, get your coat on.'

'What for?'

'You're going to the station to tell 'em the truth.'

'But if George—'

'If you don't come out with the truth this time, you could
be on the front page, next to Gina and Amanda Smeaton.'

Anita stared imploringly at Carol. 'I feel sick.'

Newall had been gloomily shuffling possibilities to and fro
along with a pile of witness statements and accumulated
notes from Kershaw and Jameson. Every time he thought
he had found a clear lead, it blurred before his eyes and he
had to restrain himself from risking any attempt to tread a
logical way across a quagmire to solid ground on the other
side. Plenty of bog; no firm footholds.

For the tenth time he ticked off names on a notepad
congested with his scribblings. Some of the doodles might
have meant a lot to a psychiatrist but were not much use to
a policeman in search of cold, clear facts.

Steve Dixon, for a start. Each time Newall came to analyse

149

the possibilities, he saw Dixon as an inadequate person, cast off by his wife and lousy at coping with life in general; but not necessarily incapable of murdering that wife. She had chucked him out, she had gone on the game and maybe enjoyed it; and when he found out, he was the sort of unimaginative slob who could be so outraged that he would go for her in murderous disgust. There were reports of him having hit her a number of times while they were married. It was only a couple of steps from there to go madly at her and this time finish the job. Newall would have liked it to be Dixon. After that assault on Carol showed what the man was capable of, he would very much like to deliver Dixon to a life sentence.

Yet he was uneasy. The original theory that the murder of Gina Dixon could be linked with the attack on Tracy — or Naomi Richards, as she now appeared in the case file — had proved a false trail. The Dez Sadiq affair was being satisfactorily wrapped up on its own. The likelihood of Sadiq murdering Gina Dixon as Tracy's rival and therefore a threat to his own pocket could not be entirely ruled out, but Newall was pretty well convinced by now that it was a dead end. The murder of Amanda Smeaton, though, did seem to follow rationally on from that of Gina Dixon. And Steve Dixon, blast him, just had to be innocent of the Smeaton killing, even though the method of strangulation was so similar. So was Dixon innocent of the first one as well? And if so, who the hell was out on the loose, slaying at random?

Or not at random?

He turned his attention to George Ferguson. They were only at the beginning of inquiries here, and he was not optimistic. The man was a shyster, all right. There were rumours of shady dealings with local authorities, especially in regard to the new Leisure Centre. Nothing that would stick, though he was certainly a sticky character in himself. And the business with him and Anita Braithwaite was comic rather than suspicious. A sleazy individual rather than a murderous one, you'd have thought: cheating the public and Council officials, and two-timing his wife, but not a big-time operator. It was emerging that he had interests in a shady credit company and in hardline debt collecting, with characters like that yobbo Simon Moore working for him; but shady though it might be, it wasn't illegal, and Newall didn't see Ferguson as being in the Mafia class, wiping people out if they didn't pay their debts. In any case, Anita Braithwaite's confirmation of him being with her on the crucial two nights seemed to stand up, and was in line with the sort of tawdry little characters they both were.

Unoptimistically Newall re-read the list of known or suspected sex offenders, including any released from prison within the last couple of months, which Jameson had wearily checked out. None fitted the pattern or the timetable, and there was no vestige of evidence against any of them. Somebody new and unidentifiable was walking the streets; somebody with a grudge, or with a mania which made his next move unpredictable.

Newall stacked the sheets of paper neatly and started again from the top.

Then Miss Braithwaite was suddenly on stage again. He could hardly believe it when Kershaw wheeled the woman into an interview room, doing a tearful, supplicatory act.

'You've got something to add to your statement, Miss Braithwaite?'

She came out with it right away. 'George. He didn't come round the other night.'

'Which night?'

'The night that other woman got killed.'

'So you lied to us?'

'Only 'cos he made me,' she wept. 'It's his flat, you see—'

'We know all that. You've already told us.'

'Yes, well. Don't you see? I have to do as he says or I'd have nowhere to live. Same as the night Gina was killed.'

Newall felt another of his suppositions splintering apart. 'You mean he wasn't with you then, either?'

'He left just after she did. Only he told me I had to tell you he was with me all night.'

Newall was tempted to put his arm round her and offer her a handkerchief. She was his favourite woman of the day – of the week. But sympathy could be allowed to go too far. First things first. He watched the tears make ugly smears down her cheeks, and set about producing a few more of them.

The plaque looked harsh and new. The raised lettering would one day be as chipped and faded as the words on the other little rectangles along the wall, commemorating those whose ashes lay in the ground below; but today it was so defiantly bright that Carol found it without difficulty. There was a white urn for holding flowers, but it was full, and she had to stoop to one side to lay her small bouquet on the grass.

There was another cluster of flowers propped against the urn, dead already. Yet the card sticking up between the stems looked quite clean, not yet pulpy with rain, and the message on it not yet smudged. It consisted of one word, in capital letters:

SINNER

Carol shivered, suddenly sure that she was being watched. Still bent over the dead flowers, she looked round. Standing beside a memorial column far across the cemetery was a man whose features were unrecognisable from this distance. He was motionless, might almost have been a statue. But he was no statue. Carol was sure, quite sure that he was watching her.

'Aren't you Emma's mam?'

Carol whimpered, and stumbled to her feet. 'God, you frightened me.' Face to face, she recognised Gina's mother, who came nowadays to collect Joanne from school. 'Sorry, it's just that there's a man . . .' She forced herself to look again at the granite column. There was nobody beside it. But there had been somebody watching, she would swear to it.

'Are you all right?' Joyce stooped to push the dead flowers aside. 'These must have been from Steve. He should have put them in some water. But that's Steve, you know.'

Carol realised she was still clutching the card. She crushed it between her fingers and thrust it into her jacket pocket.

Steve. Yes, she knew some things about Steve Dixon. But it probably hadn't been Steve who laid these dead flowers here, and she was sure it hadn't been Steve standing over there a few minutes ago.

'It's nice of you to come.' Joyce was choking back her emotions and trying to keep her voice steady. 'She didn't have a lot of friends.'

'I wanted to see where she was.' It was hard to know how much to say and how much to keep to herself, not knowing how much of the truth Gina's mother could bear.

Joyce had brought a small pot plant. She set it on the ground, looked at the plaque as if she could still not believe what it signified, and then touched Carol's arm nervously, half inviting her to walk back to the gates with her.

'I thought she was doing the makeup round.' It was more like an incantation to throw off a hideous spell than a conversational remark.

Carol said, 'I thought she was on her way home. She'd always said she'd pack it in the moment she could pay her loan off. But we'd fallen out over some money I'd nicked off a punter, and she didn't want her half – went all funny on me, said I shouldn't have taken it—'

'She's . . . she was like that. You could trust her with . . .' Joyce sniffled and looked away. 'It shouldn't have happened to her. It . . .'

'I thought she'd maybe got enough to pack it in,' said Carol helplessly, 'and that's why she just walked off.'

153

'It's not fair. She was so young. I wish,' cried Joyce, 'it'd have been me instead.'

They parted at the gates. When Joyce was well out of sight, Carol took out the crumpled card. Staring at the word gave no idea of the fanatic who must have written the letters so large and carefully.

SINNER

14

She would have to get used to being called Naomi again. She didn't want to go back to being Naomi, but it was going to be difficult to fight it off. The surroundings were closing in on her. The large oak dining table was as solid as ever, her mother's dried flower arrangements were as tasteful as ever, the faint smell from the pot-pourri bowl was as she had always known it, and the view from the window on to the garden with its sundial and birdbath was the same. It was all conspiring to draw her back into the world she had inhabited before these last remote months.

Only they weren't remote. They were real. Much more real than the dismal years she had spent here and was expected to spend here again.

She was Tracy, not Naomi. She had always hated that name. And hated her sister's name, Laura. She knew, too, that Laura hated her. That uppity, holier-than-thou face of hers had been studying her ever since she got back, criticising without a word, until those stiff little lips opened so that she could try and make Tracy feel guilty about Mum and Dad arguing after she had disappeared, Mum having to go for counselling, and Laura praying – she came out and admitted it – that when she heard her sister had been found and was really ill, she had prayed to God she would die.

When her mother came in with a summer pudding which had collapsed, blathering away about old favourites and wasn't it fun to be all together again, Tracy sat stonily contemplating the mess and wishing she could pretend to go along with the whole silly charade. But Laura was getting up and making excuses about having to get off to school and learn her lines for the play, and giving her sister one farewell glance that showed how much she was enjoying the feeling of contempt for her.

'I've been thinking,' Mrs Richards was rattling on, 'that when you're feeling better we could go on a little holiday, just a week away somewhere, together – a family do. We could get one of those last-minute savers. What do you think?'

Tracy said, 'It won't just go away, Mum.'

'I know it won't. But we have to try.'

'Laura hates me.'

'Of course she doesn't. She's your sister. I'll have a word with her when she comes home, and—'

'It's not her fault.'

'Well, whose fault is it, then?' As a kid, Tracy had always been in awe of her mother's beautiful face. It was the sort of classic face you saw in advertisements for expensive clothes and cosmetics – aloof yet inviting, very sure of itself. Only late on had she learned that there was no such assurance there: and no help or assurance for the rest of the family. Now that statuesque, remotely adorable woman was degrading herself, making a piteous appeal. 'My fault? Is that what you're saying? Because if it is, then you have to tell me, and I can do something about it.'

'Like you did last time, you mean?' It was cruel, but the pain in Tracy's head had begun again, and she didn't see why her mother had to be spared.

No answer was possible. Her mother made none.

That evening the scene was the same, the atmosphere the same. Tracy had curled up on the sofa after refusing tea and cream cakes, settling into a pile of cushions that would not press too hard on the sensitive, aching back of her head. She was drowsy. It came in waves, the ebb and flow between wretchedness and bewilderment. Closing her eyes, she wanted to forget. Not to forget the Lane and Dez and the lifters he had found for her, but to forget life here in this house and to blot out the realisation that she had come back to it.

They thought she was asleep, or in such a trauma that she wouldn't understand what they were talking about. Her father wanting to know why her mother wasn't going for her appointment with the therapist. And her mother saying it was Naomi's first night home, and surely they had to be all together. Nice conventional stuff. All the right phrases. All the wrong thoughts. And all the time her father was making a pretence of seriously considering his students' essays and conscientiously marking them. All of it just the way it had always been.

'You can be there and back before she wakes up,' he said. 'And anyway, nothing's going to happen to her. I'm here.'

'Yes.'

'And Laura will be back from her rehearsal soon.'

'No, she won't. It's the dress this evening. She's going to be later than usual. I told Nicola's mother that you'd pick them up about nine from the church hall.'

The more Tracy tried to shut out the growingly menacing voices, the sharper and more meaningful they became.

'Helen, I hope this isn't what I think it is.'

'And what do you think it is, Tim? Come on, tell me.'

'No, it's for you to tell me. I asked the question.'

Tracy knew that her mother would dodge now, as she had dodged before. 'There's a maniac on the loose,' she was saying irrelevantly. 'We've already nearly lost one daughter.'

Which had nothing to do with anything that either of them was really thinking, or avoiding having to think. Tracy eased herself into a more comfortable position, and at once there was an unhealthy silence. Drowsily she wondered what would happen if she sat up and said out loud what they all knew had gone on for so long but had never admitted.

About her father with his hand down her knickers, about the prodding and caressing and about getting a new pair of trainers for playing piggybacks with Daddy: never with Laura, but always with Naomi, over and over again. For a long time she had believed that that was what all daddies did. And when she had hinted about it to her mother, the only response had been a waving of those lovely slim white hands and 'No, don't talk such nonsense, dear.'

They must be looking at her, trying to make out whether she had fallen asleep again.

Very quietly her father said, 'It's in your head, Helen. You imagine things and then blame me. I still think you ought to go for that counselling session.'

'If it's so good, why don't *you* go?'

'Because I don't need to, that's why.'

Mrs Richards stormed out of the room, banging the door behind her. Tracy kept her eyes clamped shut, silently defying her father to get up and come a step closer. It seemed an eternity before he finished his marking and went off to fetch Laura home.

When they were both out of the way — her father out with the car, her mother somewhere in the back of the house — Tracy crept upstairs and locked her bedroom door. She still felt woozy and not really in touch with the real world, but she was sure she would get her balance back once she was out of here. No good would ever come of staying here and trying to make a go of it, no matter what they offered her. She wanted to get back to Dez and take up where they had left off. He must have been livid when he heard what had happened. She wouldn't put it past him to go on a manhunt and carve the bloke up when he found him. But it would all be all right when they were back together again. He'd probably find some way of blaming her for wandering off on her own and then letting herself be brought back to Harrogate; but like all of his moods it would only be a brief one, and he'd give her a lifter and they'd laugh and she'd be out earning money again. No way was she going to rely on her mother and father to provide for her.

She studied herself in the long wardrobe mirror. She had lost a lot of weight in that short time. She had never had much meat on her bones, but now she was positively skinny. And her hair was a mess. She would have to wear some sort of turban for a week or two to cover that bald patch at the back, and then cut the rest of it in pageboy style. No problem. Lots of punters would go for that.

Her canvas school sports bag was still on top of the wardrobe. She reached up for it, and began digging clothes out of the chest of drawers. She was zipping the bag shut when there was a knock at the door. Tracy stood very still, then pushed the bag under her bed.

'Come on, I know you're in there.'

Reluctantly Tracy opened the door. Laura looked blown up with her own importance, as she always did when it was a matter of the school play or a concert at which she had been asked to give a recitation. With the door open, a sudden spurt of argument wafted up the stairs.

'They're at it again,' said Laura. 'I thought I'd let them get on with it.'

Tracy forced herself to ask, 'How was your rehearsal?'

'Crap,' said Laura loftily. 'Nobody knows their lines. Mr Marsh gave us a right bollocking.' She closed the door. 'I'm never going to get married. But guess what? I did it last week with Lee Paget. It's funny, he got straight As in his exams, but he'd got no idea where to put it.' She allowed herself a patronising smile at her sister. 'I suppose technically I'm still a virgin, but I'm not telling anybody that.' Abruptly the smile snapped off. 'It must be horrible having sex with a complete stranger?'

'It is. But I had to do it, because we needed the money.'

'Who's *we*?'

'Dez, he's my boyfriend, we were living together and everything.'

Laura could not help looking envious. 'I bet he was upset when he found out what had happened to you. Did he come to the hospital?'

'No, because the police were there, and they'd got it in for him because he used to do drugs.'

Laura's eyes widened. She was even more impressed. 'You didn't ever take anything, did you?'

'Just a little lifter sometimes, that's all, if I got depressed. He always knew if I needed something,' she recollected fondly.

Below them the front door slammed shut. Laura went to the window and drew the curtain as a car engine revved violently.

'It's Mum. She'll come back with a bottle of brandy and drink herself stupid.'

There didn't seem to be anything else to say between them. Laura hesitated, then assumed her contemptuous expression again and went out. The moment Tracy heard the door of the bathroom open and shut, she hauled out the canvas bag and cautiously looked over the banisters. Her father had put the music centre on loud, as if to drown out everything – like the grubby memories that were by now coming back to haunt him? – with some of his favourite Tchaikovsky. She took one precautionary glance at the bathroom door, and went silently downstairs, opening the front door and clicking it shut with infinite care.

It was pelting down with rain, but she didn't care. She had found an old beret which would have to do until she could get her hands on something more provocative. It was a long walk to the station, but once she reached the centre of town there were plenty of awnings and ornamental arcades she'd be able to dodge under.

Behind her a car hissed along the glistening street. Instinctively she half turned, geared up to assess a punter and maybe get a drive to the station anyway. But the voice from inside was her mother's.

'Where the hell d'you think you're going?'

'Away!' Tracy stumbled along the pavement, the dizziness coming back and the bag weighing her down.

'Get in the car.' Mrs Richards fumbled the door open and got out to stand by it. 'Naomi!'

'I'm not Naomi.' It was no use trying to run. Better to stand her ground and finish it here and now. 'My name's Tracy. I picked that because it's what I always wanted to be called. I don't like Naomi – I hate it.'

'All right. Tracy . . . will you please get in the car?'

'No.'

'Don't be stupid.' Mrs Richards must have had a good swig at the brandy before starting homewards. 'What are you going to do? Go back on the streets, sell yourself again?'

Tracy grinned wryly. Hadn't she already sold herself when she was eleven? Sold herself for that new pair of trainers, and the other things her father gave her as presents when she had played the little games she thought all daddies must play with their daughters.

She said, 'It's no worse than what happened at home.'

Rain was streaming down her mother's face, dragging dank strands of hair across her eyes. 'Look, Naomi . . . Tracy . . . if it's true, then I'm going to have to do something about it.'

Like last time? She hadn't believed a word of what her daughter had said then, or blindly refused to believe, and now didn't believe a word she herself was saying. Tracy knew it would never come to the crunch: her mother leaving her father, conscientiously reporting his habits to the school so that he would lose his job, facing a court case and summoning Tracy as a witness to give evidence against him . . . No, that wasn't what any of them wanted.

Tracy turned and went on through the rain.

'Naomi, please . . .'

But there was no real power in the appeal.

Tracy had calculated she had just enough money to pay

the train fare from Harrogate to Bradford, but found she didn't need it. Before she could get to the station a green Renault swerved in beside her. She braced herself to say she wasn't that kind of girl, or that tonight was her night for the launderette, or something equally silly. But the driver was simply a middle-aged woman sympathetically offering her a lift to the station; and then revealing that she was actually on her way to Bradford and would be glad of Tracy's company that far. She asked the usual conventional questions, and accepted Tracy's non-committal answers without wishing to press any further. The only matter on which she insisted was delivering Tracy right to the address she wanted, rather than leave her to make her own way through the rain which had accompanied them non-stop from Harrogate.

Tracy waved gratefully as she turned towards the steps of 160 Marston Grove. Dez's car was parked on the far side of the road. Everything would soon be all right. He must be home; and she was coming home.

A dark-haired girl in her late teens answered the door.

'What do you want?' It wasn't the kind of welcome Tracy had been longing for.

'Who are you?' she asked.

'I live here. Who are *you*?'

She couldn't credit that Dez would have let another girl move in so fast. Yet deep down she was wounded rather than surprised. 'Tracy,' she said. 'Where's Dez?'

'What d'you want to know for?'

'I just do.' Tracy wasn't going to wear this sort of cheek. 'Get him for me.'

'I can't. He's banged up. In Wakefield nick.'

Tracy's stomach knotted in a convulsion of misery. 'What for? What's he done?'

'They said he hit some slag over the head. But he's getting a good solicitor, so maybe he'll be out soon.' The girl relented, peering worriedly at Tracy as she nearly tripped backwards off the step. 'I can get a message to him if you like.'

It couldn't be true. Crazy, couldn't have happened that way. But Tracy knew it had to be true. That blow on the back of her head, the whole pattern of it: hadn't she been frightened all along, that night, that Dez would come looking for her? And that was what he had done.

'Are you all right?' the girl was saying. 'Do you want me to tell him anything, or don't you?'

Tracy wasn't going to break down here, adding her tears to the relentless rain. 'Tell him Tracy's still smiling,' she managed. 'Tell him that from me.'

15

Rose took a long swig from the pint of lager which Carol had bought her. Much more of this and she would get even more maudlin than she already felt. Carol wasn't being much help, just sitting there wrapped up in her own gloomy thoughts. Jan had put on a noisy tape of some group with rasping voices over a steady thumping beat, but it made The Hustlers' Arms seem even emptier and sadder.

Rose did another lot of mental arithmetic in her head. The sum came out no better than before. How was she supposed to live and pay that bloody fine when there was so little work to be had right now? The answer had to be London. Even for an empty-headed hustler like herself, getting near her sell-by date, there had to be some work in London.

What made it worse was the thought of the years she had wasted. Because she hadn't been all that empty-headed, really. I used to read books once, she thought wistfully. There'd been *Alice in Wonderland*, *Gulliver's Travels*, and loads like that. And she had been best in the class at drawing. Where had it all gone?

She wanted to ask Carol for some sort of reassurance, but Carol was sunk in her own reverie. A right cheerful evening this was going to be. It was almost a relief when Anita came in through the side door – until you saw the rivulets of mascara running down her face and the sodden tissue she was clutching in her hand. Whatever troubles you might have, you could always rely on Anita having something ten times worse to moan about.

'George!' she cried with a fine melodramatic quaver. 'He's been doing the dirty on me.'

Carol woke up and went to fetch a drink. This sounded quite promising. Before she had even got back to the table, Anita had fixed Rose with a stare as fierce as she could make it through the blur of tears and collapsing makeup, and launched into a tragic tirade.

When George had showed up early this evening she had thought he was coming to kill her. He might just as well have done. Instead, he just stood there and said he was finished with her. He made no attempt to break the news gently. He sounded proud of the fact that he had been screwing around, screwing somebody else behind her back. 'And he said it was someone he respected – *respected!* – like he didn't respect me.' He had been seeing her for months. And that night when Gina got killed, he'd left early because he was meeting *her*. He had tried not to give her name because she was a decent, respectable woman – something Anita wouldn't know anything about. But he'd had to tell the police in the end, because of Anita dropping him in it, and now he was in the clear, and he wanted to be clear of Anita as well. It was all over.

'After all I've done for him,' she sobbed. 'I'd have done anything for him. The men I've turned down because of him. And I never asked him to leave Kathleen, not once.'

Carol pushed the Malibu and Coke across the table towards her. Anita sipped noisily.

'You've got to look on the bright side,' said Rose. 'At least you won't have to shag him any more.'

'But I liked shagging him.'

'More fool you.'

'It'll be some snotty woman off the council.'

That was probably true, thought Rose: some woman George could get something useful out of. 'Anyway –' she turned to Carol '– she's well shot of him, isn't she?'

Carol had been covertly studying a crumpled card she had

taken from her jacket pocket. Hastily she stuffed it back into the jacket, and stood up. 'You're driving me bleeding mad, the pair of you. I'm off home.'

They watched her go, stunned. Anita seemed about to ask what was eating her today, but changed her mind and reverted to her favourite topic: herself. After the better part of an hour, Rose had had enough. Sympathetic nods and cheerful assurances that everything would turn out for the best got her nowhere. The only way to distract Anita was to get her on her feet and out of here, with the promise of a chicken biriani from the takeaway.

The lamentations continued all the way along the street. 'Y'know, in the beginning when we first started seeing each other, he used to tell me that I was the only one he'd ever loved and one day we'd be together. I thought one day he'd just turn up with his bags and we'd be together, and—'

'Who's that at your place?' Rose interrupted.

Two men were close to the front door of the flat. To one side were four plastic bags bulging with unidentifiable bits and pieces. As Anita cried out 'What d'you think you're playing at?' one of the men stood back and began putting away his locksmith's tools into a small bag. The other grinned into the light of the street lamp.

'What's it look like?' It was the dreaded Mr Moore.

'That's my door.'

'And that's your lock.' Moore dropped it into her palm as she held out an accusing hand. 'And your possessions are in those bags, all nicely packed. Sorry I haven't time to give you a hand carrying them . . . wherever.'

'You can't do that!'

Moore got into his car. 'I just have.'

Anita stared helplessly at the plastic bags. 'He's got no right. No right to just sling me out in the street.' She jabbed at a bulge threatening to split one of the bags open. 'I hope my duvet's in there. I bought that myself, and my cover. And there's got to be my picture – he bought me that from

167

Tenerife, he's not having that, it's mine.' She got her fingers round the necks of two of the bags; and Rose had no option but to lug the other two along the Lane with her. They plodded a few yards without the foggiest idea where they were heading.

Suddenly Anita burst out, 'This is all your bloody fault.'

'Mine?'

'If I hadn't listened to you and grassed on George, none of this would have happened.'

'Yes it would. You said he's been screwing her for months.'

'I'm not talking about that. I'm talking about the flat. How'm I going to live? It's all right for you. You can pull a punter and get some money whenever you like, but I can't.'

'Why not?'

'Because I'm not like that, that's why.'

'Think you're a cut above us, do yer? D'you think what you've been doing with George all these years is any better? Well, you can think again, because you're just a tart like the rest of us.'

'I am not,' panted Anita. 'You don't know anything about my life, so you can just piss off.'

Which was fair enough so far as Rose was concerned. She dumped the plastic sacks unceremoniously on the pavement and marched off.

There were precious few possessions to go into the battered suitcase. Unlike Anita, Rose had acquired nothing of any sentimental value – or any other kind of value – these last few years. The only thing that mattered was a fading snapshot, curling at the corners, of her baby. She looked at it once before slipping it back into her bank book and dropping it into her bag. It did no good to look at it too often.

In five minutes at most she could be out of here. The

place meant nothing to her. It held not one single memory worth holding on to.

There was a knock at the door. The face outside was the last one she had expected to see.

'What the bloody hell are you doing here? You've only just got out of hospital.'

'It was Dez that bashed me over the back of the head, wasn't it?' said Tracy.

The kid was dazed and shaking. Rose glanced irritably at her watch – how many trains to London this late? – but there was nothing for it but to let Tracy in.

Tracy at once took in the suitcase and the bareness of the room. 'You're not leaving?'

'For London, like I always said I would.'

'I'll come with you.' Deprived of Dez, she was already looking for trust and comfort with somebody else. 'I've got enough money for a ticket.'

Rose shook her head vigorously. 'You're going straight home. You've got a good mammy.'

'How do you know?'

'Because I do. I met her at the hospital. She'll be going off her head, looking for you all over again.'

'She knows I've left. She had to let me go, because she knew if I stayed it'd all have to come out about my dad.'

Rose sighed. So that was what was behind it all. A nice everyday story of nice everyday folk. Poor Tracy wasn't the first and she wouldn't be the last.

She heaved the case up and groaned at its weight. Tracy seized the opportunity. 'I can help you to the station, if you like.'

Rose wanted no excess baggage, no added responsibilities. The whole idea of quitting Bradford was to cut herself right off, carry nothing unnecessary with her. Tracy was thin and fragile, but still too heavy a burden to be lumbered with. She was trying to summon up the courage to tell her simply to clear off and find somebody else to cling to when Tracy eagerly opened the door for her, to reveal Anita outside surrounded by black plastic bags. It was getting more and more like Piccadilly Circus here tonight.

'I've got nowhere to go,' moaned Anita, looking with dawning desire into the room beyond.

That solved the problem. Anita could settle herself in here, and be comfortable for a little while until she learned that Rose had been two months behind with the rent; by which time Rose would be well away.

She heaved her case out on to the landing. Tracy insisted on manoeuvring it down the stairs for her; and it was Tracy who spotted a taxi and hailed it, and Tracy who was right behind her at the ticket office.

Rose forced a smile. She might have guessed that Fate would never allow her to be truly footloose and free.

Carol had planned an hour or two in front of the telly. It didn't matter what was on. She just needed something to take her mind off that awful word on the crumpled card, and off Gina and Amanda Smeaton and off every other damned thing; the more rubbishy the programme, the better. The real world seemed to be shrinking, squeezing in on her head, tightening until she wanted to scream. They were all driving her mad. I wouldn't mind going mad, she thought. Must be nice to chuck everything away and lose control. She had to have a distraction, and quickly; had to have a bath, had to drink enough to send her off to sleep right away so she didn't lie in bed asking crazy questions, or have to get up in the middle of the night and occupy herself scrubbing the sink or checking on the state of the drawer linings.

She would do some cleaning before settling down to the telly.

She caught her breath. There was a figure on her doorstep.

'I was just about to knock,' said Curly placatingly.

'How many times do I have to tell yer—'

'We made an arrangement. Last week. Tuesday, you said.'

'Oh, hell. I forgot. Look, I'm not in the mood.'

'But I am,' he pleaded. 'I need to see you.'

Maybe it would pass the time quicker than the telly. Carol felt sickness in her throat; but it was true that she'd agreed on tonight, and if she wanted Curly's cash to keep rolling in she couldn't very well chuck him out whenever it suited her.

'Wipe your feet.' When he had made a great show of wiping his shoes on the mat, she demanded, 'Are they clean?'

'I don't think I stood in anything.'

He followed her meekly into the kitchen. While she was bringing her old-fashioned whistling kettle to the boil she took her council tax book from her bag and slammed it on the work surface. 'There you are. Paid, all stamped up. Satisfied?'

He beamed approval. All at once her thoughts went to him dirtying her doormat. She went to fetch it and dump it in the sink. As the kettle came to the boil she groped under the sink for bleach to add to the scalding water.

'Five denier,' Curly crooned, close beside her.

She had not noticed until now that while she was occupied with the mat he had been taking the shoes and stockings out of his briefcase and laying them lovingly on the work surface. He must be mad. She scooped them up and thrust them back into Curly's arms. Just not normal, this filthy creature. Carol reached for the bleach again, and for a cloth to rub frenziedly away at the work surface. A pounding in her head was growing heavier and more insistent.

'They're clean,' protested Curly, backing away with the shoes and stockings. Then he nodded towards the cloth and bleach going to and fro, to and fro. 'You'll spoil your hands.'

'So? They're my hands.' Carol dumped the cloth in the sink on top of the doormat. 'Right, where's me money?'

Not daring to let go of the things she had pushed into his arms, he groped awkwardly into his pocket and produced a brown envelope. 'A bonus this week, with it being Emma's birthday.'

She didn't like hearing Emma's name on his slack, soggy lips. He ought to wash his mouth out before uttering that name. 'Who told you it was her birthday?'

'You did, last time I was here. You said you were saving up for her bike. Don't you remember?'

Yes, all right, now she remembered. But he wasn't here to talk about her daughter. That wasn't part of the bargain. The sooner she got the shoes and stockings on, and chanted through the routine, the sooner she could send him out on his way.

So of course it just had to be one of those times when he couldn't work himself up to the climax. She tried the words outside the door, then came into the room and stalked up and down in front of him in her short black slip, with the black suspender belt and stockings and his high-heeled black shoes, but still he was puffing and wheezing away without result.

'You're rushing me,' he complained as she quickened her pace. 'You're making me tense.'

'It's half past bleeding ten. How long do you—'

'Make that noise.'

'What noise?'

'Like your legs are rubbing together.'

He ought to know by now that there were things she couldn't manage to do. Rubbing her legs together was one of them; they were too thin, they didn't meet.

'Come and stand next to me,' he said. 'You're too far away.'

'I've been doing it just the same as I always do.' She moved closer, impatient. 'Look, shall I just wank you off?'

'Talk to me.'

172

'I've said it all once.'

'Say something else.' His breath was hissing between his teeth. 'Something dirty.'

Something dirty . . . Everything was dirty. She wanted him out of here so that she could carry on with her cleaning. The words, and the way he had spoken them, were like muck in her ears. She wanted to dig in, scrape them clean; clean him so that he'd know better another time. Dirt. Filth. He needed a thorough cleansing.

She felt she was losing touch with reality. Everything was happening on the other side of a murky veil. 'I know what'll make you feel better,' she said, but her voice came from a long way off and didn't sound the least bit like her own.

Curly looked hopeful. His eyes widened as she took his hands and pulled him out of the chair, throwing the towel to one side. She went out to the kitchen to fill the kettle and put it back on the gas, then returned to touch his arm and steer him gently upstairs to the door of her bedroom. 'You've never been in here before, have you? Well, this is a special treat.'

She coaxed him towards the edge of the bed. He looked nervous but excited, not knowing what to expect. Carol took the handcuffs from the bedside drawer and clicked them into position in the bed head. Curly looked doubtful again, but she was saying soothingly, 'What you need is to be stretched right out, so all that tension in your chest moves down.' She pushed him gently on to the bed and attached his right hand to the handcuffs. 'It's all right, you can keep your gloves on.' She secured his left hand. 'That feels better, doesn't it?'

'I think so.' He didn't sound at all convinced.

'It's the best cure for tension. You'll feel it flooding away, right down your body. And we don't want these getting in the way, do we?' She unfastened his trouser belt and began pulling the zip down. 'We just want it all to flow.'

'What's that noise?'

Downstairs the kettle began to sing. Carol pulled his

173

trousers right down, and tugged his underpants after them. 'Don't you worry about nothing. I know what I'm doing. I've done the saunas, I've done the massage parlours, and I've done the Lane. If anybody knows what they're doing, it's me. Trust me.' She strained to lift one foot up on the bed close to his face. 'Look at these beautiful five denier stockings,' she murmured, 'going right to the top of my legs.' She undid the top of one stocking, peeled it off, and drifted it over his face. Curly moaned ecstatically, but tried to knock the stocking off so that he could see. The cuffs thwarted him. 'And now I'm undoing the other one, and guess what I'm going to do with it?' She tied his ankles together with the stocking and secured it to the foot of the bed. 'Now we're going to stretch all that tension out of your legs and way up, all the way.'

He began grunting a protest, trying to blow the first stocking off his face. She heard him continuing to ask more and more panicky questions as she went downstairs to fetch the kettle. When she came back in, he had managed to puff the stocking away from his eyes, and was beginning to sob a plea as he saw the way she was tilting the kettle.

'Please! No, please . . . !'

She looked down at his sad, grubby little penis and the rest of him, trying to wriggle out of her way. No chance. All that dirt to be washed away. It would be so good for him, if only he realised it.

'You're going to be all nice and clean,' she said tenderly.

And she tipped the kettle, and the boiling water hit him and the steam swirled up around his screams of agony.

16

Everything was larger and glossier and brighter. Even the scruffiest back street in Soho had a glamour about it that you'd never find down the Lane or anywhere else in Bradford. Tracy had spent a lot of the first week just wandering about and staring; but by the middle of the second week she had learned the best places to go, and after a month she knew the best hunting grounds for punters. Their expressions weren't all that much different from those on the faces of men in Bradford; but they were better dressed, and had more money to flash about.

You could get yourself kitted out a whole lot better, too. And there was a young queer off Berwick Street who had known just how to fix her hair to get round that shaved patch at the back, and give it a glowing tint that sent out signals to every male on walkabout.

Tracy was happy. The backdrop of sleazy sex clubs and rowdy bars was perfect. And it was non-stop: there were never slack periods, or long stretches of dullness when you were in danger of thinking about things that were best forgotten. Even now, early in the evening, the whole place was alive. You didn't have to hang around waiting for a few furtive businessmen to fit in a quick shag on their way home from the shops or the office. Here there was always somebody about, and except for a few hours mid-morning when they tidied up, the Blue Gardenia Club was open day and night.

The music in the club was so deafening you could hardly

hear yourself speak, and essential transactions were carried out in sign language. Most of the clientele could express their wishes in very few gestures, all of them easy to interpret. And while she was at it, she might as well spread the good news to punters who might find it hard to get through to the numbers they wanted. There were several cards with girls' names and phone numbers stuck on the wall above the telephone. Tracy removed them, chucked them in a waste bin, and replaced them with her own newly printed cards. Having a mobile phone made life a lot easier.

Moving towards the bar, she fought off the grope of a pimp who had spent the last week trying to persuade her he could represent her and make sure she didn't fall into the wrong hands, and smiled graciously at a little bald man who spent a fortune on champagne in here every evening without ever summoning up the courage to collect any of the girls for the half-hour he so obviously dreamed of. Tracy set her sights on a tall young man who had seen her come in and watched every step of her progress across the room. He was wearing an expensively tailored blue pinstriped suit, and the knot in his silk tie was impeccable. She would be prepared to bet that when they had finished and he got dressed again, he'd be able to retie that knot without even having to look in the mirror.

She accepted a Bacardi and Coke from him, pretended to understand the few words he offered through the hubbub, and then silently agreed that he could take her to a taxi and back to the flat behind Goodge Street.

There was a smell of fish and chips as they went past the kitchen door. Rose kept her back turned, knowing what was going on but keeping well out of it. It paid the rent, and Tracy had insisted right from the word go that she was the one who was going to provide that rent. Her punter asked no questions, anyway. He was a right smoothie, talking in a sort of polite non-committal way but then getting faster and faster with the words and the movements, until the words became the familiar four-letter urgings and then downright incoherent.

She had been right. Once it was over he was calm and in control again, flicking the ends of his tie over and into a knot without the slightest hesitation. When he asked if she could manage the same time next week, she said it would depend on her flat-mate, who was a student and might need some peace and quiet for her homework, but since he hadn't been too noisy perhaps he could give her a ring – she proudly indicated the mobile phone – and they would settle something. Mention of a student merited an extra fiver: he said that he worked for the Minister of Education, and hoped the two ladies would treat themselves to a bottle of wine with their evening meal.

Tracy thought of her father and his school and his students, and wondered whether he had offered any bottles of wine.

Still in her dressing gown, Tracy showed him out and sauntered into the kitchen.

'Them pies smell nice.'

'I just wish . . .'

Tracy didn't care for Rose's tone of voice. 'What?'

'I wish you didn't have to do it any more.'

'Well, I do. That's what we decided.'

'When I get a job,' Rose vowed, 'I'm gonna pay it all back, and then you can go back to college.'

Tracy laughed. 'I don't want to go back to college. You're the one for that sort of crap. I'm doing all right as I am.'

'You can't hustle all your life. You need something put away for later on, or you'll end up like me, with nothing.'

'You're getting along.'

'Only because of you and Richard. If it hadn't been for you two I'd be right up shit creek.'

Tracy felt a twinge of alarm. The name of this Richard character had come into the conversation a sight too often during this last week or two. She had only seen him the once,

177

when meeting Rose outside the Further Education College, but she hadn't fancied the look of him. He was one of those do-gooders, like someone who had once worked with her mother; one of those who had to do things for other people because they felt so messed-up about themselves. If Rose fell into his clutches, and wanted her out of the way, she didn't know how she would cope. Everything was fine right now. But it would only be fine if there was Rose here to rely on and talk to. She couldn't bear to let go of Rose.

And even more alarmingly, Rose was saying, 'By the way, I thought of asking him back for supper tomorrow night.'

'Oh, I get it. You want me to disappear tomorrow so you can get off with him?'

Rose blushed. Tracy wouldn't have thought it possible. 'Do what you like. He's just a friend, that's all; someone who helped me get on this business course, and this is my way of saying thank you to him.'

The thought of Rose trying to conquer the problems of a computer and train for respectable nine-to-five life in an office still gave Tracy the giggles. But if that was what she wanted, all right. Just so long as they stayed together, following their own timetables in this flat and outside it but coming together over the supper table and at weekends.

She said, 'Okay, then. I won't bring any punters in tomorrow. I'll just stay in.'

'Yes, you stay.' But Tracy detected the faint flicker of disappointment in Rose's tone. 'It won't bother us.'

The course was described as a simple introduction to modern business practice, but Rose was finding it anything but simple. Years had passed her by. Vaguely she remembered, for a short time, picking up the basics of typing and filing; but these modern screens and keyboards bore no resemblance to anything she had known, even if she hadn't forgotten half of it anyway. On her third day she had managed not only to lose the spread sheet on her own screen but to knock out

178

a terminal and destroy all the work of her fellow students. But their good humour and the patience of the instructor had kept her at it. She looked forward to going in every morning; and looked forward to the walk over Waterloo Bridge in the evening. It not only saved money on fares, it was good to stride out and feel the breeze off the river and the pulse of the city all around. And she had a learned a route that would take her past the Drop-In Centre, where Richard often worked late.

It was silly to think she was any more significant to him than any of the other drop-outs and mentally disturbed, homeless strays he gathered under his wing. Stupid of Tracy to get fretful and jealous. But he did seem to reserve a very special smile for her.

Like this evening . . .

He might almost have been waiting for her to show up, crossing the room past the two permanently unemployed youths with their feet up on the table, and past the untidy heaps of newspapers which few now bothered to search for job adverts. His hair, thinning on top to give his head the appearance of narrowing at the top, was pale brown, and the paleness of his eyebrows made them almost invisible until he turned towards the light from the window. His eyes were restless as he tried to keep tabs on everybody under his supervision; but Rose persuaded herself that they were calmer and more appreciative when his gaze met hers.

'How did your tutorial go?'

'So-so. He hated my essay, said I didn't have a "handle" on it, whatever that may mean. I think I'll pack it all in.'

She was only half serious, waiting to see how he would react.

'Pack it in?' he mocked. 'Oh, yes. My favourite pupil loses heart after only a fortnight. Shows what a bad judge of character I am, doesn't it?'

'Favourite?' she echoed.

'You've got brains. I've been in this business long enough

to recognise when someone's got something to give. I back winners, right? And you're my favourite. You know that.'

'No, I don't.'

'Rose, I don't have to spell it out. But anyway, am I still on for that curry tomorrow evening?'

She wasn't going to let her imagination run away with her. He probably had a dozen different ways of putting the homeless and the unhappy at their ease, encouraging them all the way even when it was obvious they were going to prove a dead loss. She was just one of many.

But she did wish that Tracy had decided to go out instead of sharing the curry with them. Richard looked none too pleased, either; but smiled politely and asked Tracy where she worked, which didn't help. She wondered what he made of Tracy's fumbled answers.

'All right?' She nodded at the chicken korma and rice on his plate.

'It's really good. One of the best I've tasted for years.'

'I used to live next door to an Indian woman. She showed me how to make it.'

'In Yorkshire?' Like so many Londoners, he seemed mildly surprised that people north of the Watford Gap ate anything but black pudding or chip butties.

'There were two brilliant curry houses on the Lane . . .' She saw Tracy smirking, and added hurriedly: 'Just near where I used to live.'

Richard glanced fleetingly at Tracy, then at Rose, then at his plate again. 'Masumi used to bring curries into the Centre sometimes. We all used to dive in. Did you meet Masumi?'

'Yes. We did that leaflet drop together, don't you remember?'

'He can't remember everybody, Rose.' Tracy spoke with heavy, unconvincing politeness. 'There's so many of you just "dropping in".'

'It's not often I forget somebody who's been to the Centre,' Richard assured her.

'Superman, are we?'

'That's me.' Richard blinked but matched her sarcasm with a lighter sarcasm of his own.

Tracy nodded at Rose. 'And she's lined up for Lois Lane, is she?'

'If she wants.'

'And you're going to fly off and save the world, are you? I can't wait.'

'Just ignore her.' Rose tried to keep her voice steady. 'Do you want some more rice?'

Richard was still eyeing Tracy meditatively. 'I get the feeling you don't like me.'

'Oh, I wouldn't say that.'

'What would you say, then?'

'I wouldn't say anything.' Tracy got up and carried her plate towards the kitchen. 'Wouldn't waste me breath.'

Rose pursued her and snatched the spoon from her hand before she could ladle more rice on to her plate. 'What are you being like this for?'

'Like what?'

'Like a prat, getting at him all the time.'

'He's the prat. It's just that you can't see it.'

'No, I can't, so just shut your face or I'll shut it for you.'

Tracy grabbed the spoon back, filled her plate, and marched off to her bedroom. The door slammed behind her. Rose went back into the living room, wondering what on earth she could find to say to Richard. He was on his feet, looking out of the window – maybe, she thought sickeningly, assembling a few polite words so that he could escape into the street and be off.

He smiled reassuringly. 'Do you have to read her a bedtime story? Or does she prefer horror stories?'

Rose picked up the half-bottle of red wine they had been drinking with the meal, and set it on the low table beside the sofa. She sat down, and Richard slid down beside her.

For a few moments they were silent, then Rose said, 'It's cosy here, isn't it?'

'Not bad at all. Better than your old home up north?' He edged round to look at her. 'You wouldn't by any chance have a husband stashed away up there, would you?'

She laughed. Either the wine or something else was going to her head. 'No, I don't have a husband stashed away. I've never found anyone I liked, or who cared about me enough. What about you?'

He hesitated, then said: 'I split up with my wife two years ago. Since then I haven't really had a proper relationship. I've had a few flings, but that's it.'

'Why did you split up?'

'She found someone else. Nothing I could do about it. She said I could keep the house, but I couldn't stand living there on my own, with all those memories round me.'

Rose could feel the hurt still there inside him. She put her hand on his; and was startled when he raised it and kissed it. 'Did anybody ever tell you, you've got lovely eyes.'

No, nobody had ever told her that.

Then he kissed her, and drew back; and she moved towards him again and kissed him, and this time it was longer.

'Can I stay?' he asked softly.

Rose wanted to say no. Only that wasn't true: she was sure she ought to say no, but she didn't want to. When they went to her bedroom she wondered if Tracy was lying awake, listening . . . and sneering. She was too tense. When he came into her she didn't suppose it would be any different from all those other times. Just another man, moving and hardening inside her. Only this time she wouldn't even get paid.

Then, without warning, it hit her. Somehow she was quivering round him, feeling a growing storm, abandoning herself to it and crying out because it had never been like this before. They came to a climax together, and it was the first time and she couldn't believe the force of it. When she turned away from him, she was crying, and he was kissing her neck and asking what was wrong.

It was impossible to tell him just why nothing was wrong. He wouldn't believe that it was the first time for her. The first time. Nobody could be expected to understand that. She couldn't understand it herself; and was frightened by it.

17

Carol hated going to sleep. The nurses called it a Psychiatric Secure Unit, but she felt far from secure. They were kind to her, had long sessions talking to her and trying to rationalise her phobias, but that time of evening still came when they insisted on her taking her medication and promised her a good night's sleep. Only it wasn't ever a good sleep. She had told them of her belief that someone was watching her and sooner or later would be coming for her, and agreed with their diagnosis that this was a self-induced nightmare due to the murders and one of her own friends getting killed. But that commonsense explanation didn't stop the faceless figure coming after her in her dreams, often treading towards her over a heap of dead flowers with a card in the middle of them bearing just that one word: SINNER.

Wash away all the sins. Keep washing until your body and soul are clean again.

They had done their best with that obsession, too. Rob Jones had put her on a programme of writing everything in a diary: how many times she had a shower or used the bidet, how many times she felt an urge to tidy her little cell of a room, how many times she wanted to clean her teeth. Gradually she was freeing herself from the compulsion. There had been a time when she had got through three bottles of bleach and a big can of disinfectant every week. She must have been going off her head. But as understanding grew clearer, it became more and more difficult to explain to them how it had been: how she used to think that if she didn't get showered she'd smell, that anyone who came into the house would smell it – sex, men, the whole thing. If she didn't keep cleaning herself, she would suffocate, drown in the dirt.

Impossible to tell them. Yet if she didn't tell them, they wouldn't let her out; and wouldn't let her have Emma back. She had to play it very cool, nod meekly to all their suggestions, and not blow her top with impatience.

At any rate one menace she had dreaded facing up to when she did get out was lifted. Anne Devlin, the social worker who sat in on most of the sessions with the senior psychiatrist and community nurse, had assured her that Curly did not propose taking any legal action. The women had tried not to smile when Anne broke the news. A man with a thriving business would not care to stand up in public and explain the harrowing details of the injury to his private parts.

It took four final assessments spaced out over two and a half weeks before Rob Jones said she could go out tomorrow; and Anne Devlin drove her home.

She was surprised to find Anita there, waiting on the back doorstep, looking unusually anxious to be helpful, bustling about in the kitchen and then saying she'd have to nip out for some milk. Carol only half heard her. She had seen Emma's doll lying slouched in a chair where it had been left, and gingerly picked it up.

'It won't be for long,' said Anne Devlin quietly. 'Just until you feel more settled.'

'I'd like the address of those foster parents.'

'I'll come and take you round there tomorrow, if you like. You can see for yourself they're lovely people.'

'It's because I worked the Lane, isn't it?' Carol was trying not to bristle with resentment.

'No, it's because you haven't been well and we want you to take things slowly. When Emma comes home we want you to be a hundred per cent.'

Carol clutched the doll close to her. 'I *am* a hundred per cent.'

Anne shook her head very gently. 'We'll go and see her tomorrow. I'll call for you at two o'clock – all right?'

When she had gone, Anita came in and sat on the far side of the room, sizing Carol up. 'Did you really go mad?'

'I poured boiling water over Curly's dick – what d'you think?'

'They didn't do anything to your brain, like they did in *One Flew Over the Cuckoo's Nest*? They didn't zap you with them things?'

Carol couldn't resist it. ''Course they did. What do you think I were in there all that time for?'

'I can't bear to think of it.' Anita winced. 'Did it hurt?'

'When they sawed me head in half it were a bit painful.'

'Stupid, you had me going then. You had me believing you.' Anita beamed, and said tentatively: 'I better bring my things in, then.'

'What things?'

'My bits and pieces. I've left them in your outhouse.'

Carol followed her incredulously out of the back door and watched as Anita began pulling a black plastic sack out on to the path. There appeared to be three more in the shadows beyond. 'Bits and pieces?'

'I had nowhere else to take them. I've been staying at Rose's these past two months, because she buggered off to London. Only her landlord came round this morning and slung me out.' She was gearing up for her familiar tearful, little girl routine again. 'I've been ever so upset. I've had nobody to talk to, I couldn't stop crying, you've no idea what it's like to have nowhere to live, and . . .' Her voice faltered as she looked past Carol's shoulder. 'Bloody hell, it's the flying squad.'

Carol turned to confront DCI Newall. 'What do you want?'

'I was passing, and I heard they'd let you out.'

187

Anita began lugging a bag of clothes indoors. 'I'll shove these in Emma's room.'

'Leave 'em on the landing,' said Carol sharply. 'She'll be back home soon.'

When Anita had disappeared inside, Newall said: 'So how've you been?'

'Fantastic. I've had a brilliant time. And you? Not caught him yet, then?'

'No, but we will.'

Carol sniffed sceptically and went indoors, knowing he would follow. Unsure of herself and of Newall, she picked up a cloth and began feverishly polishing a cupboard door until she realised what she was doing, and forced herself to stop.

She said, 'I'm packing in the Lane.'

'Really?' He caught her arms from behind and pulled her close. 'Tell me that again in six months' time.'

'I mean it. So get your filthy paws off me.'

'You won't last two minutes off the Lane. You can't do anything.'

'Neither can you, but it hasn't stopped you. All your bloody training and exams and promotion, and you can't catch one bloody man.'

'Look, you don't know anything. We've followed every lead, you've no idea what's been going on. We nearly charged somebody two weeks ago.'

'Who?'

'Man called Moore. He's a loan shark.'

'Really?' said Carol with exaggerated amazement. 'Well, you learn something every day.'

'We've had him in twice. We know from her mother that he was threatening Gina Dixon, and now he's at it with Steve Dixon as well. He's got form, he's been banged up for GBH before.'

'Anybody on this estate could tell you that. I could take you to three women who've been carved up by him.'

'Unfortunately he's got an alibi.'

''Course he's got an alibi. Jesus, he isn't going to knock someone off, is he? He's the main man, he'll get someone to do it for him.'

'But what would be the point of him killing the Dixon girl?' Newall had obviously gone over all this before and was still suffering a headache from it. 'I mean, he's not going to get his money then, is he?'

'He's not going to get it anyway. I mean, if she hasn't got it, she might as well be dead. As a lesson to everybody else. I know what I'm talking about. You get two warnings, and that's it. I've been on my second, and I don't borrow money any more. Maybe Gina were on her third. And Amanda Smeaton as well.'

Newall left it until after ten o'clock that night. He might be making a fool of himself, but right now he was susceptible to a nudge or a kick in any direction. He didn't really anticipate much joy from Moore, after their previous encounter, but the fierceness of Carol's challenge had got under his skin. Maybe he had given up too easily on Moore.

Jameson and a uniformed officer were with him when they burst unceremoniously into Moore's flat and on into the bedroom. And with Moore, cringing down into the bed beside him and letting out a high squeal of terror, was a rent boy who couldn't have been more than fourteen.

'Ah,' said Newall smugly. 'Get dressed.'

'What for? I'm not going anywhere.'

'You and me are going to have a little chat down the station.'

'Again? What for this time?'

'Murder.' Newall pulled back the bed cover the boy was trying to hide under. 'Oh, and buggery.'

'We weren't doing anything.'

'And my name's Kojak. Come on, get your trousers on.'

Spitting abuse, Moore scrambled into his clothes while

Jameson was taking the boy's name and address. The clock in the interview room showed eleven o'clock as Newall and Jameson sat down to face Moore yet again. He was sullen rather than defiant: one to be worn down rather than beaten down, thought Newall.

'Right. How many times did you go round to Gina Dixon's house?'

'I don't know. Once or twice, I can't remember. Anyway, I was at Ricky's bar the night she copped it. You checked that out – three times.'

'Funny. Once or *twice* round Gina Dixon's place. I've been talking to a couple of your ex-clients, and they tell me that you only get two warnings and then it's the big one.'

'Oh, come off it. We all do that. Put the frighteners on so they'll cough up. I took her telly and her video, that's all. I aren't going to bloody kill her, am I?'

'No, you're going to get somebody else to.'

'Bollocks. What for?'

'Because she didn't pay up, and you had to make an example of her to frighten all the others that owe you.'

'They don't owe me,' said Moore triumphantly. 'It's not my money.'

Newall eased himself forward on the edge of his chair. 'Well, whose money is it, then?'

'I can't say.'

'Well, I hope whoever it is'll come forward and visit you, 'cos that rent boy'll be using Grecian Two Thousand by the time you come out.'

'You've got nothing on me.'

'You want to bet?'

Moore suppressed an unconvincing yawn, then his shoulders sagged. 'All right, I'll tell you. But it didn't come from me, right?'

Carol had hurried along the street in the sunny afternoon, but found her pace slowing as she approached the school railings. It was crazy to think of herself as spying on her own child; but wasn't that just what it was? She picked Emma out at once from the middle of the crowd erupting like a flight of chattering birds into the playground; and then saw the large, motherly woman who moved towards her and swept her up in her arms.

Gina's mother was there, too, collecting Joanne, with Michelle in the pushchair and Sarah holding on to one side. She came level with Carol and looked at her, concerned.

'You all right?' When Carol could no longer hold back her tears, Joyce dug into her bag for a tissue. 'Come on, love, nothing's that bad.'

'I've been in hospital. They've given my Emma to foster parents. And she looks quite happy without me. I mean, I want her to be happy, but . . . I've been so worried, I thought she might be frightened, I've missed her so much . . .'

'I know.'

It struck Carol that Joyce was the last person she ought to be talking to about loss. But as they walked slowly away, with Carol glancing back just once at Emma disappearing down the pavement, it was Joyce who seemed to want to put her at her ease, talking on and growing indignant as she did so.

'D'you know, I had to go and ask for my job back this morning. Steve's just got hopes of a new job but there's still a lot of bills to be cleared up, and I can't go on looking after the kids all the time. So I went to see Mr Ferguson—'

'Ferguson? George Ferguson?'

'You know him?'

'A friend of mine does. Did.'

'I'm sorry for her. Hope he doesn't put her through it the way he does everybody else. Keeps me waiting, then says that I can come back if I'm a good girl and help him out. Wants to get his tender for the Leisure Centre cleaning contract wrapped up – but wants me and the rest to work longer hours and take a small cut in wages. Job security, he calls it. Bastard.'

Carol thought of the fervent endorsement Anita would have given had she been here.

'And d'you know who was there just as I came out? Sat there, doing nothing – that Inspector Newall. I nearly said something to him. I mean, they haven't been round in weeks, it's like it's not important any more. I don't think they'll get who did it, do you?'

Carol fought off the impulse to look down the alley they were just passing, or over her shoulder to see if anyone was watching from the corner. He was out there somewhere.

The house was hideously empty. She longed to hear Emma's voice, and Emma's movements about the place. All right, they would let her have Emma back if she behaved the way they wanted for some unspecified period which they would choose. But how could she show them she was a responsible mother when there was nobody here to mother?

She had told Newall she was off the Lane for good, and she meant it. But his taunt lingered. What else was she good for? What sort of job could she possibly do?

It was late in the evening when Newall arrived, looking pleased with himself. Too pleased. He tried to kiss her and get her on the couch within a few minutes of coming in through the door. She pushed him off with:

'Did you pull Moore in again?'

'Yes.'

'And?'

'It's not him.' His head dipped again, and he was nuzzling her neck.

'How d'you know?'

'He's just the heavy, that's all. It's not his money. Not his firm. It's Ferguson's.'

Carol began to take this in, only half aware that he was starting to unfasten the buttons of her blouse. Ferguson, with

all those phoney alibis and all the talk of another woman.
Suppose there wasn't any other woman? Suppose . . .

'Shall we go upstairs?' Newall kissed her between the
breasts. 'Or do you want to—'

'I'm tired.' She pushed him away, wanting time to think
about the implications of this Ferguson business. 'Really
tired. It must be these tablets I'm taking.'

'Come on, Carol, I've been thinking about you all day.'

'Better if you concentrated on your job.'

'Don't be a prick-tease. Come on, we used to be good
together.'

She remembered. She might have weakened, but the door
opened without warning. Anita stood in the opening, in a
fluffy nightgown and with a roller across her fringe like a
bull-bar on a Land Rover.

'I can't sleep on that camp bed,' she whined. 'It keeps
collapsing.'

'You'll have to get in mine for the time being. I'll be up
in a minute. Chief Inspector Newall,' said Carol sweetly,
'is just leaving.'

Newall, fuming, got to his feet. 'I'll see myself out.'

When the front door had thudded behind him, Carol said:
'You heard about your precious George?'

'A bit, as I was coming downstairs.'

Carol told her the rest, and Anita said very levelly: 'I
bloody hate him. If I only had the chance . . .'

Carol wondered how much Joyce knew about her employer;
or how much she might find it worth knowing. She would sleep
on it, and hope the idea of it would drive out dreams of the
watcher.

18

From the corner of her eye Rose knew that Tracy was hovering. She wanted peace and quiet to concentrate on this essay, but Tracy was dying to interrupt. At last it came.

'Did that Richard of yours say anything?'

'He didn't say anything about you, if that's what you mean. But I did. I said he didn't have to take any notice of you, because you were just a spoilt bitch.'

'Thanks a lot.' She clawed at Rose's attention before it could turn back to the essay. 'I bet you end up going off with him and dumping me.'

'Don't be so bloody stupid. You want to stop popping them pills, they're rotting your brain.'

'You won't leave me?'

Rose resignedly put her ballpoint down and looked up. Tracy was really frightened. She would always want someone to cling to. Rose was saddled with more responsibility than she had bargained for. 'No,' she said gently, 'I won't leave you.'

'I'm . . . sorry for being a pain.'

Rose got up and was about to put her arms round her when the mobile phone rang. Tracy grabbed it up from the window-ledge, at once alert and hopeful. Rose's attempt to get into the swing of her written words again was hampered by Tracy's answers to the caller. It was easy to guess at the sort of questions that were being asked: she'd heard it all so often.

'Yes, that's right. Tracy speaking. Eh? . . . Oh, all sorts

of things. Depends what you want. I can do straight massage or . . . sure, I do extras, we can talk about that when I see you.'

'Not now,' Rose muttered. 'Tell him this afternoon.'

'Hold on a tick.' Tracy covered the mouthpiece. 'What did you say?'

'This afternoon. I've got to get this finished.'

'I'm back,' Tracy chirped into the phone. 'Somebody were just talking to me. Mm? I don't know about that. It'll be double the price. Well, I should be able to sort something out. Give me a bit of time – can you ring back in an hour?'

It was no use trying to concentrate until Tracy was well out of the way. 'All right, what was all that about?'

'He wants two of us.' Tracy stared at the phone as she put it down, puzzled, as if she had recognised the caller's voice or remembered something similar from way back.

'No good looking at me,' said Rose firmly. 'I'm not doing it.'

Of that at least she was sure. There was no way she could just dip in and out when the opportunity arose. If she was going to give up, then that was what she had to do: give it up. Just do the odd job now and again to help out, and before she knew it she would be back on the Lane or its London equivalent. She had been on the Lane since she was eighteen, only she wasn't eighteen any more but pushing forty, and there was only one way for her to go in that direction: doing blow jobs for a half of lager and a bag of chips.

'You don't want to do it,' said Tracy, peeved, 'because of that Richard. Look,' she wheedled, 'if we do this punter, I won't have to work for the rest of the week. Aren't you always telling me to ease off?'

'Find somebody else.'

Rose was not to be shifted. In the end Tracy rang round, fixed up a mate called Barbara, and went off leaving Rose

196

feeling guiltier than ever about taking Tracy's tainted money just so she could pursue her own new career. She would repay it; but not by helping Tracy out in that way.

That afternoon's session at the college went better than she could have dreamed. Things were beginning to click. She had been granted a student loan and hardship grant. Most of it would have to be accounted for eventually, but for starters she could pay Tracy back sooner than she had thought. Even more important, she was making progress and earning other folks' respect. She couldn't believe it was all coming right so fast.

The only cloud on the horizon was Richard's expression when he showed up unexpectedly at the end of the afternoon. 'Can we go somewhere and talk?' It sounded ominous. As they walked across the bridge it began to sound worse. 'Listen, Rose, I've got to tell you something.'

She might have known something would come up to spoil it all so quickly. He didn't want to see her any more, and he was trying to find a way of saying it.

'You're afraid of things getting serious,' she prompted.

'What are you on about?' The breeze stirred his thinning hair into a wispy tangle. 'I really . . . like you a lot. That's the problem.'

Her spirits began to lift. 'Doesn't sound a problem to me.'

He took a card from his pocket and handed it to her. 'I found this shoved into my pocket the morning after I left your flat.' She stared in disbelief and then in rage at Tracy's printed card as he rattled breathlessly on. 'I kept thinking just throw it away, what Tracy does is *her* business, it's got nothing to do with you. But it was eating away at me, so I decided to ring the number.'

Disbelief gave way to bleak certainty. 'And ask if she could bring a friend along?'

'Did she tell you?'

'And you thought she'd bring me.'

Richard fumbled helplessly for words. 'No, I didn't really think . . . I mean, I suppose deep down I knew you couldn't do anything like that, but the brain gets to working overtime . . .'

'And before you know it –' Rose stared straight ahead '– I'm a fully fledged hooker.'

'No. I mean, I was so glad when you didn't show up . . .'

So he had gone wherever it was, to see if she *did* show.

'Oh, hell,' he groaned, 'this is so difficult. I just thought I ought to be honest with you about what I did, that's all.'

'And I'll be honest with you,' said Rose grimly. 'For your information, I've given it up. I don't do it any more. I did, and now I don't.' He quickened his pace, and she had to hurry to keep up with him as he turned on to the Embankment as if about to break into a punishing jog. 'What are you thinking?'

'I don't know what I'm thinking.'

'I'm still me, you know. I haven't changed. I'm still the woman you enjoyed sleeping with.'

'Look, I can deal with it. Don't patronise me.' He stopped for breath by a seat in the Embankment Gardens. 'I've worked with enough prostitutes in my time, I know how women fall into these things, but—'

'But what?'

'Well . . . It's hard for me to understand. How you could sleep with all those men. Men you didn't even know.'

'It's easy when you don't like yourself very much. You just turn off, think of something else.'

'What did you used to think of?'

No, she wasn't going to tell him that. Thinking of Hannah, a baby she hadn't seen for years and wouldn't recognise even if she saw her now. She had been so tiny then: the tiniest fingers Rose had ever seen. Weighing seven pounds ten ounces, and with a mop of black hair; and Rose insisted that she was smiling even though they told her it was too soon for that, and it must be wind. It had been Valentine's Day, twenty past three in the afternoon, when they took her away.

Her father had had such hopes for her. Thought she could become a teacher. Only now he didn't want to know, so she packed her bag and left. He had called her a whore, so she might as well become one. In six months she was on the Lane. Simple enough. Instead of clocking in you opened your legs, and if you were lucky it was over quickly. Cold rubber sex. You didn't care about them, you didn't even look at them.

'I got raped once,' she recalled. 'And when the police asked me to describe him I couldn't even remember the colour of his hair. They don't take you seriously anyway. We're just scum. You're on your own when you're a hustler.'

She tried to walk past him, but he grabbed her arm. 'It's going to be all right. We'll work this out. I mean, there's a thousand questions swimming round my head, but given time—'

'What sort of questions?'

'Well . . .' A flurry of sweet wrappings and a cigarette packet danced along the path and were lifted on a current of air into his face. He struck out pettishly. 'I mean, when did you last have a blood test?'

He had judged her and passed sentence. And it was no good him saying 'It's going to be all right' in that self-righteous, condescending tone; because it wasn't going to be all right, couldn't be all right now. She could have loved him, but in the end he was just like the rest of them.

Rose turned up into Villiers Street and headed for the flat.

Tracy was in an indignant mood. 'Guess what? That bloke didn't turn up.'

Rose went into her bedroom and hauled the suitcase down off the top of the wardrobe. Tracy, slouching after her to continue her complaints, stared as Rose began cramming clothes into the case.

'What's up with you?'

'I'll tell you what's up. That bloke on the phone was Richard.' Rose could hold it in no longer. She slapped Tracy hard across the face, sending her reeling back against the edge of the door. 'You scheming little bitch. You've spoilt everything, every bloody thing.' She grabbed Tracy by the throat and hit her again. 'You couldn't bear to see me happy, could you?'

Tracy cried large, childish tears. 'Rose, I'm sorry. Honest, I'm sorry. I didn't know—'

'Didn't know when you planted that card on him? What were you aiming at? You knew I liked him, so you set out to—'

'He was going to spoil everything, couldn't you see that?'

'You're the one that's spoilt everything. He was my way out, my way to a decent life.' Rose snapped the case shut.

'We'll be all right,' Tracy begged. 'You can keep on going to college—'

'I don't want to go to college. Not any more. I've had enough of it down here. I'm off.'

'But what about me?' Tracy tried to get her arms round Rose, who pushed her forcibly back again. 'You said you wouldn't leave me.'

'All right,' said Rose icily. 'I'm going home, and because I promised I wouldn't leave you, you can come with me.'

But Tracy wasn't prepared to go that far. London suited her. She wasn't going to make a fool of herself over a man, not the way Rose had done, and she wasn't going to go creeping back to Bradford.

Rose had made the offer, and was glad it had been turned down. So far as she was concerned, Tracy could stay down here and end up a crack head like all the rest of them.

19

Emma was being very polite, and Carol loved every movement she made, every word she spoke; yet that politeness made Carol herself seem a visiting stranger rather than Emma's mother.

'Do you want another piece of cake, Mum?' Well, at least she called her 'Mum' without too much effort.

'No, thanks. I'm full up.'

Patricia Coombes, a plump lady sitting below a framed colour print of Barbados, with which she presumably had family connections, herself looked a complete picture of maternal pride and contentment. They had certainly placed Emma with first-rate foster parents. But Carol felt unhappier with every passing moment. She was aware of Anne Devlin appraising her reactions, and made an effort to sit back and look relaxed.

'Can I give Sandy a piece?' Emma asked Patricia.

'We'll save him a piece.'

'He wants to come in here and have it.'

'I know, sweetheart, but your mummy doesn't like dogs. He's all right in the hall.'

Emma made a face.

Carol knew she must leave before something snapped. 'I'll have to be going in a minute or so. I'll just drink my tea.'

'I'll give you a lift back,' Anne Devlin offered.

Carol could not bear to be shut up in that car again, being silently assessed, even for ten minutes. There was no telling what she might blurt out, or what judgment the social worker might pass on her. She would rather walk.

She was halfway down Lambton Lane, automatically taking it as a short cut even though she had sworn to avoid the place forever from now on, when a car coasted in alongside her and an automatic window slid down.

'Hello, there.'

'I'm not working,' she said curtly from the corner of her mouth.

'You don't remember me, do you?' She looked at him for the first time. He was a quite personable man in youngish middle age, wearing a navy blue polo-necked sweater and dark blue slacks. 'Ian,' he prompted her in a slightly mannered, almost effeminate voice. 'You came to my house once. I say, have you been crying?'

'No. I've just got something in my eye.'

'Look, I'm just off to make a business call.' He leaned over to open the door. 'Do you want a lift somewhere?'

'No, it's all right, thanks. I'm just on my way home.'

'Where do you live?'

'Off Hewlett Road.'

'That's on my way. Come on, hop in.'

She was still trying to place him. He seemed pleasant enough, anyway, and she was too drained to argue. As she fastened her seat belt he said, 'You know, I nearly drove past you. I didn't recognise you at first, you look so different.'

'I've been away. In hospital.'

'Nothing serious, I hope?'

'No. Anyway, I'm better now.'

'We never did go for that drink, did we?'

'What drink?'

'I promised to take you and Gina for a drink, don't you remember?'

Now she remembered, all right. This was the punter she had robbed. Did he know she had been the one? Nothing

202

in his manner suggested that. But now she was anxious to get out of the car.

All the more anxious when they turned into Hewlett Road and she saw Curly a hundred yards away, standing outside her own front door. 'You'd better drop me here. There's someone I've got to see.'

'Anybody special?'

'No, it's nothing. Nothing special. But I'll have to go. Thanks for the lift.'

She hoped Curly wasn't looking in her direction as she got out of the car and dodged down the path between two blocks of terraced houses. How long would she have to hang around until she could be sure he was gone? She came out opposite a phone box, and was tempted to ring Newall and ask for police protection. But that would be swapping one bit of trouble for another. She must resign herself to walking around, filling in time and having a cautious peep every now and then to see if Curly had got tired of waiting and cleared off.

In the morning there was no Emma to take to school, but Carol went there nevertheless. It was crazy, wanting to see Emma and yet wanting to make sure Mrs Coombes didn't see her and gush a welcome all over her. But she couldn't help herself.

Anita was up surprisingly early. She explained it with a touch of resentment. 'If that creature from the social wants me out of here before you can have your kid back, I suppose I'd better get started looking for somewhere else.' She left the house at the same time as Carol, but made no attempt to go off towards any letting agency or to study notices in the newsagent's window. Instead, she trotted alongside Carol all the way to the school, chattering intermittently about life being a bitch, oblivious to the fact that Carol was not offering the slightest response.

At least she was fatter than Carol, and useful to shelter

behind as Mrs Coombes arrived with Emma. Carol watched her daughter skip across the playground towards her friend Joanne, turning once to wave happily to Mrs Coombes.

'Any news yet?'

It was Joyce, with Michelle in the push-chair, her voice as troubled and affectionate as if they had been the oldest of friends, with no hint of shared tragedy or guilt between them.

'I've been round. She's being well looked after till she can come home. And,' said Carol emphatically, 'that won't be long.'

'As soon as I can get myself out of there,' Anita lamented.

Carol put a hand on the bar of the push-chair and added her weight to Joyce's as they toiled uphill.

Joyce had moans of her own. 'That bastard Ferguson, he's still getting on at me to get back full-time and lead his bloody posse of cleaners on to victory at the Leisure Centre. Or else!'

'Two warnings,' said Carol, 'and then you're for the chop?'

'What you on about?'

Carol told her. Anita winced agreement, half enjoying the denunciation and half in maudlin mood over the past pleasures of George Ferguson's company.

Joyce stopped pushing. Lulled by the steady progress, little Michelle had drowsed off. Now she stirred, and Carol bent over to make comforting noises. Joyce was in no condition to make comforting noises to anyone.

'You mean *he's* the loan shark? The one who . . . no, I can't believe Gina'd go to him. Not him, of all people.'

'You don't understand. She won't have known it was Ferguson behind it.'

'He wants his mug keeping lily white,' Anita confirmed, 'for the Council tenders.'

'He's got a front man and a heavy to do his real dirty work.'

Joyce made a move as if to turn the push-chair right round in its tracks. 'I'm off to the Town Hall right away. I'll bloody well tell 'em he's a loan shark and—'

'It won't do any good,' said Anita. 'He's in with 'em all.'

'Buys his way in,' said Carol, 'with a little holiday here and a free shag there.'

They went on their way towards Joyce's back door, bumping the push-chair into the kitchen. They were greeted by a scowl from Bob, unshaven and in his shirt sleeves, champing away at a bacon butty.

'This is Carol,' said Joyce perfunctorily, 'and her friend Anita.'

Bob nearly choked on a large piece of his bacon sandwich. He tried to look away, but Carol had recognised him. Before she could pass it off casually, Anita waded in. 'Don't I know you from somewhere?'

'Did you get our Sarah up?' Joyce was asking. 'She's got to be at the doctor's at a quarter-to.'

'She's getting dressed.' Bob was on his feet, heading for the stairs with the rest of the sandwich clutched in his greasy fingers. 'I'm off to get shaved.'

Anita watched him go. 'I'm sure I've seen him before.'

'He's got one of them faces,' said Joyce. 'Ugly!'

They laughed – Carol a bit too loudly. Because of course she remembered Bob a lot more clearly than Anita did. Only he hadn't been called Bob. He was known to them all as Punter Joe, with a habit of trying to knock the price down. He and Carol, and he and Rose, had used Anita's flat more than once.

'Of course.' It had dawned on Anita. 'What a prat!'

Carol tried to kick her, but she was too far away.

Joyce thought they were reverting to the topic of George Ferguson. 'A proper bastard.'

'Oh, I'd have thought he was too feeble to be an out-and-out bastard. Pathetic old Punter Joe – up and down the Lane like a bride's nightie.'

'George Ferguson?' marvelled Joyce.

'No.' Anita gestured towards the staircase. 'That bloke you live with.'

'You troublemaking bitch,' groaned Carol.

It was too late to say it was all a mistake, Anita was thinking of somebody else, they'd never in their lives seen Bob before. No way of smoothing it over. Joyce wouldn't have believed them; she might never have faced up to the truth before, but now it had come up and hit her she wasn't going to fend it off. She asked only, bluntly, if it was true, and how many times. And where. When she could stand no more she waved them down and turned resolutely towards the stairs.

They heard a door open, and a shout of rage. 'You sick bastard.' Then the door shut; but there was still a throbbing of voices, occasionally spiralling up into a wild war of abuse. All the indications were that Joyce was winning.

When she returned she was red in the face, but buoyed up by savage resolve. 'I'm having him out of here. Should have done it years ago, if I'd had any sense.' She kept her gaze on the stairs, as if to make sure of having the pleasure of throwing Bob out bodily when he put in an appearance. 'Bloody hypocrite! He went on about our Gina, who only did it to pay off her loan – and all the time he were going with 'em himself.'

Carol said, 'Anita's got a big gob.'

'That's all right. I ought to have rumbled him long ago. Anyway' – Joyce was in glowing destructive mood – 'he's out, and so far as I'm concerned George Ferguson is out as well. I'm going to tell him where he can stick his job. There's plenty of people need cleaners. I'll go to work for meself.'

Carol felt an immediate response inside herself. This was

no bad idea. She had been thinking without much purpose about some kind of job, and now here was something she could surely manage. She had overdone the cleaning at home, let it become an obsession, shut away with herself and her phobias. But making money out of it, doing it for someone else on a proper professional basis, was a whole different matter.

She said, 'You know all the ropes?'

'I've been doing it since our Gina were three. A flaming lifetime of it. Offices, or private houses – they can't get the young 'uns to do it, they won't stand for it. But me . . . I tell you what, I've a bloody good mind to go down to the Council and ask about the new Leisure Centre contract: the one Ferguson's after.'

'You're joking.'

'No.' Joyce's enthusiasm was self-kindling. 'Look, I nicked one of the application forms, just to get some notion of what Ferguson was up to. Haven't been able to make head or tail of it yet, but we ought to be able to figure it out. And if I quit George Ferguson's team and I can get a couple of the other girls to come in with me—'

'You could give me a job,' Carol interrupted. 'I'm a damn good cleaner.' She laughed drily. 'Ask me shrink.'

'Fine. It'd be good to have you in with me.'

'But we don't know anything about contracts and all that.'

'They can't be all that awful.' Joyce rooted in her bag and produced a four-page document severely creased and dog-eared. 'I can get a clean one tomorrow,' she said apologetically, putting it on the table.

They bent their heads over it. Anita's lips moved as she read, and her brow began to wrinkle. Carol felt her earlier optimism ebbing away. There was so much to be tackled. What experience did the company have of similar contracts? State the company for which the contract applied. The said company would be approached for references.

207

'That means,' said Joyce glumly, 'they'll ask George. He's the one I've been working for all this time.'

Carol turned the next sheet towards her. There was a lot of small type about Financial Security, with several lines to fill in, followed by three paragraphs about Health and Safety.

'It's a bit complicated.'

'We'll learn.' Joyce was decisive again. 'If only to spite George Ferguson. I'd love to see his face.'

'Yes,' said Anita dreamily. 'That makes two of us.'

Upstairs there was a thud, and the sound of an opening door. Footsteps came out apprehensively on the landing, and stopped. Joyce's smile slid sideways into a wicked grin of determination. She moved a few paces at a time towards the foot of the stairs, ready for the next encounter.

'I think we'd best be off,' said Anita. 'And look, I'm sorry about letting it out like that. I should have kept me trap shut.'

'Don't even think about it.' Joyce was poised, waiting. 'I'll see you tomorrow, when I've got a clean application form. And we'll really get down to it. Right?'

'Right,' the other two said simultaneously.

20

Four o'clock in the morning was no time to be woken up by
strange noises. Carol's dreams had been nothing too horrific
during the night; but the uneven rattling and tapping that
jolted her out of sleep was frightening. She lay for a moment
staring at the ceiling, trying to persuade herself it was just the
tail-end of an otherwise harmless dream. But then it came
again: a brief but loud scraping against the window, as if
some bird or bat were hurling itself at the glass.

Or somebody throwing earth and small stones at the
window.

Carol slid out of bed and cautiously pulled the curtains a
few inches apart. The watery light of what was not yet dawn
showed nothing but grey shadows on the path and pavement.
Yet she was sure she heard movement – a dragging sound
this time – by the side of the house.

She longed to get back into bed and pull the duvet over
her head. But all that would mean was lying awake, tense,
straining to hear the faintest rustle or a footstep downstairs.
She slipped her dressing-gown over her shoulders and went
down a step at a time – wary and noiseless like an intruder in
her own house. There was somebody down there. She could
sense it. The menace which she had tried to clear out of her
mind was real again. Somebody was coming for her.

She snapped on the kitchen light and slid the drawer by the
cooker open with a grating squeal, taking out a kitchen knife
before opening the back door on the chain. Nothing appeared
in the gap. She risked slipping the chain and opening the

door a few inches further, holding on to it tightly with her left hand, gripping the knife even more tightly in the right.

'Who is it?'

The dragging noise came closer. The light from the half open door fell on a bedraggled, exhausted Rose, heaving her battered suitcase along the path.

'I've been lobbing boulders at yer bedroom window for the past half hour. Thought yer must be dead.'

'I thought you were in London.' Carol opened the door wide, and Rose carted her case over the step.

'I was, but I've come back. Can I doss down on your settee till I get myself sorted out with somewhere to live?'

'I've got Anita staying with me already.'

'I've got nowhere else to go.'

Carol sighed. Her house was turning into a bloody hotel, or more likely a dosshouse for homeless layabouts; but she was so relieved to find the early morning prowler was nobody more dangerous than Rose that she had to give way.

It took only a few minutes to make a pot of tea and two rounds of toast. Rose sipped gratefully while listening to what had happened in her absence. She interrupted Carol's story only when she had finished her cup. 'But they can't take your kid away without a bloody good reason, can they?'

'Well, they have. And these people that're looking after her, they've got a dog called bleeding Sandy, and Emma loves it. I can tell she doesn't want to come home.'

'Tell her you'll buy her a dog.'

This hadn't occurred to Carol before. It didn't appeal very much when she did come to consider it. She hated dogs. Sticky, slobbery, messy . . . She dismissed the idea. 'They keep saying she can come back as soon as I'm right.'

'Tell 'em you're right, then. Put your foot down so they have to believe you. Tell 'em you want her back and they've got to bring her home. Get on that phone.'

Carol glanced at the kitchen clock. Hardly the time of day to try ringing even the most sociable of social workers. But she promised herself she would make an effort as soon as the office was open.

And it was time she stopped talking about herself and her woes. She said, 'So how was London?'

Rose go up and put another slice of bread in the toaster, keeping her back turned. 'I'm glad I'm back.'

'Much doing down there?'

'I don't know. I packed in hustling. I'm trying to sort myself out.'

It seemed to be catching, thought Carol ruefully. She wondered just how hard Rose was finding the going.

'What about Tracy?'

'She . . . didn't want to come back,' said Rose stiffly. 'She were doing plenty of business. Blowing most of it on crack.'

The sound of voices had brought Anita downstairs, her hair sporting its usual huge roller. She rubbed her eyes, making the dark smears round them worse. 'Bloody hell.' She smiled a bleary but genuine welcome. 'The old tart herself's back.'

Rose slammed the round of toast down on to her plate. 'I'm not a tart, Anita. All right? Have you got that?'

'Sorry I spoke.' Anita's smile faded. She could not figure out what she had done wrong. 'I think I'll go back to bed and get up again.'

They were all up again after a few hours' fitful sleep. Carol lay awake most of the time wondering how soon she could get rid of them so that Anne Devlin and her cronies would pronounce the place fit for a child to live in. And on top of that there were so many questions about how she was going to support Emma from now on.

The first thing she noticed when she came downstairs was the muddy track across the floor where Rose had dragged her case along. She set to work with cleaning fluid and a mop, and was giving it a second go when she realised that it was perfectly clean by now. She had to stop herself going at it over and over again.

Anita came in, her face reasonably in order and her hair tidy. She was followed by Rose, emerging from the living room with a series of long yawns. Carol resignedly shovelled slices of bread into the toaster and got the kettle boiling again.

Before they had begun this breakfast, there was a knock at the front door. Carol contemplated not answering it. The postman never brought anything that needed a signature, or was too big to go through the letterbox. And if there was someone she had overlooked who now wanted to move in, the only space she could offer was the bath.

It was Joyce with Joanne, Sarah and Michelle.

'I wondered if you'd look after the kids and take our Joanne to school for me. Their dad's actually hoping to land a job this morning, and anyway I've just *got* to go in to work to get my hands on that application form.' She looked a melting appeal at Carol, who was about to say that the place was becoming a madhouse, until she remembered what it had been like to be in a sort of madhouse for real.

They trooped through to the kitchen. Carol deliberately kept her eyes away from any sort of mark that might be left on the floor, and introduced Joyce to Anita and Rose. The room wasn't big enough to hold quite so many human beings.

'You're sure it's all right, you dropping Joanne off at school?' Joyce went on. 'She's got her dinner money and everything. If it's too much trouble, just say.' She meant it yet didn't mean it. 'I didn't know what to do. It's the only thing Bob were good for.' She glanced up at the kitchen clock. 'I've got to go. I want to catch Gloria and some of the others about working for us. And if you want to have another look down the questions, you can still have a go at this while I'm getting the clean one.' She handed over the

212

crumpled application form, kissed the girls and hurried off. 'I'll be back about ten.'

Rose looked inquiringly at the document Carol had put on the table. 'What's all this about "working for us", then?'

'Have a read of that.'

As Rose reached across the table, Anita crowed, 'We're gonna shaft George Ferguson till his eyeballs pop out of his head.'

Joyce was as good as her word. She was back by ten o'clock, kissed Sarah and Michelle again, and then jubilantly laid an A4 brown envelope on the table.

'Here we are. But to be on the safe side, we'd better finish filling in the scruffy one first and then copy it out properly.' She glanced a silent question at Rose, not sure if she ought to be staying in the room with them.

Rose said briskly, 'I've just lately done this course in London. All about business and that.'

They settled themselves round the table after Carol had wiped it over once, and just stopped herself from wiping it twice. Anita craned her neck to see over Joyce's hand as she laboriously filled in the date at the top of the first page. Then Joyce frowned at one of the figures on the rough draft.

'I think we ought to put eight cleaners down.'

'You said six before. Watch it – we don't want to make a mess of that form.'

'We've got to get it right,' said Carol, 'or they won't take us seriously.'

'Ferguson thinks eight. He's had a proper assessment done, and that's what he said this morning. Still thinks I'm going to go along with him.'

Anita nudged closer. 'Look, there's a gap here where it says company secretary. I could be that. I've always wanted to be a secretary.'

Rose groaned. 'They don't mean like that, you daft bat; they mean like someone who takes minutes.'

'I could learn to type fast.'

'And I don't mean minutes like what's on the clock, I mean like minutes of the meetings you'll have.'

Carol liked Rose's businesslike manner. Whatever she had been up to in London, she certainly seemed to have picked up a lot of useful stuff. They could use her. Make the going less hard for all of them.

Sarah put her head round the door. 'There's a lady come to see yer, Auntie Carol.'

Anne Devlin followed her in. 'I got a message to ring you, and I was passing so I thought I'd pop in.' She looked round the congested room. 'Obviously it's a bad time, so—'

'Don't worry about me.' Joyce was hastily collecting her things together. 'I'm just leaving.'

'And I'm still here,' said Anita with an ingratiating smile, 'but not for much longer.'

Rose added herself to the list. 'I'm just visiting.'

'I can call back later, if you like.'

Carol wavered. She had not expected the social worker to show up at this time of day, without warning – and didn't like the way she looked around, sizing up the women and the two kids jamming the place up and mentally fitting Emma in . . . or not fitting her in.

Rose said meaningly, 'Carol, you wanted to talk to her about Emma, didn't you?'

'That's right. Yes, I want her back home with me.'

Before Anne Devlin could make any more polite attempts to slip away, Carol led her into the living room. They sat down as the front door closed and Joyce took the two children down the path and away along the street.

Carol tried to smile confidently.

Anne Devlin had come to tell her that they had had another regular case meeting, and of course Emma's name and hers were on the agenda for discussion. They felt they would like Carol to come in to the unit again for a final assessment '– Nothing formal, really, just anything you might want to

214

talk out and get settled now you've had time to think –'
but in the meantime they would start with Emma having
a visit home. Then if things worked out and Carol was
managing all right, Emma could spend a weekend here and
soon would be able to come home for good. There was still
a quiet but significant 'if' behind each proposed stage of
this. But the woman's voice was reassuring and friendly,
and Carol swore to herself that there was no need for any
doubts: she could cope; she'd show them she could cope.

There was nothing to do now but wait for the date to
be fixed. Until then, she had the matter of the cleaning
contract to occupy her mind. There was precious little time
to spare: Joyce's wild idea had come late on, and the form
had to be handed in complete this afternoon for tomorrow's
interview.

Anita had gone upstairs for one of her ritual hourly
inspections of herself in the glass, and a few repair jobs
with lipstick, skin rejuvenators, brush and comb. Rose was
hunched on the sofa, sunk in a reverie. Carol was sure she
had just caught the sound of a sob choked back.

'What's up?'

'Nothing.'

'What you crying for, then? Come on, are you gonna
tell me?'

Rose went on staring at the floor. 'I met someone when
I was in London. I liked him and I thought he liked me.
He acted as though he did – got me on that course and
all that. But as soon as he found out what I'd been doing,
he changed. Got leery. Not as if he hated me, but . . . sort
of didn't like the taste. You can't run away from who you
are,' she burst out abruptly, 'and what you were. That's
why I came back. I thought he'd understand. He made a
big thing of understanding everybody else. Why couldn't
he understand *me*?'

Carol sank on to the sofa and put an arm round her. Both
of them could do with some distraction to take their minds

off their troubles. It was time to go round to Joyce's place and get down to serious planning.

Next morning they were already practising looking serious and responsible as the taxi wove its way through the streets towards the town hall. It had been agreed that whatever question they were asked, they mustn't all shout out different answers. And if it was to do with money or business plan, that would be left to Rose, who had acquired the confident look of a city businesswoman along with a second-hand document case picked up at the corner shop. Carol had chosen her best light grey two-piece; Joyce wore a dark dress which Carol suspected she had worn to Gina's funeral; and Anita, squeezed in the back between Carol and Rose, was trying to apply another layer of lipstick in spite of the jolting of the cab.

'Don't get yourself all dolled up,' Carol warned, 'we're supposed to be cleaners.'

'I'm not a cleaner. I'm going to be the secretary, or the receptionist, and they always wear makeup.'

They drew up at the foot of the town hall steps.

Their hearts almost failed them. The flight of steps was so wide and went up such a hell of a long way. But Joyce had known the building for long enough not to be overawed. She led the way up and through the heavy doors into the splendour of the vast entrance hall, light streaming down from a glass dome as if into a cathedral.

Now it was a matter of finding Conference Room B. They had reached the first floor landing when Anita whimpered: 'Do you think I've got time to go to the toilet?'

'You should have gone before we came,' Rose snapped.

'Honest, I've got to find a ladies'.' Anita hobbled desperately away in search of an imposing door with the right message on it.

A man appeared from along the corridor to intercept the other three. His lip curled in faint disdain at their appearance. 'Councillor Baker and the panel are waiting for you.'

'Councillor Baker!' Carol stared at Rose in horror.

'Yes, Councillor Baker. Is there a problem?'

'No,' Carol managed to say, 'no problem.'

'First door on your right. Knock before you enter.'

As they reached the door, Joyce whispered to Carol, 'What was wrong back there? What's the matter?'

'I've done him.'

'Y'what?'

'Done him as a favour for your precious Mr Ferguson.'

'Likes his arse spanking,' Rose contributed.

They were aware of the man watching them suspiciously from the head of the stairs. Joyce hastened to rap her knuckles on the dark oak panel of the door.

'Come.'

It was an authoritative voice. And Councillor Baker looked very much in charge as they filtered nervously into the large conference room. It was only as they approached and he saw Carol full face that his magisterial self-importance began to crack. He went very white, croaked something unintelligible, and waved a hand vaguely at the woman beside him at the head of a long, highly polished table.

Surprised but immediately efficient, she said, 'Hello, do come in. I'm Glenys Minkin, manager of the Leisure Centre. This is my colleague, Councillor Baker.'

'Pleased to meet you,' they chorused. Baker forced a smile, directing it anywhere but at Carol.

'And this is Robert Price, our internal auditor. And John Scarcroft, our legal representative. Do sit down.'

They sat down, far away up the table.

Glenys Minkin had their application form in front of them. She had obviously read it fully before they arrived, and was geared to pick on the salient points.

'Well, now. Scrubbit International. That's an interesting contradiction.'

'We thought it was very catchy.' Baker had regained his composure and was anxious to reassert himself. 'Very unusual.'

'We wanted something hard-hitting,' said Joyce cheerfully.

Carol caught Baker's eye as he choked and momentarily bent forward over the table.

'A name that would say what we did,' Rose took up the sales pitch, 'but that we weren't small time. This is just the start for us: we have every intention of getting much bigger.'

Glenys Minkin pursed her lips. She was keeping things very cold and objective. 'I have to admit that that's something which concerns us. Being such a new company, don't you think it's a bit ambitious of you to go for a big contract like this? I mean, if you haven't had the experience of working together as a team before?'

'Oh, we . . . er –' Rose looked very earnest '– we have sort of worked together before.'

'But presumably that was just as cleaners, not managing a company?'

'We're not a company.' Rose was gaining in confidence. 'We're a co-op. We're all going to work together and we'll all be paid the same.'

'And do you know what the dynamic of your team is – what your strengths and weaknesses are?'

It was the sort of question you'd like notice of. Lots of notice. As Rose groped for a plausible answer, Councillor Baker thrust himself into the fray as bossily as possible, all too eager to get them out of here without delay.

'Then there's the financial side. We're talking about an eighty-K contract. Employing other people, doing the wages, national insurance, accounting for every single stamp. You'll have the whole lot to sort out. And it goes without saying that you'll need a banker's reference before we can even start to consider you seriously.'

Rose's brief spell of confidence was ebbing away. 'I've done a business course.'

'Doing a business course and operating an eighty-thousand-pound contract are not the same thing,' said Glenys Minkin.

The lofty attitude was too much for Rose. 'I'm not saying they are. But the only way we'll know if we can do it is if you give us a chance. If it doesn't work out, then you don't renew the contract next year. Somebody's got to take a chance somewhere down the line, or how else can anybody get started? All I can tell you is that we'll work hard, 'cos we've got a lot to prove and we'll do things properly.'

Baker was obviously on the verge of intervening again with something even more derogatory when the door opened and Anita sidled in. He recognised her at once; and again was stricken speechless.

'Hello, I'm Anita Braithwaite. I had to go to the ladies', and I lost the way back.' She edged towards Carol and the others. 'I'm with them.'

Glenys Minkin looked down their application form and gave a perfunctory nod. 'Yes. Do sit down.'

'Sorry about that, but you know how it is: when you've got to go, you've got to go.'

Carol winced silently. It might have been better to have left Anita at home. Better, indeed, to have left her out of this altogether. Not that any of them had much more to contribute. Glenys Minkin was at least polite, but you couldn't have called her encouraging. And Baker's face told a whole story that they ought to have taken into account right from the start. George Ferguson and Baker had got the whole Leisure Centre deal wrapped up. Consideration of other tenders was purely a procedural routine. That was why, thought Carol bitterly, Ferguson had organised Anita weeks ago to find someone to satisfy Baker's pathetic appetites. And the someone had been herself. She glared at Baker. He still wouldn't meet her gaze, but he was looking more relaxed now. An embarrassing moment for him, seeing Carol and Anita here, but no more than that. Ferguson's contract was in the bag, and Baker's rakeoff had no doubt been settled between them. Another thing that was sure this morning was that from now on his perks would not include any sessions with Carol.

Going down the dizzying steps outside as slowly as they had come up, Rose said, 'We should have known to have a bank account. I felt a right bloody idiot. We'll have to open one.'

'What with?'

'Oh, let's just forget it,' said Joyce.

'Come on, we've got this far. He said he wanted a bank reference, that's all. We can get that. No problem.'

Only when they were looking into the face of Mr Ward in his bank manager's office did they realise just how hefty the problem was. You couldn't have said he was downright rude or contemptuous, but he had had plenty of experience in turning down absurd propositions, and knew exactly how to keep things courteous, factual . . . and lethal.

Basically what they were saying was that they hadn't got an account with his bank, that they were all unemployed, and had no management experience, no business plan for this cleaning venture, and no collateral whatsoever. It was not difficult to guess that he was not going to say yes.

No bank reference, no company, no contract.

They went silently home; silently, that is, except for Anita, who had missed out on most of the proceedings in the conference room and had to be brought up to date, item by item, and then have the whole matter of bank references and collateral explained to her. Carol doubted that much of it had sunk in, and was baffled by a sudden flicker of hope in Anita's eyes.

For herself, she would have to give up hoping about the job and get back to thinking about Emma and planning for her to come home.

Rose was close behind her as they reached the front door. On the step was a bouquet of dead flowers.

Carol felt fear coming cold up her legs, stabbing into her stomach and working its way upwards to freeze her brain. He had found her. He knew where she lived, he could get to her any time he wanted now. He had killed Gina and left those flowers at her grave, and now he was closing in again.

She whimpered, trampled over the flowers, and blundered on into the house. The phone was ringing. It might be Joyce, calling to say that on the way home she had had another idea. Or better still, Anne Devlin, with a date for Emma to come round. Carol snatched up the phone.

'Hello.' She waited, hearing only a faint, dry rustling at the other end. 'Who is it?'

The voice breathed one word only: 'Sinner.'

21

Anita had taken a lot of trouble to make herself look smart and presentable. She had no illusions about the contrast there would be between herself and Kathleen Ferguson – who would have had so much of George's money to spend on the niceties of her appearance – but she was going to put up as good a show as she could manage. After all, she had right on her side; though maybe Mrs Ferguson wouldn't quite see it her way.

Anita had never seen George's wife before and hadn't known quite what to expect. When the front door of the plush Ferguson house opened, she was confronted by someone rather prettier than she had been led to believe by the treacherous George; slim, with a nice skin and an easygoing smile; though those thin lips might just as easily harden into hostility.

Hard lines. That smile simply had to be wiped off her face.

'Can I help you?' said Kathleen Ferguson pleasantly.

Anita plunged straight in at the deep end. 'I think you should know that up to six weeks ago me and your husband were having it off on a regular basis.'

It took only the slightest readjustment of the woman's features to switch from courteous interest to stony dismissal. 'I'm sorry, but I don't want to listen to rubbish like that.'

'No, but you're going to have to.' Anita wedged her foot in the door before it could close. 'We'd been doing it for nearly two and a half years.'

'I'm going to ring the police.'

'Every Thursday night,' Anita persisted, 'till he decided he wanted to screw somebody else. And then he turfed me out of the flat.' Kathleen Ferguson kicked her foot away and closed the door; but that wasn't going to stop Anita now. She put her mouth close to the letterbox. 'I expect he's moved her in there now. I've got the rent book and everything if you want to see it. And another thing, he's a rip-off merchant and a loan shark who gets his heavies to do his dirty work for him.'

She heard Mrs Ferguson's footsteps hurrying away down the hall, perhaps towards a telephone, and made a last wild attempt.

'Where d'you think he spends his Thursdays?' There was a long silence. 'He threatened Gina Dixon,' she spat through the letterbox. 'Frightened her on to the Lane. That's why she ended up dead.'

There was another long hush. Then Kathleen Ferguson came back and opened the front door. 'I think you'd better come in.'

Anita mentally chalked up one point to herself as she walked into the hall and on into the type of drawing room she had always dreamed of. The sort George Ferguson had hinted at, half promised, and let her dream of while he kept her in that grotty little flat in a part of the town whose existence would hardly have been acknowledged in a tree-lined street like this.

Kathleen Ferguson said, 'I can't believe you've got the audacity to come round here to my house and—'

'We've got a lot in common. I'm someone who's been dumped by your husband, just like you have.'

'I won't listen to this.'

'You're longing to listen to it,' said Anita remorselessly, 'because you've known it for a long time and never had the guts to face up to it. Now I'm handing it to you on a plate. Only I want something in return.'

'Is this blackmail? I have no intention of helping you in any way. What exactly are you here for?'

It came out splendid and dignified. But Anita knew from the look in the woman's eye just how much she had doubted her husband for a long time; how much, indeed, she had been growing to hate him. Basically Kathleen Ferguson was an all right sort of person, but she had been shielded from reality for too long. She must have suspected some of his carryings-on, but had turned a blind eye. She had a comfortable life, a comfortable house. It was high time she was made to face up to what it had cost.

Anita said, 'Look at this room. It's full of stuff. Must have cost a bloody fortune. Where d'you think he gets his money from?'

'He runs a very successful cleaning business, in case you've forgotten.'

'Oh, yes. So he does. On starvation wages. And on the side he's a bastard loan shark. People have been killed because of your husband. How d'you know those curtains of yours haven't been bought with blood money? Or this vase.' She picked up a piece of china with a finely fluted rim from the mantelpiece. 'Some woman might have gone to hell and back so that you could have this.'

'Will you please put that down.' She freed the statuette carefully from Anita's grasp. 'I don't know what you think you're here for.'

'To get you to help us.'

'Help you? For heaven's sake, you say you've slept with my husband—'

'You'd like to see the rent book? Check up on all those Thursday nights?'

'No.' Anita had to admire the woman's dignity. In spite of herself she wondered how George Ferguson could have given up loving anyone so sleek and attractive and with such style. 'I don't owe you anything. Give me one good reason

225

why I should help you – whatever this help is that you're asking.'

'Don't see it as helping me. See it as getting back at George. He's had you for a mug long enough, and I think you know it. All them Thursdays. I used to say to him, "Doesn't your wife know you're having an affair?", and he used to say "Kathleen? She's too thick to work it out." Don't you think it's time,' said Anita insidiously, 'that you got your own back?'

Kathleen Ferguson looked round the room as if to summon up reassurance from all her possessions, from the whole atmosphere in which she had lived for so long, sheltered – and sheltering herself – from reality.

'I still don't know what you're expecting of me.'

'Not a lot. Just that me and my friends have got only twenty-four hours to come up with a banker's reference.'

'Why should I even consider—'

'Ask him about his Thursday evenings,' Anita plugged away. 'Ask him what he's doing this Thursday. And next week. And every other week.'

'He always goes to his club every Thursday. Has done for years.'

'Oh, yes. For years. Try and see if he'll alter the timetable just for once. Just ask him to do something different for a change, and see where it gets you.'

'Banker's bloody reference,' said Joyce. 'Bloody nightmare. We don't stand a chance, really. I wish we'd never started.' She thought glumly of what George Ferguson would have to say when he heard what she had been up to. Because he would surely have heard about it by now from his toady Baker.

Steve handed her a letter. 'Look what I got this morning.'

It was fantastic. At last the job had been confirmed: a full-time job with good prospects. The only trouble was, he confessed, that he would have to go several weeks to Blackpool. Lovely place, Blackpool. But it left that same question hanging in the air which had meant so much trouble already: what was he going to do with the kids?

Joyce knew in her bones what was liable to happen. Steve would get his job, while she'd be out of one. Which meant that she would still be able to look after the kids while he was away. Sturdily she said, 'Take it, love. You've got to get your life back together sometime. We'll . . . sort out the snags somehow.'

There was a knock at the front door.

Carol and Rose stood on the step. Carol was trembling. 'Joyce, I need you to come to the police station with me. You've got to tell Newall about them flowers at the cemetery – them dead flowers on Gina's grave.'

The mere sound of her voice had brought Steve to the door behind Joyce. 'What the bloody hell's she doing here?'

'She's come to see me.'

'You're mixing with scum, Joyce. You want to make sure you don't catch summat.' He stormed past her, pushed Carol out of the way, and went down the path to his car.

Carol regained her balance. 'Hang on a minute.' She followed him and reached the pavement as he was slamming the car door. 'I want to talk to you.'

'Piss off,' he mouthed through the glass, switching on the ignition.

'I said I want to talk to you.' Carol marched round to the front and put her hands on the bonnet as he revved up. 'Come on, then. Run me over, if I'm just scum. Go on, put yer foot down.'

Steve revved up to a grinding screech, then slackened off and switched off. He got out of the car very deliberately, his lips clamped together and his right fist clenched.

'All right, you want to say summat. Say it.'

'The night you came to my house you asked if Gina was good. Well, I'm telling you now, she was good.

227

Better than you'll ever know. She was a clean, decent person—'

'Till she met you.'

'You can think anything you like about me, I don't care. But she was different, she were special. She'd have done anything for her kids, and you were lucky to have had the time you had with her.'

'She was a whore.'

Joyce was at Carol's elbow, with Michelle in her arms. 'That's my daughter you're talking about.'

'And to think I tried to talk her into going back to you,' Carol marvelled. 'No wonder she went on the Lane.'

Steve made a grab at her, but Joyce lurched between them. 'Leave her alone.' Michelle began to cry.

'I don't want my kids anywhere near her,' Steve raged.

'Then take them home and look after them yerself.'

'You know who she is, Joyce, don't you?'

'Yes, I know who she is.'

'How can you let her in yer house? How can you bear to look at her?'

Joyce drew herself up, hugging Michelle close to her shoulder. 'See this one? She's yours. Your daughter, your own flesh and blood. Just like Gina was mine. I held her in my arms, fed her at my breast, wondered what she'd be like when she grew up. It never entered my head that one day she'd be gone, gone in my own lifetime. You don't expect that. You never think you'll bury your children.' Joyce kissed the top of Michelle's head, and the baby stopped crying. 'I know one day when I go round to me dad's with his dinner, I'll find him dead and I'll be upset . . . but never in my life, not for one single second, did I think I'd be going to me own daughter's funeral. I'm not going to get over it. Never. I've just got to find some way of living with it, some way of making sense of it. And Carol helps me do that. She's the only one who's been there for me.' Joyce thrust her face close towards Steve's. 'So don't stand there asking me how I can do this and how I can do that. I'd stand on the street corner tomorrow and sell me body to have Gina back. And if that makes me a whore than I'm a bloody whore and proud of it.'

Steve went back to his car, revved up again as noisily as possible as if to show them all what he felt about them, and roared off.

'Jesus!' said Rose, awestruck.

Carol put her arm round Joyce and eased her back indoors. Joyce could almost feel the blood sizzling in her veins. She was incapable of sitting down and letting the anger drain away out of her.

Then she realised what time it was. She was due in at Ferguson's offices for the evening cleaning session. Such a short time ago she had been looking forward to marching out of there and gleefully snatching the Leisure Centre contract from under his nose. Now the brief daydream was all over. She still needed a job. It wasn't going to be easy facing George Ferguson; but she was still in his employ, and maybe she was going to have to get down on her knees not just to scrub the floor but to beg to be kept on.

She looked at her watch and then at Carol. 'I hate to ask you, but . . .'

'It's all right. We'll babysit.'

'Haven't got anything better to do,' said Rose.

Joyce set off. The adrenalin was easing off. She quaked as she went into the office, though it looked much the same as usual. No sign of George Ferguson. Maybe he had knocked off early. Automatically she set about her usual evening programme of cleaning out the sinks in the ladies' toilet. It was just possible to believe that things would go on just as they had always gone on. Regular routine was so soothing.

Until the door of the toilets was kicked open and Gorge Ferguson bellowed, 'I'd like to know what the bloody hell you think you're playing at.'

'Just doing what I always do at this time of—'

'Don't come the bloody innocent with me, Mrs Webster. What about Scrubbit International, eh? A load of scrubbers all right, but what makes you think you can go behind my back and steal my ideas?' Joyce assessed her chance of wriggling past him into the corridor instead of being penned in here; but Ferguson's heavy body blocked the doorway. 'Seven years you've worked for me. Seven sodding years. Paid you well, let you have time off when your daughter was killed. Let you have God knows how much time off, one way and another. Bloody disgraceful. You're straight with people, you give 'em a job, trust 'em . . . and this is how you get repaid. What's happened to loyalty, that's what I'd like to know?'

'Just out of interest,' said Joyce artlessly, 'who told you?'

'I have friends in high places – people who care about me.'

'I've got friends in high places, too. And they tell me that you run the loan company that my Gina borrowed money off.'

'Where d'you get that load of—'

'And you have heavies working for you, and you send 'em out to frighten people – people like my Gina.'

'Never heard such a load of rubbish in my life.'

Joyce unbuttoned her overall. It was no good thinking she could ever go on working here. It was all over; but not before she had thrown the lot at him. 'And you think people don't know,' she fumed. 'Only they do know, and if they don't know then they will by the time I've finished. Because I'm going to spread it around. The only thing you can't believe, George Ferguson, is that someone would have the guts to stand up to you. You must have told us all a hundred times that the art of being a good cleaner is being invisible.' She threw the overall at his feet. 'Well, here's one invisible cleaner. I'm gone. Keep the overall. Give it to some other poor sod who can't afford to lay out the sixteen pounds and forty pence for a new one.'

This time she made the effort to get out, and found to her satisfaction just how flabby he was, so easy to shove aside out of the way.

It had been a wonderful sensation, getting all the hatred she had felt for so long out into the open at last. But when the exhilaration had died, there was still the question of what she was going to do for a living.

She went thoughtfully back to relieve Carol and Rose of the children.

Carol was glad to get home and open the cupboard. There had been nothing to drink at Joyce's, and she was in need of a long swig of something. She opened a flagon of cider and poured it into two of the largest glasses she possessed, one for herself and one for Rose, who was sinking back into her reverie.

Joyce's house had at least had one thing to commend it. Nobody else except Steve would know she was there; and she didn't really think Steve could ever have been Gina's or Amanda Smeaton's killer. Now, at home, she was back on dangerous territory. The maniac knew where she lived. He could strike whenever he chose. And she had forgotten to urge Joyce along to the police station with her to report on the flowers and ask for some sort of protection. Waste of time, maybe. They wouldn't be too worried about protecting the likes of her against her flimsy fantasies.

Anita creaked downstairs and looked at the flagon. 'What about me?' Carol gestured towards a smaller glass. There was only just enough cider left to half-fill it. The three of them sank into a shared gloom. Carol felt the inevitability of that crank, whoever he was, drawing closer; her Emma was in care; and they had blown the cleaning contract. Like Rose's reminiscences of a new dawn in London which had darkened again so suddenly, it was a nice dream while it lasted, but it was gone. And maybe, in spite of everything, Anita still missed that disgusting slob George Ferguson.

If only . . .

The phone rang. Carol's breath seemed to lock in her throat. She was sure she knew who it would be. A faint breath, and then that one word again. How long would he keep it up before . . . well, before what?

She went out into the hall and lifted the receiver.

It was for Anita. So Anita wasn't just still on the premises, but was handing out the phone number here to her friends.

'Yes, Anita Braithwaite speaking.' It was so twee and self-conscious. Carol heard a few words but was paying little attention; though it had just occurred to her that maybe Anita was genuinely looking for accommodation somewhere else, and this was something to do with it. 'Well, if we meet there first thing in the morning.' Anita's voice had risen gleefully. 'Oh, yes, I do think you're doing the right thing.'

The cheerfulness was so untypical that Rose emerged from her sombre ruminations and raised a questioning eyebrow at Carol.

Anita came back into the room looking overbearingly pleased with herself. She enjoyed keeping them waiting, until Rose could stand it no longer.

'Well?'

'That,' said Anita blithely, 'was Kathleen Ferguson.'

'What the hell's she doing ringing you?'

'She's going to be our backer.'

'Yer liar,' said Carol.

'Straight up.' It was Anita's moment, and she was glorying in it. 'We're meeting her tomorrow morning at nine o'clock outside the Yorkshire Bank.'

22

They agreed that the Minkin woman must have been behind the invitation. Although it had been phoned to Joyce by Baker's secretary, it was unlikely that Baker himself would have invited them to come and see the Leisure Centre to calculate exactly what their commitments would have to be. Only Rose had fancied that Glenys Minkin, in spite of her unrelievedly stony expression, had been impressed by their cheek if by nothing else. And she might well be one of those who had worked long enough for, and closely enough to, Councillor Baker to have developed a distaste for him and his shady ways.

Nevertheless it was from Baker that the summons had come officially. Perhaps deliberately, he had given them very little breathing space. They were to meet him at the Leisure Centre at six o'clock, when he would spare them just half an hour.

Rose and Carol sorted through a number of dresses from Carol's wardrobe. Rose was in dire need of some new clothes, but most of Carol's things were too tight for her.

'You could have worn my blue striped top with your skirt if I could find it,' said Carol, 'but the bloody thing's disappeared. I could have sworn I put it out on the line yesterday.'

They were jostling for position in front of the wardrobe mirror when there was a knock at the front door. Carol peered out through the curtains.

Anne Devlin had brought Emma to the house.

233

Rose seized Anita's arm and urged her towards the back door.

'See you at the Centre at six. Don't be late!'

Carol nerved herself to open the door and look down into Emma's eyes, wondering what she would see there: happiness, or uncertainty, or awkward rejection.

Emma beamed. Carol snatched her up and hugged her. 'My little treasure pie. Have I missed you!'

'I've missed you, too.'

Anne Devlin said, 'I hope you didn't mind me springing it on you, but I thought if we did the visit today it might be a sort of prelim to the weekend. If you can manage that.'

'Oh, I can manage,' Carol breathed. 'I can manage.'

Emma gripped her hand, and tried to tug her on indoors.

'You'll be back in your own bed on Saturday night,' Anne Devlin was saying. 'You'll like that, won't you?'

'Why can't I sleep in it tonight?'

'Because Auntie Pat's expecting you back there.'

'It's all right, treasure.' Carol could scarcely speak straight.

'You'll be home to stay next week – and you don't want to upset Sandy, do you?'

Emma summoned up a scowl too ferocious for her demure little face. 'Sandy chewed Barbie's leg. I don't like him any more.'

Carol winked at Anne Devlin. 'Thank God for that.'

They had a happy hour and a half digging out Emma's toys and treasures from the box in her bedroom. She greeted each with a squeal of joy. Some of them she had half-forgotten, and each one merited an ecstatic reunion. The social worker smiled approval, and seemed to be enjoying every minute of it; but Carol knew that she as much as Emma was under skilful, unobtrusive surveillance. She wanted to prolong this visit until it ceased to be just a visit and Emma was really home, playing here until bedtime and then finishing up in her own bed, and Mrs Devlin had gone for good.

But there was that meeting. When Emma reluctantly left, Carol realised she had only a few minutes to get to the Leisure Centre. Hastily she wiped away tears which insisted on stinging her eyes, and called for a taxi.

She was already fifteen minutes overdue when it rolled up, and her fingers fumbled impatiently with the door lock. She had taken only three paces down the path when a figure loomed up out of the shadows beside the house.

Curly said, 'I have to see you. I've got to talk to you.'

'Not now. Look, I'm sorry about what happened, but I was off my head.'

'It's all right. I understand.'

The cab driver honked his horn.

'Look, I'm finished with all that now. I'm not doing it any more.' She brushed past him and waved to the cab driver.

'But you have to,' Curly protested. 'I need you to. I can't breathe unless you do.'

She was desperate to get away and be done with him. 'Have a squirt of yer inhaler, then. Find someone else. Stop hassling me.'

He was trotting after her. 'But you don't understand, I can't exist without you, you have to walk for me . . .'

She reached the cab and scrambled in.

As it slowed at the corner and then headed towards the city centre, she was sure headlights were following. There was no way of telling whether it was Curly in pursuit; but it just had to be. She had never expected to see him again. Now she was going to have to work at shaking him off all over again.

They had delayed as long as they dared. But Baker was in no patient mood. He clearly resented being here at all, but there were things to be said and he wanted to get them said and wrap the whole thing up. On the whole he seemed relieved rather than irritated that Carol had not shown up.

Giving her up as a bad job, the other three set off with

him on a whirlwind tour of the Leisure Centre, with its shimmering new pool, its gymnasium and work-out room, and the small theatre. Baker gabbled his way through a brief aimed at making everything sound too large and complicated and arduous for these silly women to cope with. Anita was impressed, but not in quite the way he intended. The more he ranted on about the size of the job and the responsibilities, the more her eyes widened and the more obviously she was visualising herself in positions of power, running a vast enterprise from a vast, luxurious office. But as they came breathlessly down the steps to the exit, Baker came out with dismissive words which he must have rehearsed several times before meeting them this evening.

'Look, I'll be perfectly honest with you. It's a complete waste of time, because this is not going to happen.'

His complacency turned Rose's stomach. 'What's not going to happen?'

'You getting this contract. It's impossible, so you might as well forget it. I know that . . . how can I put it . . . that things are a little delicate.' He risked one shifty glance at Anita. 'But it's no use expecting me to help, my hands are tied.'

Rose was tempted to ask if that was the way he liked it nowadays, but managed to hold her tongue.

'If the circumstances were different,' he went on with renewed glibness, 'say it was next year and the library cleaning contracts are up for renewal again, I might be able to help out. As a personal favour,' he added winningly. 'But this one's allocated, so to speak.'

'So to speak,' Rose echoed.

'Yes, I'm sorry, but there it is. Best that you let this whole thing drop, or else things could become difficult. And I mean very difficult.'

'Is that a threat?'

'Gracious me, no. More of a friendly warning.'

'Well,' said Anita, 'I think we'll have to see what Carol and our backer have to say to that.'

236

He blinked. 'Your backer? I wasn't aware that you had one.'

Rose thought it only fair to allow Anita the treat of telling him. And as his jaw dropped and he began to flail around to find the right derisive words of disbelief, all three of them wondered just how quickly he would get to a phone and just what George Ferguson at the other end would have to say.

They were jubilant as they headed back to familiar territory and into The Hustlers' Arms. 'Mr F-F-F-F-Ferguson's w-wife?' Anita mimicked rapturously. She was in fact so pleased that she ordered the drinks and began fumbling for her own money.

Behind the bar, Jan said, 'Did Tracy catch up with yer?'

Rose stared in disbelief. 'Tracy?'

'Yeh. Not twenty minutes ago, asking after yer. Told her I thought you were at the Leisure Centre about summat.'

'So we were.' Rose looked about the bar. 'But where the hell is Carol?'

DC Jameson had phoned Newall the moment the full enormity of the place dawned on him. At first it had looked a fairly routine burglary, bungled by youngsters who had made a lot of noise smashing the glass and alerting the neighbours. The owner was not at home, but it was easy enough to get in: a whole side of a french window had been opened up.

There was some valuable stuff around – some delicate religious statues, and less delicate ones of boys wrestling and water nymphs suggestively intertwined – but the burglars must have taken fright and left the lot. When Jameson switched on the wall lights in the study, he could begin to see why. And saw why the DCI would be very interested.

Newall incredulously worked his way along the photographic sequence neatly assembled on a wall panel, until incredulity gave way to chill certainty.

There were photographs of Gina Dixon; before her death,

from various studies from a distance; after her death, a hideous close-up. Then one of Amanda Smeaton's corpse, though this had a red cross scrawled across it, as if to cancel it out.

And next, a group of pictures which must have been taken using a zoom lens: all of them of Carol. She stood on her doorstep, talking to two women Newall recognised as Rose Garrity and Joyce Webster; led her daughter in off the front step; headed out into the back garden with a basket of newly washed clothes. And there was a projector with a video already loaded. Shakily Newall switched it on and stooped to view the film – again of Carol, hanging a striped blue and white top on the clothes-line.

Behind him, Jameson said, 'We found this outside, sir, in the bin.' It was the same top, but ripped into shreds by repeated slashes of a knife.

Newall said, 'For Christ's sake . . . Move.'

Jameson drove. On the way, Newall snapped instructions into his phone. Circulate the man's name and his car number-plate once it had been checked, and get a description from his neighbours. There had been headed letterpaper with a security company name on it in the desk. Ring them, but don't let them trigger off an alarm. 'Move.' He kept saying it, with a near-hysterical crack in his voice.

Outside Carol's house, Newall was out and up to the front door before the car had stopped. There was no response to his frantic knocking. He raced round the back, but there was obviously nobody at home.

She might be all right. No reason to suppose the man would be after her tonight. But if he had gone home and seen the police milling about, and thought it was maybe his last opportunity . . . She had to be warned. This time he wouldn't let her push him around. A right fool he might look, bursting in on her drinking in that sleazy bar with her sleazy friends. But until that bastard was caught, he was going to have her taken into protective custody whether she liked it or not.

The women were just where he had predicted they would be. And pretty merry about everything, by the sound of them. Newall stormed into the bar and headed straight to their table. But there were only three of them.

He said, 'Is she in the bog?'

'That's no way to talk to a lady,' said Anita Braithwaite huffily.

'Where's Carol?' raged Newall. 'Where *is* she?'

Rose looked at him, and his expression brought her to her feet. 'I've just been starting to get worried about that.'

23

The imposing plate glass doors of the Leisure Centre were locked. Carol could not believe that she had arrived too late to join the conducted tour. Presumably the opening hours for any members of the public were over; but Councillor Baker would be showing the other three around, and couldn't have finished this quickly. She wanted to be in on it. She pressed an illuminated button beside the doors, and a tinny voice from a speaker above the button said: 'Who is it?'

She was relieved. It was all straightforward and efficient. 'Carol Johnson. I've got an appointment with Councillor Baker. I'm a bit late, but he's expecting me.'

There was a buzz from the speaker. 'Push the door now.'

She pushed, and went in. The door did not swing completely shut behind her, but she paid no attention, crossing the reception area and wondering why there was nobody at the desk. The security man must have had her name on his list or he wouldn't have let her in: didn't he know that the receptionist had quit for the night and there was nobody to answer a visitor's questions?

And where would she find Anita, Rose, Joyce and Councillor Baker?

Carol looked at the battery of phones and keyboards on the desk, and wondered which one she could use to question the guard, wherever he was tucked away. She pushed open another door and found herself in a deserted bar, with a large glass panel looking down on to a squash court. They really

did have everything here. You wanted the energetic stuff,
you helped yourself to it; and your mates in the bar relaxed
and made faces at you while you played.

But it was all too deserted: empty, eerie, echoing.

'Councillor Baker!' Her appeal floated off into nowhere.
'Hello – is there anybody about?'

A flight of stairs on the far side of the bar led up to
a landing with a curved window overlooking the city and
the Centre's car park immediately below. She saw someone
opening a car door and getting in. Recognising Baker's
back, she banged on the window and shouted, but there
was no way he could hear her. Nor, shut away in here,
could she hear the faintest sound from his engine. Brake
lights winked at her from the top of a ramp, and then he
had driven off.

Nobody else but herself was making a sound in here, yet
there seemed to be a thousand sinister echoes filtering out
from the ends of distant corridors. One door had a large
square of glass at eye level, with complete darkness beyond;
yet in that darkness she could believe shadows were building
up into something solid, waiting for her. She edged further
along the landing, peering round the half-open door of an
empty room; then found herself looking down a spiral staircase which must eventually link up with the reception area.

'Hello! Can anybody hear me?'

Suddenly the lights along the landing and in the spaces
below the stair went out.

At last somebody answered. Drifting up from below came
one resonant whisper: 'Sinner!'

No, she wouldn't believe it. She turned back the way she
had come, but somehow managed to take a turning that she
hadn't noticed was there before, and found herself facing
the steely grey doors of a lift. The moment she pressed the
button, the door opened. Here at least there was an inner
light; and when she pressed for the ground floor, she went
down smoothly enough.

She stepped out opposite a small office with surveillance screens tilted down towards a desk, each showing a slow scan of different parts of the interior. There was a man slumped forward across the desk. Thankfully she opened the door and tapped the back of his chair.

'Look, I think there's somebody . . .'

He very gradually slumped further forward, and as his head hit the desk a wide, dark trickle of blood seeped down beside his left ear.

There had to be a way out. Or there had to be somebody still around who could come and help her. She started to cry Rose's name, and Joyce's. But if Councillor Baker had left, then the others must have gone too. Carol staggered away from the office and started along the endless corridor running beside plate glass windows which must offer a fine view of the city in daylight. Now there was nothing but a blur of street and house lights – and then, terrifyingly, Curly's face pressed to one of the windows.

He was pawing the glass, mouthing weird things at her. For once she'd be glad if she found herself in one of her nightmares. If only it was just that, she could grope her way out and wake up from it and find herself in her own bed, sweating and shivering, but safe. But when she touched the wall to steady herself, it was too solid and real.

She turned away from Curly's freakish grimaces – at least he was safely outside – and her feet propelled her aimlessly along another corridor which opened out into the entrance hall. The main doors were right ahead. There surely had to be a way of opening them and getting out. She pulled on one of the decorative ebonite handles, but they wouldn't budge an inch.

Aloud, just to hear the sound of a voice – anybody's at all, her own would have to do – she cried, 'Why won't it bloody open?'

'Because,' said the voice behind her, 'I haven't released it.'

Carol swung round. It was such a relief to hear a calm, nicely balanced tone. She found herself facing someone whose face she knew but hadn't expected to see in here. It was Ian, looking as suave as ever, in control of himself and everything else. She gasped a welcome. 'I didn't know it was you.'

'Life is full of surprises.'

'There's a man in the room along there. I think someone must have—'

'Did you get your flowers?' said Ian.

He looked so calm and rational. His smile was pitying rather than threatening. But she saw his fists clenching and unclenching, his fingers splaying out and then coming together again.

And at last she knew who the killer was.

She turned and ran back along the corridor. His voice followed her, raised yet still unhurried and terribly, terribly reasonable.

'There's no point in running. There's nowhere to go.'

Round the corner she found herself back facing the doors of the lift. She pressed the button; they opened again; she was inside, and the doors were beginning to close as he came implacably towards her.

'I've been searching for you,' he said. 'Now I know everything about you – who you are and what you do.'

His hands gripped the edges of the doors to stop them closing. He began to force them apart. Carol kicked out wildly, and heard him gulp with pain. He reeled backwards, and the doors began closing the last inches of the gap. His voice rose to a howl. 'Sinner!'

She went up as far as the lift would go, and stumbled out on to a gallery above the pool area. She was halfway along it, looking for another way out, when he emerged from a doorway, a bit out of breath but still quite sure of what he intended.

Somehow she had to bring him to a standstill – plead

with him, stop him, make him think. He was a pervert, a woman-hater, a man who hated himself because he'd had it off with Gina and then murdered her and murdered Amanda Smeaton, trying to wipe it all out, cleanse himself, deny any of it had ever happened. But if she could only get through to him, to the real person who must be under all that twisted rage . . .

'I've given up the Lane. I don't do it any more. Honest, I'm not a hustler any more.'

He leaned on the rail, sorrowfully contemplating her. 'You're a thief. You stole money from me. That wasn't fair. I liked you. I liked Gina. I trusted both of you.'

So that was it. Just money, not shame.

'You can have it back,' she sobbed. 'I'll give you it.'

'If only it was that easy.'

'But it is. Really it is.'

Thin creases appeared across his brow, digging in deeper and deeper as his voice grew emotional. 'You have to be punished. Can't you see that? I killed Amanda Smeaton because of you. And that was wrong. She was a simple girl, nothing to do with it at all. I made a terrible mistake.'

'Look, we all—'

'I killed the wrong girl.' His voice acquired a ghostly reverberation below the resonant roof of the swimming pool. A slight swell across the surface of the water made those creases on his face twist and turn. 'I squeezed the life out of her for *your* sins, and I'll carry that to my grave. She didn't deserve it. But you do. You're the one responsible for that as well. She'd be alive today if it wasn't for you and your greed.'

He began pacing towards her. Carol flattened herself against the rail; then knew there was only one way out, and plunged off the gallery. She hit the water on her side, knocking all the breath out of her. She felt herself going down, right to the bottom, and would have screamed if she dared open her mouth. She had never learned to swim.

Desperately she kicked out, flailing her arms to push herself close to the side. When she reached for the edge, Ian was standing above her with the safety pole he had snatched from the wall. Gasping, she raised her head further; and he slowly pushed her under again. She fought back, but he allowed her only a moment above the surface while he intoned with an almost religious fervour: 'Let it happen – breathe in the water, let it cleanse your soul.' Then he pushed down again, and she was engulfed.

Something was pounding in her ears. She had to open her mouth to gasp for air, but there was no air, only an inrush of water. Every time she tried to kick herself away out of his reach and claw her way up with nothing to hold on to, the pole thrust her back. Until suddenly there was a lull. The roaring in her ears gave way, as she surfaced, to a clamour of voices. Must be what they said about your whole life flashing before your eyes while you were drowning – only this was in her ears, not her eyes. There was a heavy splash as Ian hit the water beside her. Tracy's voice was screaming at him – which was crazy, because Tracy was miles away in London – and then Joyce's, and then another splash and an arm around her, and Rose's voice close to her ear. 'Come on, Carol, come on. Don't die on us.'

A hideous wheezing rasped in her throat. Two of them were hauling her out on to the slippery edge of the pool, and somebody was sitting on her and pounding away until she spewed up a gout of water.

All she could see, from a crazy angle, was Tracy standing with a mobile phone in her hand. 'They're on their way.' And in the distance was the wail of a police siren.

Carol coughed, and went on coughing until Rose hauled her upright. To one side of her Ian lay unconscious, with Joyce standing above him still holding the handle of a fire-bucket, as it waiting for another opportunity to swing it at him. On the other, a man was bending towards her with one hand held out imploringly. It was Curly.

Spluttering a last few drops, Carol found words. 'Jesus, I've landed in hell.'

Then she passed out completely.

She was in dry clothes, and the warm drink pouring down her throat was coaxing her gently back to life. Newall sat opposite, for once not going on at her, not saying a word until finally she found the strength to break the silence.

'He didn't get away this time?' she said.

'No, we've carted him off.'

'That'll make things easier down the Lane.'

He wasn't going to let that one pass. 'Look, you said you weren't going back there.'

'I was thinking of my friends.'

'Think of your friend Gina Dixon,' he said harshly. 'And first thing in the morning I'll want you down the station for a statement.'

She put her mug down. 'Fair enough. Glad to oblige. But one thing – *we* got him, right? Me, Rose, Anita and Joyce got him. Right?'

'I'm not saying any different.'

'Well, just don't go taking all the credit, that's all.'

'I'm not. I won't.'

'Right.' Carol got to her feet. 'I reckon it's time I went and bought them all a drink.'

'You'd be better off staying at home tonight, until—'

'Nobody's likely to come round frightening the daylights out of me any more. So, like I said, I'll be off to congratulate the girls.'

Newall sighed. 'All right, I'll give you a lift. Save you the cab fare.'

It was a clear night, and she would not have been surprised to find a full moon at one corner of the heavens and bright sunshine in another. She could breathe again. There were no shadows.

In the car, Newall said: 'There's talk of moving me on somewhere else, so maybe you'll soon be rid of me.'

She wasn't sure whether to rejoice or whether, to be honest, she had felt just a twinge of regret. All she said was, 'That's the way it goes.'

He kept his eyes on the road. 'You could come with me if you like.'

'Are you mad? How long d'you think we'd last?'

They were almost at The Hustlers' Arms when he spoke again. 'We were good together.'

'Listen, I'm a hustler. You wanted to control me – you're a copper, that's what you get off on – only you couldn't control me, so you did the next best thing: you shagged me instead. Well, that's over. I'm not a hustler any more.'

'No,' said Newall cynically, 'you're going to be a cleaning lady instead.'

'We're going to get our own contract sooner or later.' He had put her on the defensive yet again. 'Just because we've been cheated this time, doesn't mean we're giving up. Next time we're gonna fight the likes of George Ferguson and win.'

He stopped and gave her an unexpectedly genuine smile, like a fond uncle just about to hand out a very special present. 'I wouldn't think that'd be too hard. Your friend Ferguson's been under investigation by the Fraud Squad for the past two months. And before you ask, yes, they're on to Baker as well.'

She didn't wait for him to attempt kissing her. She kissed him fervently and laughed her thanks; but moved hastily out of the car before he could get any further ideas.

In the bar Rose was hugging Tracy. 'Well, yer came home.'

'Bloody good job I did – got more strength shoving a scaffolding pole through that glass than you lot could muster.'

They were all laughing. They laughed more loudly, and

more wildly, when Carol stood triumphantly in the doorway and yelled out the news about Ferguson and Baker. Scrubbit International were about to take off.

'We're gonna do it.' Joyce set up a chant. 'We're gonna do it. We're gonna bloody do it.'

'Too right we are.' Carol nodded to Jan to set up the drinks, and raised her glass towards Joyce. 'This one's on Gina.'

'To Gina.'

There was a brief hush as they all lifted their glasses.

Glancing across the pub, Carol spotted Curly framed in the doorway, his hands spread out, his gaze set yearningly upon her.

'Oh, no,' she groaned. 'No. I don't frigging believe it! Will somebody please tell him . . .'

Delirious laughter bubbled up and engulfed them all.

A selection of bestsellers from Headline

LAND OF YOUR POSSESSION	Wendy Robertson	£5.99	☐
TRADERS	Andrew MacAllen	£5.99	☐
SEASONS OF HER LIFE	Fern Michaels	£5.99	☐
CHILD OF SHADOWS	Elizabeth Walker	£5.99	☐
A RAGE TO LIVE	Roberta Latow	£5.99	☐
GOING TOO FAR	Catherine Alliott	£5.99	☐
HANNAH OF HOPE STREET	Dee Williams	£4.99	☐
THE WILLOW GIRLS	Pamela Evans	£5.99	☐
MORE THAN RICHES	Josephine Cox	£5.99	☐
FOR MY DAUGHTERS	Barbara Delinsky	£4.99	☐
BLISS	Claudia Crawford	£5.99	☐
PLEASANT VICES	Laura Daniels	£5.99	☐
QUEENIE	Harry Cole	£5.99	☐

All Headline books are available at your local bookshop or newsagent, or can be ordered direct from the publisher. Just tick the titles you want and fill in the form below. Prices and availability subject to change without notice.

Headline Book Publishing, Cash Sales Department, Bookpoint, 39 Milton Park, Abingdon, OXON, OX14 4TD, UK. If you have a credit card you may order by telephone – 01235 400400.

Please enclose a cheque or postal order made payable to Bookpoint Ltd to the value of the cover price and allow the following for postage and packing:

UK & BFPO: £1.00 for the first book, 50p for the second book and 30p for each additional book ordered up to a maximum charge of £3.00.
OVERSEAS & EIRE: £2.00 for the first book, £1.00 for the second book and 50p for each additional book.

Name ....

Address ....

....

....

If you would prefer to pay by credit card, please complete:
Please debit my Visa/Access/Diner's Card/American Express (delete as applicable) card no:

Signature .... Expiry Date ....